FLIGHT
RISK

Michael McGuire is a senior writer at *The Advertiser* in Adelaide. He has also worked for *The Australian* and the *Sunday Mail* in Adelaide. He has won awards for his journalism and *Flight Risk* is his second novel. He lives in Adelaide and is married to Rachel. They have two children, Tom and Ruby.

MICHAEL McGUIRE

FLIGHT RISK

ALLEN&UNWIN

SYDNEY · MELBOURNE · AUCKLAND · LONDON

First published in 2019

Allen & Unwin
83 Alexander Street
Crows Nest NSW 2065
Australia
Phone: (61 2) 8425 0100
Email: info@allenandunwin.com
Web: www.allenandunwin.com

A catalogue record for this book is available from the National Library of Australia

ISBN 978 1 76063 288 5

Set in 13/18 pt Granjon by Midland Typesetters, Australia
Printed and bound in Australia by Griffin Press

10 9 8 7 6 5 4 3 2 1

MIX
Paper from responsible sources
FSC® C009448

The paper in this book is FSC® certified. FSC® promotes environmentally responsible, socially beneficial and economically viable management of the world's forests.

For Rachel, Tom and Ruby

PROLOGUE

The pilot walks down the airbridge. He is relaxed, happy. In one hand he is balancing a briefcase and an iPad. In the other he is holding a clear plastic container. The flight crew are waiting for him. He is a popular figure on board; many have flown with him before and he is often a contender in their 'who's your favourite pilot to fly with' conversations.

As a tall man with black hair and sharp, strong nose, he carries himself with pride that stops just short of arrogance. You can tell he loves wearing that dark blue uniform with its golden epaulettes and peaked cap. But he is also a considerate man. Unlike other pilots, he takes the time to have a chat to the rest of the crew and he knows something of their life stories.

Inside the plane, he signals with a nod towards the container in his right hand and immediately one of the crew leaps forward to relieve him of the burden.

'Just a little treat for you all. A bit of chocolate cake,' the pilot says. 'We're going home today, so let's have a nice flight.'

The top is ripped off the container and there are many *oohs* and *ahhs* and noises of appreciation as hands reach inside to grab a slice of cake.

'Make sure you save a slice,' the pilot says as he walks on towards the cockpit. 'I don't want a grumpy first officer if he finds out he missed out on cake. He won't speak to me for eight hours.'

1

The building is one of those concrete and glass monstrosities you can find anywhere in the world. Like a McDonald's or a Starbucks, and with just as much style. Designed by architects who think they are cutting edge, paid for by businessmen with more money than imagination.

Standing on the very top floor of this cathedral to money makes me feel a little uncomfortable. Still, I stop for a look at the view of outside through the requisite floor-to-ceiling reinforced plate glass windows. The windows bow, so if you are feeling particularly brave you can lean with your forehead against the glass, place your trust in the wonders of high tensile and look down 49 storeys to the unforgiving pavement below. The real joy up here, though, is looking out over the vast expanses of Sydney Harbour. The Opera House, the Bridge. For a moment, you have the feeling you are a living in a postcard.

But I drag my eyes from the splendour below to gaze up. As ever, when I am this high, I scan the sky for planes. There are some habits that are just too hard to break. They are so ingrained, so hard-wired deep in your brain, that there comes a point where thought gives way to reflex. Like driving your car home. Ever found yourself at your front door with no memory of the journey?

Anyway, I find what I was looking for. This time it's a fat, lazy-looking Qantas A380, drifting high above the harbour as it makes its way to the airport. I am so elevated, it feels like I am almost at the same point in the sky as the plane.

But no time to dawdle. The boss is waiting. I'm not sure why this is his office. It's a little extravagant. A monument to the excesses of some now defunct merchant bank. We inherited it sometime after the last financial crash. The bank had fleeced customers, didn't pay taxes and the government ended up sending a couple of its suits to prison and taking over these offices in part recompense.

The outfit I work for is part of what people like to call the nation's 'security architecture', but in reality we sit somewhat uncomfortably in the cracks between the official and unofficial worlds. Our existence is acknowledged by government, but they don't talk about us unless it's necessary. I don't think I have heard the prime minister ever utter our name, which is mostly the way we like it. There are no speeches about our 'brave and necessary work' by ministers. No questions asked about us in parliament. We are like some unwanted stepchild. Everyone knows we are here, but it's a bit rude to talk about us in public.

It's also safer this way. We have operatives in countries all over the world. Some friendly, some not, so it's better for everyone if we all stay well under the proverbial radar.

One of the reasons we moved into this capitalist monument was to keep us away from the official government buildings that dot Sydney and Canberra. Just another level of mystery, I presume.

And there were no markers of the office's true function. We're not listed on the tenants' directory on the ground floor. There is only one elevator that can carry you to this level, and that is hidden far from the other public lifts. There's even a touchpad where you whack in a secret code to access our elevator, which will then let you in for a ride to the top floor where the boss resides.

If you ever reach the top, the first thing you will notice is how quiet the joint is. Hushed, really. Befitting a top-secret organisation, there aren't many people working up here, either. Scattered around the vast space are a few IT types, poring over some seriously impressive-looking computers, and a few other staff whose names I don't know and whose jobs are a mystery to me. I don't pop up here often, and when I do I don't tend to stop for a chat with the boffins sitting in front of their computer screens. All the workstations are isolated from each other. None of this modern, open-planned stuff where desks are jammed in and the worker bees are piled on top of each other. There's no whispered conversations between colleagues here: if you wanted to attract the attention of your closest neighbour, in fact, you would have to shout. The upside is that view. Wraparound 360-degree views of Sydney Harbour from

49 floors up makes it one of the more spectacular offices you'll come across.

Nobody looks up from their terminal as I walk across an Italian marble floor. One of the few up here I do know is Penny. She is the gatekeeper to the boss's office, which sits in the far left corner and was constructed with a dark, heavy wood, possibly mahogany. Spies don't like to be spied upon themselves. It is a huge space, presumably the one reserved for the spiv-in-chief at the old merchant bank.

Adjacent to his office is a smaller anteroom. This one is all glass. This is where I find Penny. Late forties, dark hair that just makes it to her shoulders, attractive in a severe-librarian sort of way, but her most impressive attribute is her eyes. They are an intense green and Penny has a way of looking at you as if she knows all your secrets. If our lie detector machine (I don't know that we have one, I'm just speculating) ever broke down, Penny would be the answer. She would know you were lying just by looking at you. I would hate to be one of her kids.

'How are you this fine morning, Penny?' I ask.

'Fine,' she replies. 'Where have you been? You took your time.'

'Sorry, traffic was terrible.'

'From Glebe? What's that, ten minutes away?'

'The cab was late.'

'We sent a car for you.'

It should be pointed out, I am a terrible liar when talking to people I like, so it's possible I am over-estimating Penny's skills in this department.

'He's waiting for you.'

Bob Sorensen is indeed waiting for me. He is sitting in a comfortable-looking leather chair behind a desk so big it could have been designed for six people. He's not a big chap, and he's in his early sixties so getting on a bit, and I always have this image of him curling up in the enormous seat like a cat in front of a fire and having a little sleep. Maybe I should have brought him a saucer of milk.

'How are you, Ted?' he asks.

'Okay, Bob, you know.' We like our one-syllable first names around here. 'Happy as ever to be seeing you at the crack of dawn on a Saturday.'

Not for the first time, I wonder what Bob sees when he looks at me, beyond a tall, 39-year-old secret service agent with a few too many miles on the clock. I give myself a quick once-over. I'm in my usual uniform. Blundstones, somewhat worn, new blue jeans, a long-sleeved green cotton shirt from Kmart and my faithful brown leather jacket. Not a bad ensemble for this time of the day, possibly giving me unearned pass marks in a stylistic sense.

It's true we have known each other for about five years, but I don't think that makes us friends. I am good at certain things that make me useful to Bob. I'm his stay-at-home agent. The one based in Sydney but expected to fly anywhere in the world at any time that he deems it necessary. Sometimes it's straightforward. To deliver a parcel that he wouldn't trust to anyone else. Sometimes more serious. Like when I found my way into Burma over the Thai border trying to locate a missing Australian journalist.

If I ever stopped being useful, I can't imagine I'd ever see him again. There would be no Sunday arvo barbecues at his place, no catch-ups for a quick beer after work. No cheery reminisces about the old days: *Hey, Bob, remember that time I was shot at in Burma and the bullet took away a chunk of my upper thigh? Jeez, I don't know how I survived that one. Those were the days.*

Which isn't to say I don't like or respect him. After all, he took me in when others had given up on me. From a point in my life when I'd been knocked a bit off course (always a bad thing for a pilot) and had been well and truly lost.

Bob rescued me from that spiral. Saw a quality in me that I'm not sure I saw in myself anymore, and gave me another chance. By then I had already fled the military after a spell of flying in Iraq, happy with the idea of piloting very fast planes but bored with command decisions. My wife, Melody, had died. It was a car crash and I blamed myself. After she was gone, I needed to look after my daughter and thought leaving the military was my best chance of doing that.

From the military, it was the well-trodden path to flying big commercial planes. But my problem with structure and command didn't go away, I was never home for my daughter and the planes were much slower. By the time I met Bob, I had left the commercial world. If I had still been in the air force, they would have called it a 'dishonourable discharge'. There were going to be no more flying jobs for Ted Anderson.

It was a phone call on a Tuesday morning that brought me to Bob. From Penny, asking for a meeting in this very office.

'Why?' I asked. I found it all a bit peculiar, but having nothing better to do at the time I thought there was nothing to lose by meeting him. And I was intrigued.

'He will tell you what it's about when you get here,' Penny said.

And he did. I liked him straight away. Something comforting in his manner. He was formal and old-school, but he clearly cared about the work and his people. He explained the job. Said it would start small. He was high up in the Australian Secret Intelligence Service, the nation's foreign intelligence agency. We would start with little jobs, using me essentially as a delivery boy, taking messages and deliveries to other agents in the field around the world. There were times, Bob said, when face-to-face contact was preferable to the electronic version.

'Why me?' I finally asked after he had given me the run-down.

'Remember Wing Commander Angus Sorensen?'

I did. He had trained me at Williamstown before I graduated to flying F/A-18s. He had been a hotshot pilot in Vietnam and had charisma and an enthusiasm for flying that I hadn't seen before.

'Of course. Taught me more about flying than anyone else in the air force.'

'He's my brother. Despite everything else on your personnel record, he recommended you. Said you had great potential. So don't let him down. Or me.'

Since that day I have morphed from an agent whose enthusiasm exceeded his capabilities into something a little more sophisticated, although Bob may well disagree with this glowing self-appraisal. I'm grateful to him, I remind myself as I take a seat across from his vast desk. But I'd like to think I've repaid that faith a few times since.

'Ted, a plane went missing a few hours ago,' Bob says gravely. 'A passenger plane. Flying from Sydney to Jakarta. It's early days, obviously, and probably nothing. A mechanical fault, freak weather, but I want you to keep an eye on it.'

This is not a surprise. When large passenger planes go missing, the first instinct is to crank the alert levels up to red. Since 9/11, aircraft in the minds of the public had become more than just an uncomfortable way to fly halfway across the world. They became large, fuel-heavy weapons that in the wrong hands could wreak horrible vengeance. Since that terrible day in 2001, the joy of flying left a lot of people. You can see it at any modern airport. The shuffling lines of worried people, the air of anxiety. The idea, buried deep in their psyche, that this could be the last flight they ever take.

Terrorists though have always been fond of using planes to get a point across. Think of Air France Flight 139, which when flying between Paris and Tel Aviv in 1980 was forced to land at Entebbe in Uganda by Palestinian terrorists. That was the one where the Israelis, who don't do things by half, came in with four C-130 planes, landed a bunch of special forces and knocked seven shades of shit out of the bad guys.

Hijackings in those days weren't uncommon. But 9/11 was different. It was so visceral. Half the world, maybe more, watched it happen live on television. Once you see those images, you can't forget them. It was the ultimate 'do you remember where you were' moment for the post Kennedy assassination generations.

Of course, people tell themselves they are silly to worry. That just because it happened once doesn't mean it will happen again. That security has been tightened since then, that the authorities know better these days, that you couldn't just barge into a cockpit anymore, that it would take more than just a box cutter to force a plane down . . . They take comfort from the metal detectors, the X-ray machines, the screenings for explosive materials. The taking off of belts and shoes. Surely this makes us all safe, they think. Surely this would stop the nutters.

The truth? Maybe some of the half-arsed plotters with half a brain. But for your committed, serious, intelligent nutter? Well, there's always a way, isn't there?

The plane is a Garuda Airlines A330. Flight GIA005, to be exact. There are 245 passengers and crew on board. Among that lot are 154 Australians. It had taken off from Sydney at 10.37 p.m. last night, bound for Jakarta. For five hours, everything seemed normal. All communication between pilots and air traffic control was exactly as the book said it should be. Then silence. It disappeared off the radar in both Australia and Indonesia.

All modern aircraft carry highly sophisticated equipment that tells you to the millimetre where the plane is anywhere in the world. How fast it's flying. Altitude. Fuel on board. What the passenger in seat 47B had for lunch. In addition, pilots are in regular contact with air-traffic control in whichever country they are flying through. You would expect them to communicate en route.

In short, planes are very hard to lose.

But Bob is telling me this one has gone. One second it was there, blipping away on radar, the next it had vanished. And for the last four hours, no one had a clue where it has gone. It has disappeared into the wild blue yonder.

'How can we not know where it is?' I ask. 'It's a big thing, a A330. They aren't easy to lose.'

'We don't fucking know, smartarse, okay?'

Now I start to worry. Bob isn't one of life's natural swearers. He's too proper for that. It's not that he's refined, or much of a snob, he was just born with a deep-rooted sense of decency. He wears that sense of decency like a shroud. Or a well-pressed suit. Take today. Saturday morning, early. You would think he would have stumbled into work in jeans and a jumper. Like me. But no. Full grey suit, white shirt, royal-blue tie and the shiniest black shoes you'll see this side of the military academy.

Funnily enough, though, he's not military like his brother. He's much more a man of the shadows for that. He's secret service, all the way. He always strikes me as someone a little out of step with the times; he would have been happier in a le Carré novel or running around Cambridge looking for Russian spies.

'Sorry, Bob, but seriously, where is it? How do you lose a plane like that? It's got electric gadgets hanging off each rivet, every move is tracked by satellite. If not ours, then the Indonesians, and if not theirs, the Yanks . . . The Chinese are probably having a sneaky peek as well.'

'Ted, I know, I know. But take it from me: we haven't a clue. One second it's there, the next nothing.'

I utter the unutterable word: 'Bomb?'

'It's certainly one option. It would explain the sudden loss of communication. We had the air force up there in the very spot it went missing at first light, but so far there's no sign of any debris.'

'Weather?'

'Flying conditions were clear as you would like. There is always the possibility of some freak turbulence event, but that's highly unlikely. We are not jumping to any conclusions; there could be any number of explanations. None sinister. The Garuda was half an hour off the coast of Western Australia when it went missing. It could have gone in any direction once we lost it, travelling at God knows what speed. It could have covered a lot of sea and there's a lot of water out there. It's going to take time to have a proper look.'

Bob is right. There is a lot of land and water out there. A lot of remoteness.

'Where exactly was it when it went missing?' I ask.

Bob rearranges himself in that large chair. Lifts himself partially out of it, reaches over to the large iMac screen on his desk and swivels it in my direction. He shows me a map. In the bottom right-hand corner is the northwest tip of Australia. I can see Darwin and Broome marked on the map. Above that, a lot of empty blue ocean until the scattered islands of the outskirts of Indonesia come into view.

Bob points to a section of the map a few hundred kilometres off the northwest tip of Australia.

'It was just about here when it vanished,' he says. 'As you know, radar doesn't work like an invisible force field that surrounds Australia. Once off that coast, coverage is patchy. Operators need to be told what to look for, and if a plane does something beyond the bounds of the expected, it can be tough to track.'

'Yes, but what about satellites? What about the bloody Americans and their whizz-bang stuff out at Pine Gap? Nothing's shown up?'

'Not a thing, Ted. It's like it never existed,' he says, raising his right hand to his face, rubbing his thumb into one eye, his forefinger into the other, before sweeping it back over his scalp in a gesture suggesting he is deeply worried about the fate of this aircraft.

2

I leave Bob's office. The plane may have crashed due to pilot error, action or malfunction, may have been hijacked or blown up. May have just taken a wrong turn at some roundabout in the sky. But I'm not the man whose job it is to find debris floating on a lonely wave somewhere in the Indian Ocean. There are other people for that. I'm here for the worst-case scenario. I'm here to find out if there is some badness at work.

The first question is who? Which means working through the usual train of lunatics to figure out if one of these fuckwits has actually slipped through the net this time. These guys—Al-Qaeda, Jemaah Islamiyah, ISIS, whoever—like to present as all-knowing, all-powerful groups of immense cunning and subterfuge. They define themselves this way, just as they define the West as weak, degenerate, incompetent and fearful.

It suits their world view and their view of themselves. The reality is different. Sure, the odd one gets through, but only because someone like me has made a mistake that has never been picked up. Until it was too late.

Even 9/11, that great triumph of this kind of statement terrorism, should have been knocked down before it reached its ultimate, terrible conclusion. In 1998, someone in the CIA was writing reports that Osama bin Laden was planning to hijack planes in New York and Washington. But then this same someone in the CIA forgets to mention it to their friends in the FBI, and the report slips through the cracks. The next thing you know there are planes heading towards the Twin Towers and the Pentagon, and there are a thousand US intelligence guys with their dicks in their hands, wondering where it all went wrong.

They are competitive buggers, these terrorists. Osama bin Laden sat at the apex for a while because he had pulled off the big one. The moment that made the world go 'fuck me'. But that wasn't necessarily a cause for celebration among all the brotherhood. In some, it provoked intense jealousy and a desire to replace bin Laden at the top of the tree.

Don't underestimate the narcissistic element in some of these fuckers. They want to be noticed, and they want to be feared by some and loved by others. Islam itself has very little to do with it. Just like everyone in the West, they are chasing their own little bit of fame. They just do it with guns and bombs.

So, Al-Qaeda begat Al-Shabaab, which begat the spectacularly evil ISIS, and the story goes on, with each new chapter prompting an even bigger bout of brutality as their hackneyed quest for world attention continues. I suspect many of them didn't get the love they needed as children.

And now a plane is missing. An aircraft with 245 people on board. They could be dead, they could all be alive, they could be at the bottom of the sea, or floating somewhere, praying to be rescued.

So far there has been no claim of responsibility. If we are not dealing with an accident, there are some who would be shouting it from the rooftops by now. But there are others who will keep quiet, hope for the fear of the unknown to build and build, for the panic and the chaos to develop. They're the scary ones. It's hard to guess at the motives of people you can't find and won't tell you who they are.

But it's still only a few hours since the plane went missing.

I make my way from the glass monstrosity. With such little information, finding a place to start is always a challenge, but Bob reckons I may as well head to the centre of the search area. Just to keep an eye on things. To Western Australia it is, then.

* * *

I emerge from the office into one of those Sydney days that makes you never want to leave the place. A day when the sun is high, the light is bouncing off the harbour and flinging rays against the Opera House. The water lends the soft wind a salty tang, which this morning is free from the taint of the diesel fumes of the ferries. It's even a bit early in the day for the usual miasma of eager tourists, looking everywhere except where they are going.

But today is not a day to stand around and admire God's handiwork. There is a car waiting. Standard-issue secret service. Black, with black windows, black seats and a white driver. We are heading towards Sydney Airport. I am travelling with nothing, something that seems to happen quite a lot to me. Dressed in my hastily assembled morning outfit, mostly picked from the floor of my bedroom after Bob called. If you didn't already know me, there's a fair chance you would assume I'm a single man. And guess what? You'd be right. The air of raffishness I like to tell myself I project is more likely interpreted as carelessness and laziness by those with a more studied view of such things.

I have my Ray-Bans, my iPhone, my wallet with $67.25 and some credit cards dangerously close to their limits. Happily, there is also my 'work card'. That one has no limit, although Bob does like to pay particularly close attention to any bills I run up at the taxpayers' expense. On another of these trips, Buenos Aires, I think, I treated myself to a haircut and a shave on the company card. Because Bob reckoned my hair would have grown whether I was at work or not, he decided I should pay for it myself. So, the taxpayers were reimbursed that $35.

So that's me, all tooled up and ready for work. No gun. Not yet. Don't like them and never carry them with me if I can help it. I expect Bob has arranged for one to be on the plane I'm about to board. That's another perk of this job. You do get to take guns on planes. They are, I suppose, a workplace necessity.

Don't get me wrong. I'm not some New-Age agent who believes I can solve all the world's problems over a cup of green tea and some gentle persuasion. When you're facing down some suicidal lunatic armed with an AK-47, you want more than words at your disposal. And while I can shoot well, as more than a few souls have found out over the years, I'm no death-cult fetishist for guns like some in my line of work. I don't sleep with a gun, or spend hours cleaning and polishing them. I don't have a pet name for my gun. It's an implement needed in this line of work, nothing more, nothing less. Accountants carry a calculator, special agents usually carry a gun.

* * *

Even on a Saturday morning, the traffic around Sydney is something to behold. We crawl out through the city, heading towards Surry Hills and Redfern, and through some of the suburbs I lived in as a kid. Dad drove a truck that would deliver bread all over the inner-western suburbs of Sydney. His day would start at two in the morning and finish about ten, so I never saw him as much as I wanted.

I remember trying to go with him on his rounds once when I was in primary school. I thought it would be an adventure. I pestered him for weeks. When the time came, he had to drag me out of bed. I slept through most of the delivery run and wasn't invited back.

My mum had a part-time job behind the counter in one of the small corner shops where Dad delivered the bread, but mainly she stayed home to look after me. I was an only child. Both my parents were in their early forties when I came along. 'A miracle,' according to my mother. 'An accident,' according to my father.

We moved around places like Newtown and Alexandria, places that have acquired a trendy sheen they didn't have 40 years ago. Cramped houses with tiny backyards where I would climb onto the back fence to see if I could spot planes heading to the airport. That was when inner-city grime was a reality, not polished up as a fashion accessory for the hipsters.

It wasn't far from there, in Erskineville, where I later lived with my wife and daughter. Both gone now, but in different ways. As the car bumps slowly up Elizabeth Street, I realise we're headed towards a spot I have not been back to in more than eight years. It's where my wife, Melody, died. The corner of Elizabeth and Devonshire Streets in Surry Hills.

I had been in the pub at 3 a.m. again for no good reason. I was back from Iraq where I had been flying F/A-18s for the last time, telling myself I deserved to blow off a little steam. But one night led to two, then three, then four, then for a while I just stopped coming home.

That night Melody had come to find me, an act of mercy, while our nine-year-old daughter, Eliza, was strapped in the back seat, when a drunk broker in a four-wheel drive blew a red light and killed my wife. From the window of the pub I saw it all happen. By some miracle, Eliza was unharmed, but she never forgave me. And I can't blame her for that. She went to live with Melody's mum when she was thirteen and it's been six years since

I saw or even talked to her. I don't even know where she is anymore.

I stare out of the window as we cross the intersection, finding the exact spot where the cars collided and a life ended. A million memories, many more regrets. I think about Eliza and all that we have missed together. I make a vow to try to find her when I get home. To try to make amends.

3

After that unhappy trip down memory lane, I try my best to stow away all the pain in a rarely accessed part of my brain, and when we finally arrive at the airport I find the excuse I need to concentrate on the job at hand. Here's another upside of this gig: you don't have to go through the front door of the airport. Instead we skirt round the edges, along Joyce Drive until we come to a closed-access road, which in turn leads to a guarded tunnel, and then we're driving to a hangar tucked away in a disused corner of the field. Waiting inside is one of those gorgeously sleek private jets that usually find their way into the hands of the unworthy. Billionaires, oil sheiks, Russian robber-barons.

I am greeted by the pilot, Reg Wilson. He's an old hand at these flights. He has guided to me to more than one trouble spot in the past and, more importantly, he's got me out again. He's another I have to trust my life to and I don't even know whether Reg is really his name.

'Hi, mate,' I say as I climb the metal stairs into the plane. 'Good to see you again. Ready for adventure?'

'If you mean am I ready to rescue your sorry arse from whatever mess you find yourself in—again—I suppose I have to be. It's what they pay me for.' Reg laughs. 'Nice to see you too, Ted. Welcome aboard.'

I don't want to give the impression this is my personal air force. The crew do ferry others around as well. But they are good people to have on your side in a crisis. Reg picked me up from my ill-fated Burma trip. I was delirious and half-gone from the bullet through the thigh, but he managed to find an old World War II base near the Thai border and took me to safety.

Reg is ex-Royal Australian Air Force, but today he looks more like Royal Flying Corps circa 1917. He's wearing heavy cotton khaki pants, a similar coloured top and a sheepskin-lined brown leather jacket that has seen better days. He even has a white silk scarf.

'I see you're going for the Biggles look today, Reg. Are we taking the Gulfstream or your Sopwith Camel?'

It turns out to be the Gulfstream. A new one. I assume we have confiscated it from some reprobate or other as it seems unlikely the agency would spring for the $40 million or so it would take to release it from the showroom. The smell of new leather hasn't even left this one. There are ten seats inside the narrow fuselage, upholstered and padded to within an inch of their lives. Seats that you don't really sit in but instead descend into on a cushion of air and never want to get up from again. The interior is all-calming beige. You do get the feeling any show of excitement would be frowned on in such an expensive setting.

Up front with Reg is his co-pilot. I don't know her name. She has taxied me a few times here and there, but all I have seen is the back of her head. Not that I haven't tried to sneak a look. But somehow Reg always manages to cut me off at the pass, like a protective father looking after his favourite daughter.

The last person on board is Liz. Always there to help is our Liz. I'd call her the hostie, but she'd probably kick me in the nuts for applying a label that demeaning. But she is the only one dressed in uniform, an air force one, blue and smartly pressed. I am particularly taken today by the headwear worn at a jaunty angle. Liz is mid-thirties, tall and attractive, short brown hair and brown eyes. A nose that seems too small for her face, but a wide, expressive mouth.

'Ah, Ted,' she says. 'Welcome back. You look like you have been keeping bad company again. Have you been getting into trouble?'

'Not so much,' I reply. 'I'm steady these days. Each morning I rise clear-headed for some toast and coffee and read the paper. I like to take lunch by the harbour and dinner in the city. Then straight to bed. Very civilised, really.'

I give her a smile that suggests I am not being overly serious. She knows me well enough to know my habits, the good and the bad.

'All on your own?' Liz attempts a sad face. 'That must be lonely for you.'

'No, it's good. Gives me time for meditation and contemplation. Makes me think of all the bad things I have done in my life and how I can improve myself. Life-affirming, really.'

'All the bad things? That would keep you busy, I suppose.' The right side of her mouth and her right eyebrow lift in concert as she contemplates this frankly unbelievable claim.

'Thanks, Liz. Lovely to see you again as well.'

'Wheels up in ten, so take a seat. Anything I can get for you?'

'A coffee would be good. And I just realised I haven't had a thing to eat today. Any chance of a sandwich? Toast? Maybe some caviar and crackers?'

* * *

It's going to take around four hours to get to the search hub in the far reaches of northwest Western Australia. We are heading for RAAF Base Curtin, known as 'bare base', which is about as far from civilisation as you can get in Australia. No permanent unit is allocated there, just a few barren buildings and a three-kilometre-long landing strip.

I contemplate a snooze, but soon reach for the iPad in front of me loaded with the information we have so far on the Garuda. It's updated in real time so when I land I will have as much information as possible. Whether I will be able to do anything with it is another matter entirely.

Bob's mindset was leaning towards the 'accident' category, but my early feeling is that there is a human hand at work here. Something more sinister than a busted rivet.

The lovely Liz drops off some scrambled eggs on toast, slightly runny, full of Tabasco, perfect. I'm impressed. She gives me a small smile and disappears back to her hiding spot at the back of the Gulfstream.

I am the only passenger. This is always a slightly disconcerting experience. I find it a bit quiet. All you have for company is the background whine of the jet engines. It also seems a bit self-indulgent. In theory, I could just lie back, call for a beer and flick on *Flying High!* on the movie channel or something. But, despite the comfort of my surroundings, I am supposed to be at work.

I give life to the iPad by holding it up about ten centimetres from my face. It scans my eyes, likes what it sees, and switches itself on. It provides me all the usual top-secret guff, warnings about this and that, but after a few judicious swipes and electronic promises not to reveal anything to anybody I am through to the actual useful stuff.

Most of it reiterates what Bob told me an hour ago. The aircraft just disappeared. There is a replay of the last five minutes of satellite tracking. I see a little green circle with a cross stating designation *GIA005*. It's one of hundreds of flights I can see on my screen. Even after all this time, I am surprised by the amount of air traffic happening at any one time. You sometimes wonder how more of the buggers don't just fall from the sky.

I perform some finger exercises on the iPad and narrow my focus down to GIA005. There it is. Blinking happily away. I see it cross the Australian coast on its designated path towards Jakarta. It's flying at 38,000 feet. It's travelling at 880 kilometres per hour. All so very normal.

Then it's gone. Just like that. About on the border of where Australian airspace becomes Indonesian. And I wonder about that . . . If you wanted to take an aircraft out of circulation, the hazy border between one country's airspace and another's is the perfect place to start.

The final conversations between pilot and air traffic control are also on the computer. According to my file, the captain is Soraya Notonegro and his first officer is Rizky Dayak; Dayak has the last conversation with Australian traffic control.

'Garuda zero zero five, we are now handing you over to Jakarta radio to continue your journey,' comes the Australian voice out of my iPad.

'Thank you, Melbourne control,' replies the Indonesian voice from the cockpit. 'This is Garuda zero zero five saying goodbye.'

Prophetic last words?

In this job, the tendency to overanalyse everything is taken as a given. Sometimes, the smallest details can lead you to your destination. If you don't pay the fullest attention, you can miss a lot. Of course, the downside to this is that you spend a lot of time looking for stuff that really isn't there.

I replay the audio of the Garuda's last few minutes, listening and re-listening to those last words. But it tells me nothing. No stressed voices, no hidden messages. The little we have managed to cobble together on the background of the pilots doesn't raise any alarm bells, either.

The captain, Notonegro, is a long-standing Garuda pilot. He has been with the airline for fifteen years and his conduct has been exemplary in that time. Before working for Garuda, he had flown F-16s for the Indonesian Air Force; again, he was seen as one of the good guys. According to the file, he was regarded as an ultra-professional, never involved in any of the shenanigans as the corrupt Suharto regime fell apart in the late 1990s.

Information was scarcer on Dayak. He was only 31. Been through various flight schools in the United States and Australia, worked at a couple of smaller Indonesian regional airlines before starting long-haul flights for Garuda six months ago. Dayak was the product of a rich Indonesian family, but no flags were being raised. No dodgy friends, no indication of radical leanings.

There is no information on the rest of the crew. It's possible one of them was involved, but if you are looking at who has the capability to crash or lose an aircraft, the pilots are still top of my hit list.

But it's still early. No doubt both the Indonesians and the Australians are already digging away to make certain there's nothing untoward in either pilot's history buried away some-where. What would become of any information unearthed was another matter—if the pilots had been responsible for disappearing the plane, it would mean they had slipped through the net of the Indonesian security forces. That may be information our neighbours won't be keen to share.

The Indonesians don't exactly have the greatest of records when it comes to cutting off terrorists at the pass. The Bali bombings, followed by another attack at the Australian Embassy in Jakarta, made many of my colleagues wary about how much the Indonesians were really doing to stop these kinds of threats. There was even a belief that the Indonesian security services were quite happy to see a few Australians blown up from time to time: some of those blokes were said to still be holding grudges after we made a nuisance of ourselves over East Timor back in 1999.

Our high-up spooks, of course, would be pushing people like me to find out as much as possible about what the fuck had actually happened. Whether any information discovered would ever see the light of day is another matter again. That would be a political decision. One taken by people way above my head and for reasons that generally only pissed me off.

A decision would be taken. It would be either: Do we want to piss Jakarta off today? Or do we need to suck up to Jakarta today? Concepts such as security, justice and vengeance would be in the mix somewhere, but hardly priorities of the first order.

No doubt plenty of people think the work I do is a bit murky, a bit underhand, maybe even lacking in ethics and morality. But there is a certain honesty in my dishonesty. Those who know me, friends and enemies alike, know what to expect. They understand my motivations, they know my goals. High-up spooks and politicians? Well, who the fuck would know?

4

We are 36,000 feet above Australia's red, dead centre. I can't tell you how many times I have crisscrossed this desert, but I have still yet to set foot in it. Uluru is down there somewhere, the Olgas, places I have been reading about since school but have never managed to visit.

I am a fringe dweller in as much as I hug the edges of this great continent. Sydney is my natural home. As such I have the Sydneysider's distrust of the great interior; all those vast open spaces make us city folk raised on a diet of films such as *Wolf Creek* and *The Cars That Ate Paris* a little jumpy. Still, it's probably better than visiting Melbourne. A grey, wet and miserable joint filled with self-important intellectual misfits. A place where football passes as culture and coffee is a high point of civilisation. Spare me.

Of course, that still makes it an improvement on Brisbane. A shiny place full of shallow souls. Perth is too far away for anyone on the east coast to care about. Strangely, I quite like

Adelaide. Good wine. Decent food. Never even bothered going to Hobart.

The iPad beeps. It's a message from Bob.

'This may be something or nothing. We've been checking the cargo manifest of GIA005 and something doesn't add up. According to the official papers, that aircraft was only carrying around 500 kilograms of cargo, which is ridiculous. That flight averages around 15,000 kilograms of cargo each day. Something doesn't add up.'

I ping back a quick acknowledgment of the message. Two scenarios come immediately to mind. The first: that the Indonesians were carrying something lethal, or at least dangerous, in that 'empty' hold (a big no-no on an aircraft that was carrying that many passengers) and it exploded. It could be anything from lithium-ion batteries to undeclared ammunition or some sort of radioactive material. Or, of course, a bomb. This would suggest we were now looking at an official cover-up. A mid-air explosion would explain the sudden disappearance of GIA005 from all known radars. But if that is the case, we will soon spot quite a bit of wreckage in the vicinity of the aircraft's last known position. Sure, the ocean is a big place, but an exploding A330 would make a mess difficult to miss with half the Australian Air Force and most of the world's satellites now looking for the thing.

The second option is scarier. It still involves a lot of weird shit being down in that hold, but of even more concern is the idea that some fairly bad dudes have discovered what GIA005 was carrying and decided to take it for themselves.

But to do that they would also need someone so familiar with the Airbus A330 that they knew exactly which buttons to push to make it disappear from the most sophisticated radar systems known to mankind—and to do so in a way that aroused no suspicion from anyone until it was far too late.

It's with these thoughts banging around in my head that I finally nod off. But it's a brief and unsatisfactory nap. One where I feel suspended between sleep and wakefulness, and I jolt awake because in my dream I kick a kerb and stumble, almost falling, leaving me with a strange sensation in my left big toe and no sense of balance.

* * *

There is something relentlessly barren about the far reaches of Western Australia. The dirt is red, the vegetation sparse and the sky seems to stretch to infinity. I struggle to believe this place and the Sydney I left a few hours ago are part of the same country. Each living thing, animal or plant is a testament to fortitude and persistence.

The air force base is just a few windswept huts. No doubt one day the earth will reclaim what is rightfully its own and the mark of man will be blown away. If you ever think humanity has dominion over the earth, pop out to the desert some time—that should help convince you that we're really only a temporary stain on the face of the planet.

The long grey landing strip was built in World War II when the whole country was paranoid about those deadly Japs sweeping down over the horizon and invading our lucky country. Today, the enemy is far more ill-defined, probably deadlier, and coming at you from all directions.

After the cool interior of the aircraft, it's a rough return to the land of the living. There is a piercing quality to the midday sun, penetrating my sunglasses to launch itself into the back of my eyeballs, making me blink, raise my arm and take an involuntary half a step backwards as if warding off an unprovoked aggressor. At the bottom of the stairs waiting to greet me is a severe-looking gentleman in an air force uniform. He's also wearing a cap with the RAAF logo and those black mirrored sunglasses that make me think of a redneck cop.

No salute is offered by either of us. Any rank I once had has long been swept away. Technically, I am now a civilian, so he thrusts out a hand and introduces himself as Colonel James Summers, the commanding officer guiding the search.

'What's the latest, Colonel?' I enquire. 'Any sign of the A330?'

'Not a skerrick, I'm afraid. We've had four P-3s up since dawn. The navy are out there as well and the coast guard has been flying its planes and drones too. I would estimate we've looked at 5000-square kilometres of ocean. Not a thing. I know it's early days, but if I had to bet on it I would say it's not out there. Or, if it is, it's not where we're looking. We'll keep expanding the range. It has to be somewhere.'

Despite the colonel's confidence, the uneasy feeling in my gut is starting to gnaw a little harder. The feeling that this is not a tragic accident; that it's not something exploding by mistake in the cargo hold, or some faulty ten-cent door seal blowing out and bringing down a plane. A conclusion is building. Somehow, someone has taken control of this aircraft and disappeared it, as well as the 245 people on board. And anyone who can make an A330 disappear without a trace is going to be terrifyingly smart and utterly ruthless. Not a good combination.

I walk into one of the bigger buildings on the base to find it's only the top deck of a far larger complex, most of which has been dug deep into the desert floor. I have to say I'm impressed—even I didn't know this stuff was out here.

The colonel and I take a steel-doored elevator trip down one level. When the doors open I am confronted with a square-shaped room, perhaps 50 metres by 50 metres. There are four people in here, but there is the most fantastical array of computer technology I have ever seen. One wall is taken up with an enormous video screen that shows the positions of all the aircraft currently searching for the Garuda. Off to the sides are separate screens showing live feeds of what those aircraft are seeing—which so far reveals the same large, empty grey sea.

Summers points the way to a door at the other end of the room.

'In here. There's a phone call for you.'

It's Bob. And not only can I hear him, I can see him sitting behind his desk in Sydney. He appears not to have moved in the last six hours.

'What's happening over there, Ted? Anything new to report?'

'I've just landed, but it doesn't look too promising. I'm sure you've seen the latest. Lots of planes looking at lots of ocean and seeing nothing that resembles a broken Garuda. What have you heard?'

'Only that it gets more mysterious. We've been digging

deeper into the radar signals. They reveal that the Garuda goes off the chart. The radar responder just drops out. You have seen it yourself. This could be because the thing has suffered a catastrophic failure, or because someone has switched it off.'

Transponders, I remember from my flying days, are easy to turn off and often are for all sorts of reasons, many not nefarious. If a pilot is sitting at the gate at Sydney Airport, there is no need to have your transponder turned on. You can safely assume everyone knows where you are. It's switched on again when taxiing out to take off and switched off again when you dock again at the other end. So, if someone has done it at 38,000 feet, that is worrying.

'It's too early to be definitive,' Bob continued, 'but Global-sat, one of the private operators, had some of its hardware pretty close overhead at the relevant time. Its reading shows just the one ping about nine minutes after the Garuda fell off the radar 100 kilometres due north of its last reported position. Now, there is no certainty this is our plane. The technology isn't that specific. We can't even be sure it's an aircraft. It just tells us an object of some sort was in that area, flying anywhere between 20,000 and 55,000 feet. But there was no other traffic we could pinpoint in that area at the time.'

'And that's it?'

'I'm afraid so.'

I sigh. 'It's not much to go on. And what does it really tell us? That maybe it turned due north the moment after it vanished from the screens? Then what? Maybe it turned due south after that. Maybe west, maybe east. Maybe anywhere.'

The pained look on Bob's face 4000 kilometres away tells its own story. He leans back into his big leather chair, pushes both his hands through his hair and groans.

'What else are we doing?' I ask.

'Every piece of satellite information we can get our hands on is being scrutinised and scrutinised again. The Indonesians are sending down their hardware. We have offers of help from the Americans, the Japanese.'

I feel my frustration and anger growing, but I do my best not to let Bob see that I think he is playing this all wrong.

'Bob, it's not out there,' I say in a calm voice. 'It's gone elsewhere and far away. We are wasting time looking for something that's not there. I know that radar hit is the plane we are looking for. So we need to be looking at the pilots, crew, the passengers, the airline, even the baggage handlers at bloody Sydney.'

'Ted, all that stuff is beginning. It just takes time. So while we're waiting, and while the odds still tell us the most likely explanation is the simplest—that it crashed—our efforts need to be directed to finding it.'

I don't know what to do here. I finished the call with Bob and return to the square-shaped control room. The official part of the operation is swirling around me, the search-and-rescue phase, but as I told Bob I'll be stunned if that finds anything. This is not an accident, which means my job isn't here. My job exists in the cracks between the official world and the criminal one. And that's where the plane now lives.

My problem now is the lack of intel. A quick stocktake tells me: we don't know where the aircraft is; we don't know why it's disappeared; despite my gut feeling, we don't know whether it's been stolen or crashed; and if it has been stolen, we don't know by who or why.

That's a lot of stuff not to know when you're trying to figure out whether 245 people are still alive.

If one thing is clear, however, it's that the best place to start looking is in Indonesia. But that's tricky as well. The Indonesians aren't going to want me pitching up on their doorstep. Australia and Indonesia are nominally friends these days, but it doesn't mean they appreciate someone like me showing up for an unescorted and unannounced look around. The idea doesn't thrill me, either. I will have to travel with no gun, no backup, and will probably be abandoned by my own people if things go horribly wrong. But them's the rules. I prefer working alone, but it does carry the odd risk.

It's the pilot's wife I really want to start with. The airline industry isn't keen on talking about pilot suicide, but it happens and it is one of the live options to me. The bigger question is: if he has topped himself, has he done it because of his own demons or has someone else inspired him to do it? Possibly by promising a glorious afterlife romping around with 72 virgins . . . So, I need to know a lot more about Notonegro. After all, the easiest way to get to an aircraft is to get to its pilot.

Bob will be cautious about it, especially as he is clinging on to a belief that it's all one big accident. I contemplate not telling him, but I need that nice private plane to get me down to Perth, then on to a commercial flight to Jakarta. This is not a trip for the company jet. I'll need to stay off the Indonesian radar as much as possible and there's nothing that says 'Hello, I'm here' quite like turning up in the Gulfstream.

Bob takes a little convincing when I call him back. He wants me to hang around a bit longer until the wreckage starts to surface. But I start with the premise that there is nothing for me to do here in the wastelands of Western Australia and I slowly turn him around. I tell him at this point we have to play the odds. If this really is some vast conspiracy then the chances are that the pilot or the co-pilot had some say in it. If I'm wrong, and the plane has buried itself somewhere in the Indian Ocean, well, what's the loss?

'But what are you going to do?' Bob asks. 'Turn up at the grieving widow's house? Knock on the front door and ask if her husband is in cahoots with international terrorists?'

'That will be my starting point, but I hope to develop my theory from there. I know, it's a long shot, but what do you call sitting here in the fucking desert waiting for rain?'

With that, he gives his assent and I am back on the Gulfstream heading south to Perth. Bob has promised to find me a seat on the next available flight out of Perth to Jakarta. It looks like there is one at 7 p.m. Perth time, which means I should just be able to get there in time. Then it's off to the teeming, chaotic city of Jakarta. A place where I had never had very much luck.

5

Jakarta is not the place to go if you want a bit of peace and quiet. More than ten million people live here and it feels as if at any given moment around half of them are trying to share the same road space as you. The nearly five-hour flight from Perth, though, is pleasantly quiet. It's a half-empty plane and I have managed to secure three seats in economy to myself. A rare luxury.

I try not to take too much notice that I'm travelling on a Garuda plane. I try not to think of words such as 'omen' or phrases such as 'lightning striking twice'. But I had no choice. The Garuda was the first scheduled flight to Jakarta after I made it to Perth and the only one to fly direct to Jakarta. I try to sleep, but my brain is buzzing. It's the adrenalin rush of the step into the unknown. It's like jumping out of a plane, but with the added thrill of knowing there is a larger than usual chance that someone has been hacking away at your parachute with a Stanley knife before you launch yourself into the void.

But this is what I do. Nothing beats the unknowable. Nothing beats being unaware of what is coming around the next corner—even if it is a bloke with a gun and bad attitude. Boredom is bad for me. I look for my fun in other ways, occasionally drinking ways, and that never ends well.

It's 9.30 p.m. local time when we touch down at Jakarta's Soekarno-Hatta International Airport. I'm doing my best to look inconspicuous, which is not that easy when you're a shade over six foot four inches. I walk with the other Australians from the plane, trying to stay close enough to make it look like I could be part of a group, but not so close that they take me for a pervert or a thief.

Back in Perth Airport I had a costume change. I wanted to look less like a potential drug smuggler so I picked up some conservative chino pants, a long-sleeve blue polo shirt, a plain lime-green jumper and some lovely tan shoes with those tassels on them. Clearly this is an outfit I would normally vomit over rather than parade in public, but so be it. Such are the sacrifices you make in the defence of your nation. I bought a small suitcase and another change of clothes. This is my version of being undercover.

I needed the suitcase as there was no way I was abandoning my beloved leather jacket. But, more importantly, nothing alerts your average customs official to something odd about you than trying to get into their country with no luggage. I didn't really want to end up having to explain myself to an over-inquisitive official and end up on the

Indonesian equivalent of *Border Patrol*. I think we all know that this a big no-no in my line of work.

I progress through customs with no drama. A little man behind a desk takes my passport, which is under the name of Sean Docherty, and waves me into the country. And, by the way, it's not accurate to say I'm travelling under a false passport as it came off the official government printing press, just like all the others I own. The better news is that it comes with another matching government Visa card. I always like to give that a bit of bash if I can. I had left all indications of my true identity back in the government jet; I didn't want to be searched by customs and have them finding how I prefer to travel with multiple personalities.

I emerge from the airport into the drenching humidity. Even well into the evening the temperature is above 30 and the moisture settles on you like a second skin. Jakarta is not a lovely city. Tourists here are sparse, but expats are everywhere. There are quite a few Australians who work and live in this monstrous city. The money is good and, like many other third world cities, those of a certain disposition can indulge their colonial-master fantasies by riding roughshod over the poverty-stricken masses that cram into every space Jakarta has to offer. They spend their weekends in their little expat enclaves having dinner with each other. Or they play golf at some of the city's beautifully manicured golf courses, throwing out a few rupiahs here and there to pay for someone else to carry golf clubs worth more than these servants will see in a decade. They play footy and cricket against each other, drink and eat with each other, have local drivers and maids. Some of the blokes will have local girlfriends. Some acknowledged, some not. In some ways, it's probably like living a privileged existence in Australia a century ago.

There's a peculiar and unlovely tang to the air tonight. Some expats call this place the Big Durian in tribute to the world's worst-smelling fruit, which doubles as a local delicacy. Like Jakarta, I guess, it's a bit of an acquired taste. The ever-present clove cigarette, permanently attached to millions of mouths, the fuel of fleets of taxis and cars with poor combustion belching fumes into the air, and the canals built by the long-departed Dutch oppressors that have been turned into open sewers all lend to the odour of Jakarta being more or less out of control. But it does give the joint a bit of an edge. Like you are leaving one world—a safe, knowable, friendly place—and entering another, a danger-ous, swirling mess where anything is possible.

In theory, none of the locals should know I'm here. But neither are they daft. It wouldn't take a lot of thought for them to imagine that we might send someone up to have a poke around. The early thoughts in officialdom may still be leaning towards this all being one big accident, but they must know we are going to be suspicious of the airline, the pilots, the passengers on the missing plane. Given most of the principal players have direct links to Indonesia, there is a fair chance that whatever answers there are to explain this mystery will be found here. The fact that there is possibly 154 dead Australians means they also know we're not going to leave it to them to discover what happened.

I have no doubt they will have people posted at the airport looking for suspicious types. People like me. Lone travellers, speaking to no one, travelling light and appearing to be in a hurry. My build and military haircut may not help either, but I didn't have time to grow my hair before I left.

Still, I'm hoping my faux-business attire is mild enough to let me escape any close scrutiny. My Sean Docherty passport is also clean, but not too clean. Its history will show a trip to Los Angeles two years ago and a visit to Singapore six months ago. Not that I took either of these journeys, but someone, somewhere, was kind enough to enter them into a computer. I am the ghost in the machine.

The military goons dotted around the airport with machine guns casually hanging off shoulders don't give me a second look as I stroll towards the exit. But they are not the ones I'm worried about.

Eventually I emerge into the Jakarta night. I join the queue for the taxis. I plan to head for the Marriott. It was a place that was blown up in 2003 and then again in 2009, so on the assumption that lightning won't strike three times I settle on going there. It's also not too far from the Australian Embassy in case I need to make a quick departure or require refuge. It's not the hotel I told customs I was staying at, but if they ever come looking for me it won't take too long to unravel that tiny ruse. Still, as I have discovered in this game over the years, sometimes a matter of seconds really does count.

It's while waiting in that long line of tired travellers that I become aware of an Indonesian man leaning against the wall near one of the airport's exit doors, newspaper in hand. He wasn't there a moment ago and I can see no reason he should be there now. He is dressed in the local garb—long linen trousers and a short-sleeved shirt. He has no baggage and he has no one with him. I try to keep an eye on him without looking at him, but I get the sense he's trying to do the same to me.

The taxi crowd shuffles slowly forwards, doing its usual impersonation of an asthmatic caterpillar. The bloke by the door doesn't move. Finally, it's my turn and I prepare to jump in the waiting Bluebird taxi.

From behind I hear a voice. An American accent.

'Buddy, where you off to?'

I look around. A tall, rake-thin man. Blond hair. Maybe late thirties, wearing a crumpled linen suit. I comfort myself with the thought that at least I'm not being picked up by the Indonesian cops. But it's worrying that I hadn't already noticed him waiting in the taxi queue.

'Hotel' is my one-word answer. He may be harmless, but I'm not here to have long conversations or make new friends.

'Yeah, but which one? Maybe we can share a cab. This heat is killing me.'

In the background, I can see the bloke who first grabbed my attention taking an intense interest in this conversation. He has come up out of his slouch against the wall, newspaper down by his side.

'Sorry, I'm at a different place,' I shout and jump in the back seat and slam the door.

I hear a plaintive 'Fella, but I didn't say . . .' through the window as the driver takes off like every other Indonesian driver: at high speed and with little regard for whoever else may be wanting to share our island of tarmac. But as we bolt into the traffic, I twist around in my seat trying to spot my shadow. He's lost in the crowd. I have been in Indonesia for about half an hour, but there is a strong possibility they already know I'm here. Maybe not who I am, but certainly what I represent. A foreign agent landed in their country unannounced and is here to have a poke around in their backyard. Clearly my powers of disguise aren't as good as I thought.

The taxi driver, talking on his phone, lighting a cigarette and changing the radio station simultaneously as he drives, looks around to me in the back seat and asks, 'Where to?' as we rocket out of the airport and onto the highway. I'm starting to think just getting into the centre of Jakarta is going to be the most dangerous part of my mission.

'Marriott,' I reply. 'And can you please watch where the fuck you're going?'

* * *

Even at this time of night, it will take a good 45 minutes to get to the Marriott, so I settle into the journey, try to tune out the awful Indonesian pop music belting out from the tinny speakers, and begin to figure out what is going to happen next. When we swing past the enormous Merdeka Square with the 132-metre-high National Monument poking into the permanent smog and lit up against the darkness, I know I'm getting close to my destination.

I'm not being followed. Paranoia can help keep me on edge, but it can't stop me doing what I need to otherwise I'll never leave the hotel. Still, I find it a useful emotion. As long as I keep thinking they're all out to get me, I won't be disappointed when it turns out to be true. It's also better than the alternative: *not* being paranoid. Feeling comfortable and believing everything is under control can only lead to a sense of complacency, swiftly followed by crushing failure.

The Marriott is more heavily fortified these days. Getting bombed twice will do that to you, I suppose. There are now blast walls and gates with armed security guards holding those mirrors that look under your car. There are sniffer dogs on patrol and you have to show ID before you're allowed in. I suspect if you weren't nervous before you checked in, you certainly would be by the time you had been through all this rigmarole.

I pay the cab driver, thanking him for getting me here in one piece, despite the best efforts of most of Jakarta's drivers to run him off the road. Unusually, we have made it this far without having to sling one of the local cops a few thousand rupiah just to use a slip road, make a U-turn, or sometimes just turn a corner. Maybe my luck is on the improve.

I had made a call from the airport to book in at the hotel, figuring it would help smooth my way through security if they already had my name on file. Like every other five-star place, the Marriott likes to project an air of calm superiority. This extends to the staff, who seem to believe 'unflappable' is the best adjective to describe their approach to the job. You could ask them to send a sheep, three bottles of gin and the *Sex and the City* box set to your room and they would undoubtedly reply, 'Yes, sir, we'll see what we can do. White sheep or black sheep?'

The immaculately groomed Indonesian woman standing behind the check-in counter greets me with the kind of smile I would expect from my mother if I hadn't seen her in a decade. Clearly, my checking-in is the highlight of her day.

'Sean Docherty,' I say cheerfully. 'Just checking in.'

'Mr Docherty,' she effuses in lightly accented English. 'Welcome to the Marriott and to Jakarta. I do hope you enjoy your stay with us. Is this your first time here?'

'Yes, to both,' I say. It's certainly the first time I have been here as Sean Docherty.

'Well, you are very welcome and I hope you enjoy your stay. You will let us know if there is anything we can do for you. Now, how many nights will you be staying?'

It's a good question. In an ideal world, it will just be the one, but there are so many things I don't yet know that it's hard to predict how long I'll need.

'Three,' I say, figuring if I'm here more than two I will probably be either dead or locked up somewhere. 'Is it too late to get something to eat?' It's now after eleven and I'm starting to feel the onset of hunger.

'Not at all, sir. The restaurant has just closed for the evening, but room service runs 24 hours. You will find the menu in your room.'

As I leave, I notice a pile of *Jakarta Post*s lying on the marble top with the headline *Mystery of Missing Garuda*. I snaffle a copy and head up to my room.

6

The room is on the fourteenth floor and looks out over the front of the hotel, but apart from that it's the usual bland, anonymous room with the ghosts of its thousands of previous inhabitants assiduously wiped away.

I figure I better check in with Bob. It's after three in the morning in Australia, but there is every chance he will still be sitting at that desk where I left him nearly a full day ago. I fetch the iPad from the suitcase and turn it on, perform the eye security check, select the secure transmission channel, and press the name *Bob Sorensen*.

The link bounces off one of our satellites in the heavens and I am soon staring at Bob. He is still in that chair, although he appears to have changed suits, so I assume he has been home in the last few hours. This one looks charcoal with a hint of chalk lines, and he is wearing a red tie. He seems grumpy.

'Where have you been?' he demands. 'I've been trying to reach you for the last hour.'

'Lovely to see you too, Bob. Just got here. An hour ago I was standing in the taxi rank at the airport. I didn't think whipping out an advanced piece of telecommunications equipment was the way to go. Sorry about that, chief.'

'Don't be a smartarse. Another plane has fallen off the radar. We don't know what to think. It's possibly a co-incidence, more probably it's not. All I am asking you to do is keep an open mind at this stage. Ted, you know this: there are 100,000 commercial flights every day around the world. When you think about it, it's not even that much of a stretch to believe that two of them could crash on the same day.'

There is a momentary silence as I try to take this in. I understand the words Bob has just used but for some reason my brain won't accept their meaning or his rationalisation.

'What are you telling me?'

'A Lufthansa A340 flying between Munich and Singapore has disappeared. Somewhere near the border between Turkey and Iraq. As with the Garuda, everything seemed normal right up until the point it wasn't. Communications with traffic control. Normal. Transponders. Normal. Then nothing. Three hundred and three people just gone and no evidence left about what might have happened.'

Apart from two missing planes, I think to myself. But instead I just ask, 'When did it disappear?'

'I found out about 90 minutes ago. It went AWOL about fifteen minutes before that.'

'Has anyone claimed any responsibility for this? I hear what you are saying about keeping an open mind, but let's be realistic. This is no coincidence.'

'Nope, no one has owned up. Which is one of the reasons why we're not ruling out that it's all a coincidence.

Bob's tone is puzzling me. I understand the risks of leaping to obvious conclusions, but sometimes there are reasons the conclusions are obvious.

'I don't buy it,' I say. 'Everything is pointing to someone systematically taking planes out the sky. We don't know why. We don't know who. We don't know how. And we don't know if it will happen again. So unless we start to get serious about finding out who is behind it, more are bound to go.'

'We need to keep a level head and keep all options on the table, Ted,' Bob says sharply. 'Planes have been known to go missing before. You're there because we need some eyes on the ground. As I said, I'm not ruling anything in or out at this stage. We need to remain calm and rational. What do you want to do? Shut down the global aviation industry? The economic consequences of that would be appalling.'

'But imagine all the greenhouse gases we could save.'

'Don't be glib,' says Bob, taking off his glasses to rub his eyes, something he always does when he's feeling the stress of the moment and that makes him look about ten years older.

'I'm not talking about shutting the whole thing down,' I reply. 'That's the sort of cause and effect the people behind this would be aiming for. For the West to look weak and inept. But you can't seriously be saying this is a coincidence. Bob, it's not. And don't tell me the Yanks are sitting idly by, watching this unfold. I'd have thought they would be big-footing everyone and everything in sight by now.'

'Well, there are rumblings the agency isn't buying the official line and has gone stratospheric on this one,' Bob admits. 'They have field agents in every city across South-East Asia, the Middle East and Europe investigating who might be responsible. They think all those recently vacated cells out at Guantanamo are about to be filled again.'

'Fucking marvellous,' I say.

When the CIA is in this sort of mood it does nobody any good. Let's just say they don't tend towards subtlety. They will kick down any doors, smash as many heads, and threaten as many women and kids as they deem necessary to get the job done.

Look. It's a bad world. I know that. And I'm not adverse to a bit of the old ultra-violence if the situation demands it. But I don't think it should be the first sock out of the drawer—first time, every time. There's still a lot to be said for a more sophisticated approach. Occasionally you can do better by knocking on the door rather than kicking it down.

'What do you want me to do over here? Or is there even any point in me staying? Because if you really think those planes have crashed, that it's all an accident, why not leave it up to the experts and I'll catch the next flight home? Wouldn't mind a snooze in my own bed tonight.'

Even as I say the words I know I am not going anywhere— not yet. It's just a matter of office politics. A calm Bob is more pliable than an angry Bob.

'You stay, Ted,' the boss says. 'There has to be at least part of the answer in Indonesia. They have a dodgy safety record, after all. Remember the AirAsia plane that went down a few years back flying from Surabaya to Singapore? One hundred and sixty-two souls were lost that day. So it's not like it hasn't happened before . . .'

'Okay. Have we found out anything more about the pilots or the passengers?'

'Bits and pieces. A few anomalies, possibly. I'm sending you the file.'

'Right. I'll let you know what I find.'

And with that, Bob hangs up.

7

I open the file called *Garuda5*. It's a run-down on every-thing our agency has discovered in the last 24 hours about everyone on board the missing plane. But before I start to read it, I realise those hunger pangs need to be sated and an offering made to the god of food. I order a nasi goreng from room service and take a lemonade from the minibar. After I've eaten, I plan to have a snoop around the new widow's place before the sun starts to rise at five. There's a lot to be done over the next few hours, but I need the strength that a decent plate of food will provide.

While I wait for the steaming plate of rice to arrive, I dive back into the file. At the top of my list of inter-ested and interesting parties is Captain Soraya Notonegro. Most of what is in the file I already know from the earlier briefing. He is ex-air force, a long-serving Garuda pilot, seen as reliable and relatively clean. Married, but no mention of any children. But a few barnacles have since been added to the captain's hull. There is a rumour of an affair with a much younger cabin attendant. He'd had an official reprimand for turning up for work with a hangover eighteen months ago and there are suggestions he owed money to a gambling syndicate around the same time. It's something to keep in mind.

Information is still scarce on the co-pilot, Rizky Dayak. As far as we know, he was conscientious, hard-working, something of a rising star in the aviation world. Engaged to be married. He was religious and was a regular at his local mosque, a moderate place where the imam regularly spoke out against the evils of extremism. The place had been bombed more than once.

The anomalies Bob had spoken about seemed to live in the passports of two passengers: it looked like they had been stolen. They had been taken in Hong Kong, but the owners, one Italian, one Spanish, hadn't discovered the theft until a few hours ago. This explained why the passengers had slipped through the net.

The trade in stolen passports and identity documents is enormous in South-East Asia and around the world. The file told me Interpol has a lost and stolen passport database with 40 million entries. Of course, most airports don't bother to consult it, making it easier for the bad guys to avoid detection. The 9/11 terrorists got as far as they did partly because of stolen passports.

There are plenty of others to whom a clean passport is a valuable possession. Think of drug smugglers, people smugglers and your general illegal immigrants. It's not just terrorists who find them handy. A new passport is a new identity, at least for a while, and it can unlock the front door of most countries.

As I'm reading the file, there's a sharp knock at the door. I momentarily move into alert mode, then remember the nasi goreng. Still, I check the room's spyhole before opening the door, and I only let the young man, wearing a brown and white uniform, into the room when I spot his delivery cart and my mouth starts to water.

I devour the meal. Say what you like about Indonesians but they do wonderful things with a packet of rice and a fried egg. After eating, I decide it's time to get moving. It's now pushing one in the morning. The night is heading into its quietest hours—always a good time for anyone whose job relies on a bit of snooping around.

After a shower to freshen up and wipe away the grime of my long day, I change out of my faux businessman clothes into something a little more me. Jeans and a white T-shirt. It's as close to a uniform as I've got. My trusty leather jacket is stuffed at the bottom of my backpack, which is the only thing I am taking with me on this excursion, along with my mobile, the tablet, a wallet and my dodgy passport. Nothing can be left behind that will identify me or my mission in Jakarta.

Without a gun, however, I've nothing else to protect me apart from my wits and a trust in good luck. It's not enough. The bigger bag with the rest of my clothes is left behind and as I set out the door I wonder whether I will be back to pick it up.

* * *

Back into the hot Jakarta night. After the artificial cool of the hotel, stepping out feels like getting slapped around the head with warm, wet towels. I don't know how anyone can stand living here.

It's past midnight by now, but the place is still bustling. There's a line of taxis waiting outside the hotel perimeter security. I give the driver the address in Tangerang I saw in the *Garuda5* file. It's a suburb west of here, not too far from the airport—handy for a pilot and home to Notonegro.

His place is a residential tower block attached to a shopping mall, so getting in and out unseen won't be easy. But the mall may provide an element of cover that I can use. I will need as much help as possible as I'll almost certainly be the only white man strolling these suburban streets. I have to also assume there will be at least a token security presence in the apartment block itself. This shouldn't provide too much of a problem. Not that I want to blow my own trumpet too much but if I can't outwit a couple of pretend Indonesian cops then I should probably start looking for a new career. The bigger question will be whether the real Indonesian cops and military have beaten me to the punch.

One of the advantages of the time of night is that even if they have already paid Mrs Notonegro a visit, they may well have packed up and left for the day. Or taken her to some airless room somewhere for questioning. Either way, it leaves me a small window of opportunity to try to find a way inside.

As I sit in the back of the cab, I'm still worried about the possibility of being followed. That the bloke I spotted back at the airport was some sort of Indonesian spook who had taken me for what I am and was keeping an eye on me. But I try to park my paranoia for a moment and concentrate on the task at hand. The traffic thins as we head out into the suburbs, and I haven't see anything so far to cause me any concern. Anyway, I figure if someone really is following me, I will find out soon enough. Possibly via some blunt-force trauma to the back of the head.

I have the driver stop a block short of the Tangerang City Mall. The building is in darkness except for the neon sign on the roof. The driver gives me a wary look as I pay the fare. I suspect he hasn't dropped too many tourists off in these parts, and certainly not in the night's dangerous hours. He probably thinks I'm up to no good and I give him an extra tip to buy my way into his good graces, not to mention his silence.

The entrance to the apartment block is about 300 metres away. From where I'm standing, it's around the other side of the mall. Getting inside is going to be tricky, but this kind of thing is never easy in a part of the world where you're a stranger. You don't know the lay of the land, you can trust no one, and you know that unless you're extremely careful you're going to stick out as something foreign and therefore something suspicious. Especially out here. This is what passes for regular suburban Jakarta. This is not a place where the expats live; I would be surprised if this place sees many tourists.

It's not all bad, though. The streets are utterly quiet as I skirt through the shadows. When I reach the start of the road leading to the apartment tower entrance, I find a small footpath running alongside it. It's all dark and dingy and dotted every few metres with a series of giant concrete columns holding up the shopping mall. The road is about 40-metres long and with some discrete manoeuvring I find myself in sight of the tower block's front door. It pokes 30-odd stories into the sky. The apartment I am looking for is on the fourteenth level.

The dirty yellow light from the lobby spills out into the darkness, chopped up by the slowly spinning revolving door that serves as the entrance. I can see a single security guard sitting behind a desk, but there appears to be no police presence or indication of military forces inside and no official-looking vehicles on the street.

I wait. It's now pushing 2 a.m. I estimate dawn is still three hours away—not a lot of time, but enough for what I need to do. Break in to the Notonegro abode, wake up the wife is she is still around, and if not, have a scout around and try to find something that tells me why an airline captain would either deliberately disappear or destroy his plane, and get the hell out of there.

The guard is doing what guards all over the world do at 2 a.m.: reading a newspaper, intermittently checking his phone and looking as bored and lonely as any worker on a midnight-to-dawn shift. He's behind a curved wooden desk, visible from the waist up. I keep watch for nearly an hour, and just as I'm starting to consider clearing that desk myself, he abruptly stands, leaves the desk, turns left and disappears into a corridor. He has tucked the newspaper under his right arm. He's going to the toilet, and given he has taken some reading material with him I assume it's not just for a quick piss.

I cover the 40 metres into the lobby quickly, ease through the revolving door and find myself in front of a bank of four elevators. Stabbing the up button in repeated succession brings the door on the far left to life and I jump inside.

I take the lift to level fifteen. From there I will figure out if I can find a discreet way back to the apartment. My paranoia is in full bloom now. While there has been no sign of any Indonesian security forces so far, I don't want to emerge from the lift into level fourteen only to be confronted by a group of men with large guns and not have a sensible explanation for being there.

On fifteen, all is quiet. I walk out into a corridor. The floor is tiled the colour of dark sand, like where the ocean meets land, and the apartment doors seem to be made of the same type of material. Big, wooden, double affairs with old-fashioned, pull-down handles that open inwards. The doors are key operated, not electronic, which will also make it simpler to break in if the wife isn't home.

At the end of the corridor is a green door with the word *Keluar* in a neon box above it. Exit. It's the door to the stairs. The handle creaks but the door opens. Inside, it is pitch black. I carefully guide myself down the stairs using the feel of the handrail. I spot the door to level fourteen by the light from the corridor seeping beneath the crack. I'm about to ease it open when a voice behind me whispers, 'Not so fast, buddy.'

I freeze. The words are uttered in such a low tone I can't tell the accent. I'm still staring at the door, but I don't feel a gun in my back or in my ear, which doesn't mean there's not one handy. The voice comes again.

'It's okay, I'm a friendly,' and this time I detect an American accent. 'Turn around.'

As I turn, my new friend opens the door to the corridor and allows light into the dark stairwell. I assume he has already checked to make sure there are no unfriendly types waiting out there. I am confronted with a face I have seen before but for a moment can't place where. Then it comes to me. The American who wanted to share my taxi from the airport.

'Hello again,' I say.

'This would have been much easier if you'd let me share that cab, you rude asshole.'

The accent is from somewhere in the north of the States. Boston, maybe. He sounds like a younger version of the former US Secretary of State John Kerry. You know he's American, but he's still trying to hang on to some of those pre-revolutionary British vowels.

'I was wondering when I'd bump into you again, Ted,' he says.

It's a worry that he knows who I am. He's certainly better briefed than I am. I haven't a clue who he is, beyond the likelihood that he works for the CIA.

'Yes, well, here I am. Nice of you to wait for me. But I prefer to work by myself, so I'll be seeing you . . .'

'I'd heard you were an arrogant shit. Rude *and* arrogant. Your typical *Ossie*.'

'Coming from a Yank, I won't take that insult too seriously,' I reply. 'You know that whole theory of American exceptionalism is something only Americans believe. The rest of the planet thinks you're a bunch of pricks.'

This seems a strange time to be discussing international relations. Especially when it's happening between two blokes talking in whispers, camped half in, half out of a darkened stairwell in the backblocks of Jakarta, with two aeroplanes still missing somewhere in the world.

Maybe it's time to exhibit a bit more professionalism. I mean, we are on the same side . . . technically.

'Look,' I say, 'who the fuck are you? And what are you doing here?' I open the door and walk fully into the well-lit corridor, expecting him to follow me, which he does. In keeping with his rakish frame, he has a razor-sharp nose, prominent cheekbones and a chin that tapers to a point. But there's something of a crumpled look to him. He's wearing dark linen trousers with a long-sleeved dark linen shirt.

'Alan Miller is my name. And I suspect I'm here for the same reason you are. To get into the Notonegros' apartment and see if I can find anything useful.'

'Been here long?'

'A couple of hours. When I arrived the military was all over the place, but I reckon they have now snatched the good widow and taken her away. There's nobody outside the door anymore, so I think it's time for a quick peek. You coming? It's now or never. I don't know when the locals will come back.'

I decide to try to drag more information out of him before I join whatever plan he thinks he is about to execute.

'What's your thinking about these planes? My people are still not ruling out the whole accident and coincidence theory.'

'Really?' He seems surprised. 'And is that what you think, Ted? Because if it is, then why are you here about to commit a burglary on the home of the nice woman who has just lost her husband in a terrible plane crash?'

'Look, I didn't say I was buying into the theory, just that it was one certain people in my organisation are clinging onto. My question to you is: what is your lot's current operational theory?'

Miller suddenly looks exasperated.

'Can we do this later, Ted? We're running out of time here. But, yes, we are thinking, like you, that there are no coincidences this big. Okay?'

'Fine, sure.' I nod down the corridor. 'What's your plan?'

'Just the usual. Knock on the door. Ask if we can come in. The American way.'

'I thought the American way was to kick the door down, shoot everyone in sight, then ask if you could come in?'

'Do you have a weapon?'

I'm embarrassed. Like a kid realising it isn't cool to be taking your teddy bear on a school camp. I try to bluff it out.

'Don't need one, mate. Got this under control.'

Miller gives me an incredulous look. One that seems to be saying, 'These Aussies are fucking amateurs.'

'Fine. But if the shooting starts, don't get in my way, and don't use me as your shield.'

We walk down the corridor. It's about 30 metres long, doors sprinkled on both sides. The only cover—and that is a generous term—is the large terracotta pots that break up the gaps between the doors. I feel horribly exposed. It will take just one person to open a door, spot a couple of white guys who clearly don't belong here, and the whole jig will be up.

The apartment we are aiming for is No. 1414. It's about halfway along. There's no point in trying to hide behind terracotta pots, so it's just a quick, soundless march to the double doors. Fingers crossed, hearts in mouth.

Miller gives the urgent whisper: 'Keep an eye out. I'll get us in.'

He begins fiddling with the old-style lock. He has a couple of picks in his hand and he's jiggling about. A minute later I hear the click of the lock and the door swings open. It's perhaps not the first time Miller has broken into a home.

At first, there's nothing to see. It's like standing at the opening of a cave not knowing if the bear is still at home. There are no lights on in the entrance hall, although a dirty-orange glow is drifting in through some open curtains in what is presumably the lounge room. The floor is made up of the same tiles as the outside corridor. The place feels abandoned.

Miller takes the lead, gun arm extended, and we quietly enter. I pull the heavy door closed behind me. The foyer opens out into a living area. There is a big television hanging on the nearest wall facing a well-used couch in the middle of the room, an aged recliner chair with cracked imitation leather cushions beside it. I take it to be Notonegro's favourite chair, where he kicks back, puts up his feet and relaxes after a hard day's piloting.

Just to the left of the living area is a local Javanese dining table with four chairs. Off to the left is a small, narrow kitchen. A sideboard under the window with family pictures on it. I had seen a small headshot of Notonegro in the file, but it must have been taken for his security pass or passport.

It was a serious, dark, unsmiling face of a man in his late forties. Black hair, black eyes, neatly trimmed moustache. These photographs are of a younger man dressed in a colourful red jacket with black pants, both adorned with what I assume is a traditional design. There is a matching hat and a long necklace stretching down to his waist. He is standing beside a woman I assume is his wife. Younger, somehow gentle-looking, wearing a matching outfit with a more elaborate headpiece. Make-up that gives her the appearance of being made of porcelain. It's a picture from their wedding day. While the wife looks happy, Notonegro has the same serious, almost sinister expression that he carried many years later to the picture in my file. It seems to me that he is not someone who has enjoyed a sunny disposition through life.

On the far side of the apartment are three closed doors. At a guess, two are bedrooms and the other the bathroom. The room is all very still. The neon glow of the Jakarta lights and the shopping mall falls into the room—we don't have to do anything silly such as switching on a lamp or flicking on a torch. Something that could be noticed by anyone watching from below.

I breathe out for the first time since entering the joint. It's clear nobody is here; what is not so obvious is how long we've got before the boys in blue, black or green come back.

'Okay, what now?' I say to Miller before realising I am starting to treat him as the leader of this impromptu expeditionary force. That is something to avoid. I'm not here as his sidekick. I'm not here for the Americans. I'm here to find out what happened to a bunch of Australians who suddenly disappeared. There are no guarantees that what

Miller wants and what I want will coincide. I still know nothing about this bloke or why he is here.

'You take the door on the right, I'll take the left. But let's not hang around,' Miller says. 'Let's be back on the street before anyone knows we were ever here.'

Again, I wonder how much he knows.

'Any idea what we are looking for?' I ask.

'I guess we'll know when we see it.'

Before I hit my assigned door, I have a quick peek around the rest of the place. The kitchen is too small and too narrow a place for anyone to hide. I rattle through the cupboards; nothing out of place. I approach the bathroom door with a degree more caution. I reach for the handle, knock it down and take a step back as it swings open. Nothing. I step into the doorway. The bathroom is small. There is a toilet, a sink with a vanity unit above it, and a shower stall. It's empty. Another quick rifle, this time through the small cupboard. It is mainly populated by white pill bottles. The labels are in Indonesian and I can't tell what they have been prescribed for, but I can make out 'Notonegro' on many of them.

I move to my designated door. Miller has already disappeared into the other room. I haven't heard any screams or gunshots, so I assume he's fine. My door leads to the main bedroom. I repeat the move from the bathroom and the door creaks open. It is warped at the edges and a spider web of cracks runs from top to bottom. Another victim of Jakarta's punishing humidity. The room is a reasonable size, over twenty square feet. There's a double bed covered in a neat batik quilt, a wardrobe, two bedside tables.

The curtains are pushed back and the window is open to the world outside, bringing the smells of the fetid city into the room.

At first glance there is nothing to note. I rifle through the wardrobe. On one side I find a couple of pilot uniforms, a collection of shirts and trousers, three pairs of shoes and two lots of sandals. On an overhead shelf are towels and sheets. I pat down the clothes, rifle through the uniforms but find nothing that stirs my curiosity. The other side of the wardrobe holds the wife's clothes. I give it the same treatment but again come up empty-handed. Then it's through the bedside tables. Nothing. Under the bed. Dust.

Miller's voice. 'Find anything?'

'No.'

'Well, then, you'd better come in here. It's kinda interesting.'

He is standing inside the doorway to the second bedroom. It has about the same dimensions as the one I have just been in, but there is only one piece of furniture, if that is the correct word, in the room. It's an odd, almost octagonal shape. From where I'm standing, it could be an early-scale model of the Sydney Opera House, around three metres long. It's not a seat or a couch but a kind of model. The back is open and some of a seat is visible. In front of this seat are three blank screens. I turn to Miller.

'Is that . . . ?' I start to say, my voice rising in surprise.

'Yep. It's what it looks like. A homemade flying simulator. Curious, wouldn't you say?'

'I don't know. Maybe he just likes to bring his work home. He could be the dedicated sort, our Notonegro.'

'Shall we turn it on?'

Without waiting for an answer, Miller takes two quick strides to the four-pronged extension cord on the floor and flicks the switch. The three screens inside the console come to life in a flicker of green and black. A multitude of dials below join the party. Closer now, I can see it's a very professional set-up, mirroring the cockpit layout you would find in an Airbus A330. Just like the one Notonegro was flying when he disappeared.

But more interesting are the maps displayed on the screens. His last logged session has the simulator taking off on a Sydney–Jakarta route, but he has also enacted some form of emergency procedure that has listed a bunch of small airports in the Indian Ocean where he could land if things went wrong. One in the Cocos Islands, there is the US base at Diego Garcia, Christmas Island, and even the far-flung destination of Saint Denis near Mauritius, right over the other side of the Indian Ocean.

That would be too easy, though. If he had ended up at one of these places, we would have heard about it by now. They are well-covered, well-connected points on the map. But there are hundreds of other airstrips through Asia where he could have landed. Places devoid of radar and scrutiny. Places where even something as big as an A330 could land and be hidden.

I spot a USB port under the altimeter gauge. This would be where he loads his maps. Thinking there was likely to be a lot more stuff on his hard drive than we could see on the screens, I grab a thumb drive from a side pocket of my backpack and whack it in the slot.

'Hey, what the fuck are you doing?' demands Miller, losing his cheerful demeanour.

'What's it look like? I'm trying to find out what else this fucker might have on here. Okay?'

'No! Did I say you could just charge in there like that? We don't know what we're dealing with here. We could be leaving our fingerprints all over this place. This is supposed to be a "quiet" operation, remember?'

'Fine. But two things. One, you are not my boss, so don't presume you can order me to do anything. Two, there are two fucking planes still missing, so I think the time for caution has passed. What do you think?'

'What I think is you would still be standing in that corridor with your finger up your ass if I wasn't here to get you in. So show a little gratitude to your superiors.'

'Fuck you. You think you're the only one who can pick a lock? I thought you were a little on the slow side, actually. Out of practice?'

There is silence as we both have a go at perfecting our macho stares. I claim a win on points as he mutters: 'Can we just get back to business here? We don't know how long we have got.'

A wash of red and blue decorates the bare white walls of the bedroom. We creep over to the window and, sure enough, it appears the Jakarta police are making their usual low-key entrance. It looks like there are about ten cars down there and some worrying types in black uniforms, black helmets and rather large guns who look poised to storm into the building. It's clearly departure time. We don't want to be caught prowling around the apartment of someone who may be a main suspect in a rather large act of terrorism.

My mind flashes back to my paranoia about being followed out of the airport, then to the cab driver who dropped me over this way. I hope I didn't waste that generous tip. Miller looks at me.

'Seems we're back on the same team. Unless you want to hang around and have a word with the local authorities?'

Not an inviting prospect, all things considered.

'I think I will take my chances with you, if it's all the same.'

He grins and heads for the door. I grab the USB and put it in my pocket, hoping I managed to download something useful, and follow Miller. A pause at the front door, but no sounds are detected. Miller opens it just far enough to poke his head out, declares the coast is clear and bolts towards the fire escape door.

8

I hesitate for one second. Make a quick decision and go in the opposite direction. There is another exit sign at the other end of the corridor, and I figure if the Indonesians do know we are here then they probably know the way we came in. Anyway, I figure it's always harder to find two fugitives than one. If I'm really lucky, they will pick up Miller first and won't bother looking for me.

I hear Miller shout at me from the other end and I reply over my shoulder, 'Hotel, mate, see you there.' I have no doubt he knows where I'm staying. A bit of separation will give me time to stream back to Australia whatever is on this USB before the Americans get a chance to interfere.

I throw open the exit door as a ping sounds from the elevators. As the doors roll back, I hear a lot of loud and excitable Indonesian voices. I don't hang around; I have to keep moving. It's hot, dark and stinking in the stairwell.

Either a sewer has burst or someone has been using the place for toilet practice.

It occurs to me that it could be wise to wait it out in here. But I also don't know how long the police will hang around. Being stuck in here for hours and then making my way out in daylight seems an even riskier proposition. And as I mentioned to Miller, time is not our friend here, and if they do broaden their search of the building to the stairwells, I'll be trapped with nowhere to run.

With this in mind, I make my way down as slowly and quietly as I can manage. All seems still. There are no enquiring voices, no sudden stabs of light to indicate anyone is coming for me. Once I reach the ground floor I come up against the exit door and again consider my options. Heading back out the way I came in is verging on the suicidal. I press my ear to the door, trying to listen for any movement, trying to detect the presence of heavily armed security forces on the other side.

I hear nothing. The stairs keep going down. There must be a basement or a car park down there. It raises at least some possibility of an escape route.

At the bottom of the canyon of stairs, all is still apart from the splashing sound I make as I step into a large puddle, which I'm hoping is water. I grab the handle, gently put my shoulder into the door and try to ease it open. Not much chance of that: it moves with a grind, a screech and a vibration strong enough to rattle my fillings.

Still, there is nowhere else to go. I squeeze through the tiny gap and step cautiously into the car park. A shadow looms from my left and I brace for impact, but all that hits me is a voice.

'Hi, Ted, nice to see you again.' He is breathing heavily. The product of running down fourteen flights of stairs or the stress of the situation. But he is doing his best to project an image of a man fully in control of the situation.

'You bastard, Miller,' I manage. 'You scared the shit out of me. How did you know I'd be here anyway?'

'Where else would you be? I didn't think even you'd be stupid enough to walk into reception to say "g'day" to all the cops walking through the front door. I was just on my way out when I heard you open that door. You really should try and be more subtle. But I guess that's just not your way.'

'So how were you planning on getting out of here?'

'You want my help?' he says with a touch more enjoyment than I think is strictly necessary. 'I thought I'd take a car.'

'Any in particular?'

'The one I came in should do. This way. It may be a bit of a crush, though.'

* * *

We make our way across the car park. All is still quiet. No one is charging down here, guns at the ready, looking for us. I'm starting to think the police's return is just a coincidence and that they have no idea about either of us being in the building. Miller is leading us to a dark corner.

'Our limo for the evening,' he says. 'And our driver.'

It's a silver Toyota Yaris, ten years from new, a little shitbox hatchback, the kind that is everywhere in Jakarta. At least we'll blend in.

'This is Budi,' says Miller indicating to a short man in a light blue shirt in the driver's seat. He doesn't turn around to greet me. 'He helps us out in these parts.'

'Always good to have a little help,' I say. 'But doesn't the ramp to the car park bring us out just past the main entrance? There's a fair chance we'll be spotted. I can't imagine the guards likely to be stationed there will cheerfully wave us through. Even if they don't know we're here, they will be stopping everyone coming and going from the apartment block.'

'We might have to take a few precautions,' Miller says with a small smile.

'Such as?'

'Simple. We are both going to hide in the trunk until we clear this place.'

I lift the boot. It seems cramped in there, especially for two large, unfriendly blokes.

'We're not both going to fit in there.'

'Will you stop whining and get in?'

I do as I'm told, reluctantly, and wonder how I managed to get myself into this position. Inside it's snug and I'm thinking Miller will never fit in here as well when the boot slams shut. Immediately, I feel my anger and humiliation rise as I sense Miller jump in the rear passenger seat and bang the door closed. From the movement in the suspension, I guess he's lying down on the back seat. I understand what he's doing, but it's not making me any happier. I'm trapped in here and have to trust this fuckwit isn't going to dump me in one of the canals that pass for a sewer in this hole and leave the rats to fight over my carcass.

That's if we ever get out of this basement.

The road rises beneath our wheels and I start to fear what is going to happen next. Some light is seeping in through the corroded rubber seals at the back of the Yaris, but I can't see out, and I start banging on the parcel tray above my head, though it seems to be made of steel rather than the usual plastic.

It's apparent we're not going to sneak out of here quietly. Budi takes the revs somewhere beyond the red line before changing gears and we pick up the pace. There was a metal security arm on the side of the road that delivers cars to the apartment building, but I can't remember if there is one on the exit lane. We could be driving a Yaris convertible before too much longer . . .

It could be my imagination, but it feels as if the Yaris becomes briefly airborne as we reach the top of the ramp. There is a squeal of tyres, a lurch to the right that painfully bounces my head off the internal wheel wall, then we straighten up and I assume we're out.

But we are not alone. Our hasty departure has attracted attention. Sirens. I can definitely hear sirens. They don't seem too distant, either. The Yaris picks up another gear. It's not a vehicle built for speed; I can't imagine we will outrun whatever tricked-up speed machines the cops around here favour. Although we are certainly moving fast.

The sirens are not falling behind. I haven't a clue where

we are, which direction we are going, or what the plan is. For someone who hates being out of control, this is as bad as it gets.

Amid all the bouncing and the thumping, I manage to dig out my mobile phone. I switch on the GPS function, and somewhere in the fuzzy fog my eyesight has been reduced so I can determine we're heading northwest from Tangerang on a major road that looks to be called JL Raya Mauk. It looks like it will take us past the outskirts of the airport. This might be our destination, although given we are currently carrying a convoy of half Jakarta's police force, this would be a risky manoeuvre. I consider calling Bob and giving him an update, but the prospect of telling him I'm in the boot of an American agent's car isn't that appealing. Bob can wait. I probably couldn't hit the right keys on the phone, anyway. It feels like I have just been shoved into a washing machine on spin cycle.

I can still hear the chasing pack. We take a sharp left, travel about fifty metres, take another left without braking, then a right, another sharp burst of acceleration that pins me against the boot's back rim, and soon it feels as though we have left the tarmac altogether. Then Budi drops the anchors with such force I smash face-first into the back seat. It's possible I momentarily lose consciousness, but my next recollection is of silence. I hear the passenger-side door open. The boot is gently released and Miller leans in.

'You can have a swing at me later, but for the moment shut your mouth and don't say a word.'

I comply. I hear the chasing wolves approaching. But there is no change in the note in any engines. No sense they're slowing. No skids, no squeal of tyres. They pass like a storm and leave only the quiet behind.

'They were watching the exit and didn't like the look of us,' says Miller. 'We had to shift a little, but Budi knows all the highways and the byways in these parts. We were in good hands.'

'Wonderful news. Where the fuck are we?'

'Just a hideaway we use in emergencies. It pays to have a few dotted around the city. Don't tell the locals about them, obviously.'

'No. I don't suppose you do. What now?'

Miller smiles. It's the smile of a man who considers himself in complete control, a man having the time of his life. It's a smile that only increases my own state of nervousness.

'Our next adventure is to try and get into the airport and get out of this goddam country. Want to come along? The Indonesians may not know exactly who we are, but they will have a good idea. Probably best to move along while we can.'

'Slow down. Back to the start for a second. How are you planning to get into the airport? Every cop in Jakarta is going to be looking for us and most of them will probably be at the fucking airport by now!'

'That's the problem with you Aussies. You think small-time. No ambition. You have too much respect for the opposition here. I'm American. We have ways, we have means.'

I have no idea what he has planned, but I need a moment to clear my head. I look around and take in my new surroundings, which must have once been an old garage.

Cracked concrete floor with a million years of dropped oil, dirty, bare wooden beams, corrugated-iron walls and a roof with a broken skylight.

Miller went on. 'They're not going to stop an American car with American diplomatic plates from entering the airport to depart on an American aeroplane, are they?'

I now see where he is going and it's hard to argue with his logic. There's no way, with the eyes of the world on them, that the Indonesians will risk further damage to their international reputation by arresting an American who will claim diplomatic immunity. And who will then tell the world he was doing what the Indonesians wouldn't: investigate what had happened to its missing aeroplane.

'Okay, okay. Fine. You may be right but can I just get one thing clear here? Who are you?'

'Alan Miller. Didn't I mention that already?'

I give him my best exasperated look. 'Yes, you told me your name. But who are you? Who do you work for? Why are you here in Jakarta?'

'You don't know? Come on, Ted, it can't be that hard to work out.'

'From your general air of arrogance and belief that you are in possession of all the world's wisdom, I'm going to take a stab in the dark and say you are the CIA's man in Indonesia.'

'Ten out of ten, Ted. I can see why you are so highly valued at home.'

As I start to ask him another question, a black car, one of those long Chryslers designed by a bloke with a small penis and no sense of style, pulls up outside the tumbledown garage. Budi pulls up the battered iron door with a long line of chain to welcome the newcomer.

An enormous black man in a stiff black uniform emerges. I wouldn't call him anything as demeaning as a chauffeur; this is a man who carries a level of threat in his every step, which suggests driving a car is only a small element of his daily duties. Miller steps towards him and stretches out his hand.

'Nice timing, Dwayne,' he says. 'Let's not hang around here for too long.' Then, pointing at me: 'This is Ted. Our Australian work-experience kid. He'll be coming along for the ride.'

Making an internal vow not to rise to the bait, I walk towards Dwayne. He's a good four inches taller than me and looks like he could crush me like a gnat if the mood took him. But he seems like a handy bloke to have on your side in an emergency so I decide to play nice, at least to him.

'Good to meet you, Dwayne. My commiserations on having to rescue this bastard, but I suspect it's something you have to do on a fairly regular basis.'

Dwayne gives a deep-throated chuckle. Up close, I can see he has a scar. It looks decades old, running from the outside of his left eye all the way down to the jawbone. His dark brown, heavily lidded eyes give the impression he's someone only a minute or two away from an afternoon nap, but I have the definite sense that Dwayne is someone you don't want to be underestimating.

'Yeah, well, Alan here does have the propensity to leave his ass swinging in the breeze from time to time. Occasionally I have had to catch him before he falls.'

Miller steps in. Good humour apparently evaporating.

'Lovely, lovely. We're all friends here. Can we now get the fuck out of here before our friendly cops realise they have lost us and come back for a closer look? You coming Ted? I'll let you ride inside the car with the grown-ups this time.'

Lacking any other options, I take up the offer.

9

The car carrying diplomatic plates does offer us a decent level of protection. Miller is right about that: the Indonesians won't be rousting an official American car, no matter what they think we may have done or what we might have in our possession. We carry on through the last of the Jakarta night. Dawn is swinging into action; the blacks and purples of deep night are giving way to a soft light blue with undertones of orange. I check the dashboard clock: 5.01 a.m. I glance at the Longines on my left wrist, see that it's still telling me Sydney time and wind the hands back.

We arrive at Soekarno-Hatta Airport unmolested and carry on through the entrance without so much as a second glance from anyone. It's only about seven hours since I was waiting for a cab here, but it feels like several days, and now as the adrenalin that had been flooding my system starts to leak away I feel suddenly exhausted. My head is also bursting after the hammering it took in the boot. I can hardly keep my eyes open.

Uncharacteristically, Miller hasn't said a word in the fifteen minutes since we left our temporary hideout. It's time to ask a few questions from the back seat of the Chrysler.

'Miller, what did you expect to find back there?'

'Nothing specific. I just wanted to have a look.'

'But what's your take? Accident or arranged?'

'The missing planes? As I said, I'm not a big believer in coincidences. Something is going on, but I don't know what and I don't know who.'

'You think Notonegro ditched the plane on purpose?'

'See, I'm not sure about that. It's a big world out there, but I think some fragment of wreckage would have shown up by now. Either from the Garuda or the Lufthansa.'

'Unless we are looking in all the wrong places,' I mutter.

'If we're both ruling out accidents, which I think we are'— he turns to look at me and I nod—'then it's either a deliberate crash or someone is stealing aircraft. What's your take?'

'Same as yours. The longer we go without finding some debris, the more I tend to think something sinister has occurred.'

By now we are skirting the main terminals. We zip down an access road or two and find ourselves at a large hangar, drab in grey. Its two massive doors are open just enough that I can see the shadow of an aircraft inside.

'Okay,' says Miller. 'Decision time for you, Ted. I can get you out of here now on a nice official US government aeroplane. Or I can tell Dwayne to drive you back to your hotel and you can take your chances from there.'

Staying in Jakarta is not appealing. The Indonesians will be much less worried about diplomatic niceties when it comes to picking up a renegade Australian wandering their streets. If they do find me, it could get quite ugly. Still, offering myself up to the Yanks isn't exactly at the top of my to-do list, either.

'Where we flying?'

'Good question, Ted. I'll tell you on the plane. But before I do, there is a price to pay. This is not a free ride. The US taxpayer expects something in return for its generosity.'

I know what's coming next. The phrase 'over a barrel' comes to mind.

'The download you took from the simulator. I'm going to need to take a look.'

'Fine,' I say. 'I was going to show it to you anyway.' A lie.

'Good. Let's get the fuck out of here.'

Inside the brightly lit hangar is a private jet, even sleeker than the one I took from Sydney to Western Australia. It looks like a Bombardier Global Express. It's a jet with an enormous range, so it makes me slightly nervous about where our destination is likely to be. You can cover a lot of ground in one of these things.

It is silver, about 30 metres in length, with no markings beyond its registration, swept-back wings and a nose elegantly arching towards the ground. There is a set of eight steps leading to the aircraft's interior. Inside it is half luxury private jet, half flying command centre. The back of the plane is taken up with a multitude of electronic gadgets. This is an aircraft plugged into the higher echelons of US intelligence.

There are four uniformed men and women operating the technology. I can see the pilots at their station through the open cockpit door, and two further uniformed types are acting as cabin crew. Miller briefly introduces me to the pilot. He's a grey-haired, lean-looking bloke who must have signed up to the military on the day he was born. His name is Colonel Harry Connelly. He gives me a stiff hello and we make our way back to the cabin.

Miller takes one of the two-seaters, nicely upholstered in white leather, and indicates that I should take the one facing him. Between us is a polished black table on a sliding track.

'So,' I begin. 'Any chance you can now tell me where we're going?'

'Los Angeles. We have a neat airfield there.'

I sigh. 'Mate, I'm trying to figure out why planes full of people keep dropping out of the sky. And now you want us to be sealed off from the hunt and fly to the other side of the world? Los Angeles is a long fucking way from here and I'm not in the mood for a holiday.'

'You know, you don't have to come along with us,' Miller says smoothly. 'We haven't taken off. Dwayne is still outside. Stay in Jakarta as long as you please.'

This is getting seriously annoying.

'Look, you know quite well that staying here is not an option,' I snap. 'And why is LA the next best destination, anyway?'

'The truth is after today it's going to get a little hot around here for me, so I have to take myself off the playing field for a little while. Shame. Just when things were getting interesting, too.' Miller looks at me, eyebrows raised in a querulous manner. 'But we also might not go all the way to LA . . . Once we are up, let's have a look at this USB, find out if there is anything worthwhile on it, and if there is we can make another decision from there. It may take us in a new direction. It may even tell us where Notonegro is hiding the plane.'

I consider the proposition.

'Okay, that seems reasonable.'

Miller gets up from his seat, walks to the cockpit door and tells the pilot to 'get this bird in the air'.

'Here, put these on,' he says when he returns, handing me a pair of wi-fi headphones. 'It lets us listen in to the pilots and air traffic control. Just want to make sure the Indonesians don't try any funny tricks on the way out.' I put mine on, noticing his set appears to have a little microphone, presumably to allow him to talk to the pilot, where mine is for eavesdropping only.

We trundle and bump out onto the apron and start to make our way towards one of Soekarno-Hatta's two runways. From my seat, I can hear the chatter between the pilots and the controller. He is guiding us towards runway 07R/25L, trying to line us up between a variety of landing and departing passenger aircraft.

The relief of those landing will be immense. Two planes going missing on the same day would certainly sharpen the senses of anyone in the air today. The thrill of survival at touchdown, the letting go of the fear that their plane could be the next to go missing would be overwhelming. Those about to take off, on the other hand, will be trying to convince themselves that it couldn't happen again; that there is no way a third plane could go missing in less than

24 hours. They will be telling themselves that there are thousands of planes in the sky at this very moment, making the odds in their favour.

Out my window I can see Garuda planes, planes from Singapore and Hong Kong, even a flash of a red Qantas tail. I feel a pang for home. To be there, in my own bed, and not about to take off another continent, chasing God only knows what.

We are finally coming around to line up with the runway when an urgent Indonesian voice comes through my headphones.

'AX001, AX001, do not proceed, do not proceed. Authorisation to depart is withdrawn, return to terminal. I repeat, return to your terminal. You are not cleared for take-off.'

Miller is on his feet before the controller has finished and at the cockpit door. He's shouting at Connelly. He didn't need that mic after all.

'Ignore that. Take off, take off!'

Connelly seems to briefly protest, but Miller cuts him off.

'Don't argue with me, colonel. This is a direct order, so listen carefully. Take the fuck off and do it now.'

The captain's voice is in my ear. Uptight and American.

'AX001 is taking off. Please warn surrounding aircraft. AX001 is preparing for take-off.'

And, with that, we lurch forward. There is no gradual build-up of speed; full thrust is applied, the jet engines scream, and I am pinned back in my comfortable seat. Miller stays where he is. I can see his white knuckles grimly clinging to the frame of the cockpit door. We're hurtling down the runway, while in my ear I can still hear Indonesian voices.

'Stop. Stop. You are not cleared for take-off. You can't take off. You are breaking international aviation law.'

But then we are airborne, climbing almost vertically. I glance out the window and see a Cathay Pacific 777 that must just have landed moving slowly off our runway. I don't know how close it was, but there couldn't have been much in it. I fancy I can make out tyre marks on the roof of the enormous jet.

Through the headphones Connelly is trying to pretend things are normal, that he hasn't broken one of the basic rules of the sky.

'AX001 is climbing to 35,000 feet, heading 013. Thank you, Jakarta, we are on our way. Apologies for any misunderstanding.'

There is no reply. Only static in my ears, and I get a bad feeling the Indonesians are not quite finished with us. Miller looks back at me. He's still holding on tight to that frame of the cockpit door. The plane is climbing at what I would describe as an alarming angle. It's more rocket launch than aircraft take-off trajectory. He gives me a little smile as if to stay 'told you I would get us out of here'.

Then the aircraft lurches swiftly to the right, like we are avoiding a small child who has chased a ball onto the road. The pilot's voice. Urgent. Worried.

'Jakarta? Jakarta? What is going on?'

The violence of the sudden manoeuvre has sent Miller tumbling down the narrow aisle and smashing into the bulkhead that leads to the back of the jet where all the fancy computers are kept. It's a fearful impact, but he's still conscious, although the smile has been wiped from his face.

Out of my window, I can see the threatening grey shape of an Indonesian military jet. It looks like a Russian-made Sukhoi. There's a new Indonesian voice over the radio.

'AX001, this is Captain Alatas of the Indonesian Air Force. I request you turn around and follow me back to Halim Perdanakusuma airfield as a matter of priority.'

Our captain does not reply. I can see him looking around for Miller who is slowly starting to make his way back up the aircraft, stumbling like a drunk climbing a steep hill in a gale. His headphones have come off in the tumble. They are lying under the seat next to me, so I grab them and pass them to him as he makes his way past.

As I do I point out the window and say: 'The Indonesian Air Force, they'd like us to follow them. Big guns on that plane, by the way.'

He puts on the headphones and continues towards the pilot. This time he straps himself into the spare seat behind the captain. I take this as a sign that things are about to get rough. He makes a 'keep going' signal to the captain.

Connelly speaks. *'That's a negative, Captain Alatas. We are unable to follow you at this stage.'*

'I must insist, captain, that you follow me to the base. You are wanted for questioning by Indonesian authorities. You are under suspicion for stealing material pertinent to that ongoing investigation.'

'I repeat, captain, regretfully, we are not following you anywhere. We will soon be out of your airspace and out of your way. Thank you.'

'This is your last chance, captain. You will follow us to Halim base or you will suffer the consequences.'

I can now make out three, maybe four fighters. There could be others, but it's hard to tell. Not that it makes much difference: it would only take one of these fuckers with an itchy trigger finger to blow us apart.

Another voice in the headphone. This time it's Miller talking.

'Captain Alatas, this is Alan Miller speaking. I am a representative of the United States government. This is a registered US government plane. We are currently assisting your government in the search for the missing Garuda aircraft. Any act of aggression on your part would bring all sorts of unpleasant consequences to your own nation. Is that really what you want, captain?'

I notice Miller makes no reference to me during his little speech. Perhaps I'm a secret, though more likely I just don't count. I realise I'm holding my breath, waiting for the Indonesian to answer by either shooting at us or by replying to Miller.

I look around at the military types working in the back of the plane. I hope they are telling Washington exactly what is going on, but they all seem frozen to the spot, fingers not touching keyboards, trying to look out the windows at what is happening around them.

Alatas's voice comes over the speaker again.

'My orders are to return you to Halim, by whatever means necessary. You will follow me. You will not defy me.'

'Don't take this personally,' Miller replies. 'But we are defying you. Goodbye.'

Outside, one of the jets peels away from our plane. I wonder whether they are leaving us or moving to an attack position. It banks right and circles behind us until I lose sight of it. Then another Sukhoi rockets by us. This is looking ugly.

An explosion from the front. I don't need my headphones to hear Miller screaming, *'Fucking hell!'* Through the cockpit door I can see the front window has turned grey. It looks like a jet has cut in front of us, missing by metres. Then another jet, and another.

They are trying to force us down without shooting us down. Maybe they think they can make it look like an accident. The Global Express flies into the disturbed air created by the Sukhois. We are being battered and buffered by the wake turbulence as our wings struggle to find enough smooth air to keep us level. The right wing points up 90 degrees and the plane, in slow motion, starts to tip. Anything loose in the cabin is thrown around. A coffee cup whistles past my nose and smashes itself into the fuselage just above the window.

Then the pilot has lost control and we are tumbling back towards the dreaded ocean. There's no room for error, or time for Connelly to regain control. We couldn't have been more than 25,000 feet when we started to fall. In all the swirling confusion, I can't make out the cockpit; I'm pinned to the seat and my eyesight is blurred. It's impossible to distinguish up from down. I hope my seatbelt holds otherwise I am going to pinball all the way to the back of the aircraft.

All I can hear from the cockpit are sounds of struggle. Somehow my headphones have remained in place. The pilot is doing everything he can to regain control. Elongated seconds pass. We're about to smash into the ocean. Plane versus ocean. It's not a fair fight.

There is nothing in my mind except fear and a certainty I don't want to die. Not here, not like this. There are no great flashback moments, no sudden regrets about loves lost or family spurned. Just a desire to keep living. A feeling of hopelessness envelopes me as I realise my future is entirely out of my hands.

Then there is a wiggle and a twist. A roar from the engines. The rolling and tumbling slow. The nose of the air-craft starts to rise and we are again heading back towards the sky.

Miller lets out a terrific '*Yeahah*' while Connelly, out of breath and still tense, is asking, '*How is everyone back there? Any casualties? Any damage?*'

As far as I can tell, the crew is still in one piece. There is debris everywhere as everything that wasn't nailed down has found a new home, but there appears to be no major structural damage. Maybe it is my lucky day after all.

But the euphoria of survival fades fast as the memory of who put us in this situation returns. Where are the Indone-sian Sukhois? They will have followed us down, wishing us to disappear into the foam, but since we survived they may just decide fuck it and finish the job . . .

Back in control of his aircraft, Connelly is wasting no time climbing for height. We are still no more than a thousand feet, which makes me wonder exactly how close we came to an ocean burial, and heading at full tilt via what I assume is the quickest way out of Indonesian airspace.

Suddenly one of the ugly grey beasts fills the view outside my window. It's not exactly like seeing an old friend again. I look across the aisle: there's a second on the other side of our aircraft. Through the cockpit, I can see another just in front of us.

The Indonesia captain again.

'That was some lovely flying, captain. You nearly had a tragic accident, which would have been terrible luck for you. But you can go now. We will escort you from our airspace. Please don't come back.'

Connelly doesn't say a word. Just opens the throttle wide open and tears away into the blue sky.

10

Once we are out of Indonesian airspace, and once the Sukhois have left us, Miller unbuckles from the cockpit and comes back down to see me.

'That was a little hairy,' I say.

'That it was, my friend, but Connelly up there is one of the best. If you had to rely on one man to get us out of that hole, it would be him.'

I run a hand through my hair. I realise my fingers are sore from holding on too tightly to the armrests as the plane was struggling for its survival.

'In all the excitement, I couldn't tell how close we came to the floor. Was there much in it?'

'It was close,' Miller confirms. '*Too* close. As an old Aussie friend of mine once said, today is a good day to buy a lottery ticket. If Connelly had taken another second to get hold of this baby, we wouldn't be having this conversation.'

There is a brief pause as I absorb this information. I decide there's no point in worrying about how close I just came to death.

'Okay, so what now?'

'Ordinarily we would find somewhere to land—this machine just took one hell of a battering. But Connelly reckons she feels okay, so we're going to press on to the US. We have enough fuel to get us to LA.'

'I thought we were going to have a gander at the USB first,' I say.

Miller heads towards the hardware at the back of the plane. I assume I am supposed to follow him. He takes a seat at a large, high-definition computer screen. Superficially it could be a device you would find in any office or home, but there's something about it that screams military, all sharp edges and expensive-looking, and that's not because of the US government screensaver, decorated with the coat of arms with its high-minded motto *E pluribus unum*. Out of many, one.

Miller sits in the king of large, high-backed leather chairs, the kind I'd expect to see in a chief executive's office, and I pull over another from a nearby terminal.

'Let's have a look at this USB of yours, then.'

I hand it over to Miller with a 'I want that back'. He slides it into a port on the side of the computer and a box pops up in the middle of the screen. There is a bunch of folder options down the left-hand side, a neat little graphic with revolving sheets of paper showing which documents are on the drive at the top, and under that a list of the same items. Disappointingly there appears to be no file called *How to make a Garuda disappear*.

I point to the cluster of folders named *Today, Yesterday, Last Week.*

'Let's start there?' I say to Miller.

There's not a lot in *Today* or *Yesterday*, but in *Last Week* things start to become interesting. There's a file called *Indian Ocean airports* and another labelled *Radar.* Miller quickly scans the rest of the files on the USB, but those two appear to be our lot.

He opens the airports' tab and sure enough there is a list of the nearest airports to that northern tip of Western Australia. There looks to be about a hundred or so. Some are reasonably large, like Diego Garcia, others are tiny specks in the ocean in places I have never heard of. Malé, for one. There are hyperlinks contained in the document through to satellite images of the runway layout, terminals and nearby roads.

Neither of us says a word. Transfixed by the list and its possibilities.

Miller hits a couple of commands and transposes Notonegro's list onto a map so we can see exactly where each airfield is. Little red dots appear everywhere. Not only in the Indian Ocean but as far afield as Thailand, Yemen and even Saudi Arabia. And then it turns out we are looking beyond the Indian Ocean. Markers appear showing Kovykta field in Russia and Harbin in China.

'This is fucking hopeless,' complains Miller. 'According to this, he could be headed almost anywhere. It's needle-in-a-haystack stuff.'

I am still staring at the screen. I share Miller's worry. Desperation creeps into my head. Two planes are missing,

I am somewhere high over the Pacific Ocean, heading further and further away from home, and we have nothing here but an endless catalogue of obscure airports.

'Open the other file,' I command Miller, pointing to *Radar.*

He does as he's told and again we are confronted with a mass of information that could mean everything or nothing. But there is also a map that shows the vast swathes of the Indian Ocean with no radar coverage.

After a plane leaves the west coast of Australia, it doesn't have far to travel to be beyond the reach of all land-based radars. So, if Notonegro had deliberately turned off his transponder system, it would make him very hard to track. Especially if he had taken the plane down low, beneath whatever other satellite systems might have been nearby. Satellites are useful, but they need to be told where to look. He had already mapped out radar coverage in the area: he knew exactly where to take the aircraft if he wanted to hide from all those searching eyes.

'Does any of this help us?' I ask.

'It's hard to see how,' Miller replies. 'Though it could also be a deliberate diversion to drown us in misinformation. If Notonegro is responsible for disappearing the plane then he would also know we'd come after him. He knew we would find the simulator so why would he leave anything that gives his plan away?'

Not a happy thought. Especially after all we went through to get it.

'But I'll give this to the geeks and we will begin to check whatever we can on every airport on this list,' Miller continues. 'We'll dig out satellite imagery, use our global surveillance systems—some acknowledged, some not—talk to our people on the ground. Try to find out if anywhere is suddenly hosting a Garuda A330.'

'What's your gut on this?' I ask.

'That we have to get back to looking at who has the capability to pull off something like this. We could be talking about one of the bigger terror groups. Is it a state? Syria? North Korea? What if it's someone we've never come across before. I mean, we didn't stop Al-Qaeda before 9/11, but at least we'd heard of them. If it is a group we've no idea about it will just make them that much tougher to track down.'

'So, you're totally ruling out this as just some sort of weird coincidence? Planes have been known to fall out of the sky from time to time. Maybe it was just a bad day.'

'You don't believe that?'

'I think my boss is clinging onto some hope that it's all a series of unfortunate coincidences, but no, I don't. I guess people in our line of work need to be partial to the odd conspiracy theory. Although I'd be more than happy to be wrong.'

'You'd rather over 500 people were dead because of a mechanical fault?'

'At least we'd have an explanation.'

There is some relief in Miller sharing the theory. It helps me believe I am something other than a grandiose purveyor of conspiracy theories. It also makes me trust him a little more. That despite his outward arrogance, he is someone I can work with on this. Which makes me think of home and my doubts about who is behind me in Sydney. It's been quite some time since I last spoke to Bob. It further occurs to me he's not going to be happy with this long silence. I delve into the backpack I have managed to cling onto despite all the fun and games and pull out my battered iPad.

'I better call home,' I tell Miller. 'Mum will be getting worried.'

'Do you want to use one of our satellite phones? I promise it's secure,' he adds in a way that makes me instantly suspicious.

Now technically, we're all friends here. The Australians and the Yanks have some history on the same side of some of the bigger conflicts going around. A couple of world wars they eventually joined in with, a couple of regional wars—Vietnam, both Iraqs, Afghanistan. But I don't know Miller well enough yet. Not well enough to entirely trust him, at any rate, even if we do share some common theories on disappeared planes.

'Thanks for the offer, but this thing should still do the trick,' I say, waving the iPad in his general direction. 'It will ping into one of our satellites.'

A lot's happened since I last spoke to Bob. Since then I have broken into an apartment, evaded Indonesian security forces, been shot at, met an American agent, been shoved into the boot of a car and nearly died in a plane crash. It's been a busy morning. As far as I can tell, I have managed to cram all that activity into about six hours. No wonder I feel as if I'm ageing fast. I glance at my watch. The small hand is just resting on the seven, which makes it around ten in the morning Sydney time.

I go through the process of firing up the iPad, do the whole eye-scan thing and in a literal blink I'm connected to Bob. Still in his office and, if anything, looking even worse than he did last time. It's creeping towards mid-morning now in Sydney and Bob is wearing the same suit and tie combination he was sporting last time we spoke. Has he been home to sleep? It doesn't look like it.

I don't stop to give a thought to my appearance. I haven't seen a mirror on this plane, but presumably I can't be too flash. Bob starts as my visage appears on the screen in front of him. I think he has a dedicated iPad for each agent in the field spread on that enormous desk of his. When I was in the office yesterday—was it really only yesterday?—he had four on the mahogany table. I suspect there will a few more on there today, but from my angle it's impossible to tell.

'Ted, where the hell are you? Are you still on planet Earth? Or have you just fucked off entirely?'

I note the swearing.

'Nice to see you too, Bob. I—'

He cuts me off. 'Are you on a plane? Your iPad has you tracking somewhere over Borneo heading towards the Philippines. What happened in Jakarta? Where are you going?'

I try to keep my voice as calm and neutral as possible because I know the next bit is really going to freak him out.

'Bob, I'm on an American military plane. It's very nice actually, much better than ours, and I'm heading towards Los Angeles.'

It's hard to describe the look that forms on Bob's face. Pained? Perplexed? No, neither are quite right. Remember the expression on Luke Skywalker's face in *The Empire Strikes Back* when Darth Vader informs him 'I am your father'? Well, it was something like that.

'*What?*' he splutters, unable to process the information.

'I'll speak more slowly for you, Bob. I'm on an aircraft full of Americans on my way to the States.'

'Well, I hope they have kidnapped you because if you got on that plane of your own free will, without at least having the courtesy to inform me of the situation, you will be fired. I'll take you back to that dive I found you in and you can finish that earlier mission of drinking yourself to death!' Bob is so upset by my apparent betrayal I can't see him anymore. Too angry to stay still he has left his chair and is pacing is office.

It's now my turn to be riled.

'Fuck you, Bob' is what I think to myself but manage to stop myself from saying. 'I'm only on this plane because the fucking Indonesians were after me. If I'd been caught I'd either be dead or in prison. In comparison, getting on a plane with my nice new American friends didn't seem like such a tough choice. And while we're at it, the only reason you pulled me out of that pub was because I was your last chance. Every other agent you have is either dead, in prison or fucking useless. You need me as much as I need you.'

Bob is back in his seat by the end of my little tirade and there is a heavy silence on the other end of the call. A staring competition when the opponents are separated by several thousand kilometres may seem childish, but for a moment or two there is no chance of either of us backing down.

Miller breaks the tension. He sticks his head around the partition, drawn by the raised voices, and raises a quizzical eyebrow. His intrusion brings me back to reality. I give him a nod and he backs off. I take a breath and return my attention to Bob.

'Okay, now we have that out of the way, do you want to hear what I have been up to since we last spoke?'

A calmer Bob replied that he would.

The truncated version of the yarn takes about ten minutes to run through. During that time, Bob doesn't utter a word except for the odd 'goodness'. I am just about to wind it up when Miller again sticks his head over the partition, this time with a look of panic on his face.

'Another one has gone. Another fucking plane has fallen off the radar. And this time it's one of ours. An American Airlines flight heading to Brazil vanished five minutes ago.'

A wave of nausea sweeps over me. I glance at Bob, not sure if he had picked up what Miller was telling me.

'Did you catch that?' I ask him. 'A third plane has gone.'

'Oh dear. Fuck. No, that hasn't reached us. Maybe you are in the best place after all. Okay, Ted, tell me what you plan to do.'

11

The gentle background noise on the plane above the thrum of the engines has been replaced by a roar of activity. The military types are rushing around, from one computer to the next, gathering at terminals before breaking up and going their own way. I could be wrong but it feels like panic is only barely being constrained.

I had told Bob I would get back to him before ending our conversation over the iPad. I turn now to find Miller hunched over one of the computer screens at the back of the plane. I stand up and head his way. Beside him is a young woman in air force uniform, fingers flying over the keyboard as Miller barks instructions.

He jumps as a I place my hand on his shoulder. The lightness on his face only a few minutes ago has been replaced by something much darker. I make a mental note that this is a good time to stow my usual glibness someplace far away.

'What do we know about this new plane?' I ask him.

'It was an American Airlines Flight 991, flying from Miami International to Belo Horizonte in Brazil. An A330 with 235 passengers and 15 crew aboard. Seven-and-a-half-hour flight. Last radar was over the North Atlantic 30 minutes from crossing the coast at Suriname. All was tracking normally, right up until the moment when it wasn't.'

'Who's looking for it?'

'Every piece of hardware the US military has even remotely close to the area is heading there as we speak. Remember, this thing has only been missing for around ten minutes—there is still a chance it will blip back into life. Maybe a careless pilot knocked the wrong switch. Maybe there has been some sort of screw-up on the flight deck. Maybe a fuse just blew.'

'You ever heard of something like that happening before?'

'It happens,' he mutters, but it's unconvincing and he knows it.

'Do we know anything about the pilots?'

'Nothing as yet.'

'What does it mean for our plans? Do we change our route and head that way, or stick with Los Angeles?'

'We'll press on to LA then assess from there what to do next.'

I feel helpless. Frustrated and annoyed. We are so far from anywhere that I can't see the next move. I'm trapped in this tin can, 35,000 feet in the air, heading for the US. It doesn't feel like the right direction, not that I can think of a better option, but it's out of my hands. I'm struck by the random thought that I hope I don't have to go through customs when we land in LA. I still only have the forged document to prove my identity as one Sean Docherty. Still, I'm sure Miller will look after me.

'I can't just sit here for the next eight hours,' I tell him. 'What can I do to help?'

Miller smiles. 'Thanks, my friend. I'll get you a terminal.'

He leads me to the back of the plane and finds the one space that isn't occupied by a frantic American. We both stand beside it.

'Who is doing this?' I ask him.

Miller is serious now. He is rubbing his hands together like he is washing them. 'I've a bad feeling about this one,' he says. 'In general terms, we know who it is. It's a variant on the same story we have been reading about for years. It's a terrorist organisation, probably with roots in the nutcase version of Islam. They will be brutal and ruthless and take great delight in taking on the West to fulfil whatever notions of moral supremacy they carry with them.'

I nod, agreeing with him, and continue the theme. 'But this time it's a bit different, isn't it? We don't know who these guys are. They haven't revealed themselves, and we can't find them. We don't know if they want anything at all, except to expose our weaknesses. But there must be some clues somewhere. They can't be totally invisible. There will be traces, suggestions, speculations. It's just that no one has joined all the dots yet.'

Miller has stopped rubbing his hands. He looks calmer, more thoughtful. The act of thinking his way through the problem, trying to find an answer to it, is soothing some-thing in him.

'Okay, Ted. Get cracking on it. We have some time before we land. Find something, anything.'

* * *

First, I call Bob back. He's still relying on Australian intelligence for any updates on the latest plane, and they are probably glued to CNN or the BBC World Service like everybody else. My respect for our own intelligence services isn't enormous.

Bob appears paler and greyer. The life is being sucked out of him by these terrifying developments. The fight has gone out of both of us for the moment and we talk in low tones about what may happen next.

'Have you retired the theory of this all being one big coincidence?' I ask, though gently; I don't feel the need to play the 'I told you so game' at this stage.

'It's starting to stretch beyond breaking point, but no one is claiming responsibility either. No bits of broken aeroplane have been found anywhere. We haven't a skerrick on the Garuda. There is still a full search-and-rescue mission being mounted off the coast of Western Australia, but there's nothing there that anyone can see.'

'What about the passengers with the dodgy passports that you mentioned? Anything come of that?'

'Well, we isolated the pair through CCTV taken at Sydney Airport. They have been identified. Not terrorists, but the federal police were happy enough. Turned out they were drug dealers they had been on the lookout for for quite some time.'

Bob looks away from the iPad. Something has caught his

eye somewhere in the background of the office. He holds up his hand in the time-honoured gesture that means 'just be quiet for a second'.

'It's just come up on CNN,' he murmurs. 'American Airlines plane missing off the coast of South America. No other details at this stage.'

I glance up to a bank of four TVs just above my head and see the same words scroll across the bottom of each screen. There's a silence between Bob and me. Another tanker full of petrol has just been thrown onto an already raging inferno. Three planes down and the world in full-blown panic. The modern-day fad for interconnectedness and globalisation, which we love because we can all swap information instantaneously, is now going to share fear and hysteria at the same rate.

'I have to go,' says Bob. 'No doubt I am about to be summoned to more meetings with the defence minister, the national security chiefs, the federal police, and sit around pretending we have a clue what is going on or who is behind this.'

Bob is ageing before my eyes. This is a bloke who has been in this dark counter-intelligence world for much of his adult life, yet he has seen nothing like this. I worry that it's starting to get to him.

He offers one more thought before signing off. 'Sometimes I think I prefer the old days when a hijacking was a relatively simple matter. You knew where the plane was and you knew which group of nutters had taken control of it because they wanted the world to know how scary they were. Then you would send in the Americans—or better yet, the Israelis—to blow the whole lot up. I don't know anymore, Ted, I just don't know.'

And with that, he flicks a switch and my screen turns back to black.

I look over my shoulder and spot Miller hunched over a terminal with two of the crew. He has a mobile to his ear and is conducting an animated conversation. I return my attention to my iPad me to see how the rest of the world is coping.

Badly.

I flick over to the BBC website, the *Guardian*, the *Australian*. The world is sliding into chaos.

Third plane missing in 24 hours.

Calls for global air fleet to be grounded.

Who is behind this madness?

UN calls emergency meeting.

The top global trends on Twitter are #wherearetheplanes and #neverflyingagain. By the looks of it, there will be no need to ground airlines—passengers will do the job for them. Into the void jump the mad, bad, deranged and scared. The right-wing media nutjobs who tell us this is what we get for allowing Muslim immigration and placating terrorists; the left-wing newspaper editors trying to draw a link to US imperialism; the political opportunists sensing a chance to bash the government; the lawlessness of social media and its community of the professionally outraged. The background chatter has grown to a roar and the noise is squeezing out rational debate and the sense that any of it will help.

A story in the *Guardian* says Heathrow, the world's busiest airport, could become a ghost town as people cancel bookings in the tens of thousands. For a second I enjoy that mental image, a deserted Heathrow. What sweet relief. I was stuck there for 24 hours years ago after a snowstorm closed the place and it was a circle of hell that Dante didn't have the imagination, or pessimism, to invoke. In spite of this, it looks like airlines are struggling on for the moment, with no official order to ground anyone at this stage.

The US president and the UK prime minister have both made speeches in the last hour urging airlines to keep flying and not be scared by 'these terrorist cowards'. That this was ever a coincidence seems to have flown out of the window.

'We will find them and we will bring them to justice for their crimes,' President Arnold Baynes intones. 'Don't give in, never give in, go about your lives without fear. If you are booked to fly, then fly,' he concludes, as only a bloke who has his own 747 on standby can. 'We are working relentlessly to identify these wrongdoers. They may be keeping silent now, but I have a message for them as I know they are listening. We will find you and our vengeance will be swift, just and brutal. The brightest and best of our security forces are looking for you. And they always get their target.'

12

Three planes gone. No one knows where. It feels inevitable a fourth will go as well. And a fifth? And a sixth? Where does this stop? How does this stop?

And, most of all, who is doing this and why? And what can I do about it?

I track back and try to put some logical sequence into the last day and night. I can feel the rising tide of panic inside me as well. It's as if I can taste it at the back of my throat. But I can't let it overwhelm me. It's time to get back to work. Back to first principles. I start to make notes. Just to bring some order to my own thoughts and feel as if I'm doing something.

The answer has to lie with the pilots. We need to know more about them. It's inconceivable that three aircraft can go missing without pilot involvement. I begin making my list.

Aircraft number one. Garuda Airlines flying Sydney to

Jakarta disappears off the Western Australian coast. Airbus A330. Captain ex-military. Notonegro. Indonesian national. Has built a flight simulator in his home. Missing 28 hours.

Aircraft number two. Lufthansa Airbus A340. Flying Munich to Singapore. Disappears somewhere near the Turkey–Iraq border. No new information on captain's background. Missing seven hours.

Aircraft number three. American Airlines Miami to Belo Horizonte. Boeing 777-300. Captain still unknown. Missing one hour.

I am shocked by how little information I have in front of me. But the act of sitting down and trying to apply logic is settling. The brain is starting to kick back into action, emerging from the deep freeze the shock of the last day has induced.

I look around for Miller. He is heading my way and flops down into a seat to my right.

'What do we know about the other pilots? We have something on the Garuda captain, but nothing on the Lufthansa or the American Airlines blokes. I can't help but think they're involved. Nothing else makes sense.'

'The Lufthansa pilot was a fella called Gunther Kroos. Out of the German military a decade ago, married but no details on his family life. Still early days on the AA front but the captain was a Franck Dupree. Canadian.'

'Can I ask you something, Miller? How in the loop are you? Are your CIA bosses in Langley keeping you up to date on this? What's their theory at this stage?'

'I'm in touch with them. They know all about you. I told them about the USB and that's being examined.

Even so, they're not particularly happy I gave you a ride, but I explained you're more hostage than passenger.'

We both start to laugh. It's a relief to actually have something to laugh about. It momentarily breaks the oppression of the deep-seated feeling of dread that I have been carrying with me for most of the last day and a half. I look more closely at Miller. In all the chaos, this is about the first time we have both been still in each other's company. He's older than I originally took him for. Maybe late thirties. In the darkness of the Jakarta stairwell, my first impression had been of a painfully thin young man who carried the physical threat of a celery stick. Now I can see what he has is well-honed leanness. Lithe, suggesting the capacity for swift, and perhaps deadly, movement. He tries to contain all this behind the mask of an easy-going frat boy, but you don't have to look far into those black eyes to find the menace of the man. I tell myself Miller is not someone to take lightly; he's probably not someone to trust, either.

I wonder what he sees when he looks at me. The battered Australian? A man kicking towards his forties but who has clearly been around more blocks than a lost taxi driver. He's wondering if my height lends me strength or just a level of clumsiness. He hasn't seen me do much of anything useful in the last few hours: just chase him around like a lost puppy and follow orders with the alacrity of any grunt in the army. No doubt he thinks he has the better of me and for the moment I am happy to let him have this moment of superiority. In my book, it's always better to be underestimated than overestimated.

'How long had you been in Jakarta?' I ask him.

'A couple of years. The usual kind of thing. Attached to the embassy, but spent most of my time on the streets talking to anyone and everyone. Nice people, the Indonesians, even if more than a few still mourn the passing of the old strongmen in Sukarno and Suharto. They forgave their corruption for the sense of solidity and national pride it gave them in return. It was a rotten deal, but everyone seemed to like it. Well, close to the end . . .'

'So, this could be the end of that particular assignment, then?'

'Yep, it will be a while before the Indos let me back in their country. I'm just sorry I didn't get a chance to say goodbye to my wife and kids.'

'What?' I exclaim before realising he is winding me up.

'Sorry. This game really isn't built for family men, is it? I'm guessing you're like me. No attachments. Well, none of the permanent variety, anyway.'

I hesitate. The peculiar atmosphere of our situation almost prompts me to spill my guts to this stranger. Something about plane travel always plays with my emotions. The number of times I have made a surreptitious wipe to a leaky eye while watching some godawful film is more than a little embarrassing.

But, no, now is not the time and Miller is not the person, either. I'm not in the mood to share my story about the tragedy of Melody and the heartbreak of Eliza, or about the destructive streak that saw me wallow in the bottle, trying to drown my self-pity after Melody died instead of caring for my daughter who ran away to her grandparents in search of some stability in her life.

I ran away, too. I left the air force after Melody died, hid my problems from my next employer. Flew all over the world with Qantas. Was rarely home to look after the one person who should have been my only concern in the world. The memories flood through me. They cause me pain. I look back up at Miller.

'Yes, mate, all alone,' I say. It's not a lie.

Miller, though, wants to keep pressing. He's either somewhere on the autism spectrum when it comes to reading the emotions of others or he is just pumping me for information he thinks may come in useful down the road. Ours is not a profession for normal people. I'd suggest that if you did a thorough analysis of everyone in this line of work, a good 80 per cent would have a 'syndrome' or a 'disorder' or be 'borderline' this, that or the other. More than a few doctors over the years have tried to pin some sort of label on me.

'So, tell me your story,' Miller says. 'Where you from?'

'Born in Adelaide,' I reply. 'That's down near the bottom of Australia. Headed to Sydney as most bright folk do soon after. Dad drove a truck that delivered bread very early in the morning, Mum mainly looked after my sister and me. School followed, university after that. University led to the military. The military led to flight school. Flight school, funnily enough, led to aeroplanes and a bit of flying over Iraq. A bit of death and destruction. Home. Discharge. Flying for Qantas. Left in disgrace. Here we are.'

Miller looks at me. Unimpressed.

'I can't help but get the feeling you may have left a few things out.'

'Maybe. But why should I be telling you anything?'

Miller smiles. 'I suppose it doesn't matter. I've already had a peek at your official record, anyway. It isn't pretty. As far as I can tell, it's just a long line of insubordination and reckless-ness. You have been given more chances than most because, occasionally, you show a glimpse of what might have been. The one you could have been if you exercised a little more discipline, and I'm wondering if there was more to you than what I read on that screen?'

This is annoying. Standard operating procedure would be to tell him to fuck off. Instinct over intelligence, I suppose. I make an effort to compose myself and have another go. I'm also keen to have a look at my official US record. That could be fun.

'What else do you want to know? I'm sure whatever you found stashed away in the files is accurate. Your intelligence is flawless, I'm told.'

He flashes me a grin.

'I want to know your version of your life, not the version some pencil pusher in Canberra or Langley who has never left the office makes of it. I'm old-fashioned; I still believe the best way to gather information is to actually talk to people.'

'Look, don't take this personally,' I say, 'but not today. Maybe not ever. Or maybe when we find these fuckers, we can have a jolly night in a bar somewhere.'

He shrugs his shoulders. A gesture of acceptance.

'I'll let you get back to it then,' he says and walks back towards the front of the plane.

I look at the terminal in front of me. I can barely focus.

Exhaustion is washing over me in big crashing waves. I stand and follow Miller's footsteps, find the well-upholstered leather chair I was in earlier and crash down into it. I close my eyes.

13

I wake. Not with a start, but like someone emerging from an anaesthetic after an operation. Fog lies heavy in my brain and the dream I was having just a moment ago is already gone, leaving behind only a sense of vague discomfort.

The cabin is brightly lit and I shield my eyes with my hand as I adapt from the dark of sleep to the light. Miller is sitting opposite me.

'Welcome back.'

'How long have I been out of it?' I ask.

'Almost seven hours,' is the surprising reply.

I look at my watch, which is still set to Indonesian time and telling me it's coming up for 9 p.m. in Jakarta. Midnight at home in Australia.

'Don't worry, I had a few hours shut-eye as well. Got to take it while it's going, I reckon.'

'Did I miss anything?'

'If you mean have any aircraft fallen out of the sky in the last few hours then happily the answer is no. Going by the timetable of the last day and a half, we could have expected another disappearance. But now somewhere around 30 per cent of the world's airlines have grounded themselves in the last few hours, including Lufthansa, Garuda and American. Say they won't go back up until this thing is resolved. It could be that there was another one planned but the plane is still stuck in a hangar somewhere with the "flight cancelled" sign blinking in an unknown airport.'

'And no fresh leads? No breakthrough discoveries from the boffins?'

'Ah, no, you didn't miss anything in that sense while you were sleeping.'

'How long till we land? I'm getting sick of being stuck here with you.'

'Less than an hour, I'm told. We've had some nice tailwinds. And remember, Ted, we're not the only two people on the face of the earth trying to find a solution to this nightmare. There are teams of people in Munich, Belo Horizonte, Istanbul and God knows where else trying to find the answers. There are literally thousands of people on this case.'

A silence lies between us.

'Don't give the company claptrap, Miller,' I grunt. 'I may have only known you five minutes but I could have spotted your ego from Sydney. You want to be part of this as much as I do. I have the feeling you are trying to elbow me out of the way. That you don't want a rogue Australian getting to the bottom of this before your lot do.'

'Oh, Ted, park the paranoia for the moment. I'm not

trying to push you out. I'm just trying to be a little real. Tell me, if I'm so good, why the fuck was I stationed in Jakarta? Sure, it has a few things going for it. A few mad bombers, an attractive extremist element and all that, but it's not exactly the number-one posting sought by the bright young things the agency tends to hire.'

'So why were you there?'

'Call it time off for bad behaviour.'

We both lapse into quiet contemplation, perhaps thinking about all the wrong moves that had brought us to this point in our lives, until Miller breaks the silence to ask, 'You hungry?'

I realise I am. Starving, in fact. The last time I ate was in my hotel room in Jakarta, however many hours ago that was.

'Yes, very. What you got?'

Miller signals to a uniformed man at the back of the plane.

'Yes, sir. What can I do for you?'

'Can we get a quick breakfast before we land?'

'Of course, sir. We have just enough time to serve you a meal before we touch down in Los Angeles.'

'Excellent. Two breakfasts, please. Eggs, bacon, hash browns, mushrooms and tomatoes. Coffee. Lots of coffee. That okay with you, Ted?'

'Great,' I say. It sounds like the best meal I have ever eaten. Just the thought of it is making my empty stomach growl and my mouth water. When it arrives, it's as good as advertised. Miller and I concentrate so fiercely on the plates in front of us that we don't say a word until we are done.

'Man, that was good,' he finally offers.

I nod and rub my stomach, close my eyes and think it's time for another nap. Instead, I reach for my iPad and tell Miller I am going to find a quiet spot up the back to check in with Sydney. To see if they have anything useful to contribute.

Seconds later I'm back with Bob. It seems Bob has popped back to his Woollahra haven for a rest and despite everything it's mildly shocking to know the boss has a human need for a sleep and a shower just like the rest of us, even if it's gone midnight in Sydney.

From what I can remember of Bob's house, from the one time I was allowed to visit, it looks like he's in his study. There's a big oak desk from the eighteenth century that he paid some ridiculous price for at an auction and matching bookcases mainly populated by tomes on politics and war, although there is a row of George Pelecanos detective thrillers in there as well. The French doors open out into a shady garden where an assortment of vines just about holds together an ancient pergola. It is his sanctuary from the seriousness of the rest of his life. As far as I know he lives there alone. There's never been a suggestion of a Mrs Bob or even a Mr Bob. What Bob gets up to outside office hours is a complete mystery. I find myself grinning when I see him on the iPad. Maybe it's just the need to see a (relatively) friendly face again.

'Ted, nice of you to check in,' he says in a voice heavy with sarcasm, and I feel some of my childish bonhomie start to fade. 'Still enjoying the company of our American friends?'

'It's not a bus, Bob. I can't press a button and ask to be let off at the next stop.'

'Quite. I guess you're not too far from LA, so at least you will be on the ground again soon. When you are, wander over to the Tom Bradley Terminal and find a Qantas counter. They'll have a boarding pass ready that will bring you home. Economy. Hopefully in a middle seat between a couple of obese passengers.'

This wasn't what I was expecting. I can feel the red mist descending. It's a struggle not to let my fury show.

'Now, Bob, hold on . . .'

He cuts me off before I can begin to make even the outline of a point.

'No, Ted. I've had enough of this nonsense. You work for me. Not the Yanks. And not for yourself, which I suspect is what you really think you're doing most of the time. So get on that plane and I'll see you tomorrow. From there we can decide what is going to happen next.'

I'm doing less and less well at containing myself. I thought in our last conversation that I was making progress with him, convincing him my theory was the right one. My mind flicks to my conversation with Miller. The one where he was trying to convince me that we were less than crucial to this operation.

'Have you been speaking to Alan Miller?'

'Who?' Bob is not much of an actor and seems puzzled by the question. I'm still suspicious, though, that a scheme is being cooked up to take me from the field. I can't remember now if I've mentioned Miller's name to him or not, but it wouldn't have been difficult for him to contact a counterpart at the CIA and make some inquiries.

Either way, I'm not happy.

'Bob, that's shit. How does me getting back on another plane *help*? Planes are falling out the sky. We have to know what the fuck is going on.'

'But what's your big lead, Ted? What's your theory? Where are you going? Who are you planning to interrogate? If you're there, if you're not, does anything change?'

That's cold from Bob but I can offer nothing in return. I am regretting sleeping so long on the plane. I missed my chance to find something, anything. A card to play. Still, I'm not ready to stop, or go home. Logic and instinct tell me that whatever is going on, there will be an American hand to be played at some stage. It makes sense. America is the number-one enemy of most of the mad nutters, therefore it is also the number-one target as well.

'While you have been wasting time travelling the world, we've been working pretty hard at this end. We are having a much closer look now at those stolen passports and we think they hold the key. If you had been here, perhaps you could have done so. Turns out Jakarta could be the key to the whole thing. You should have stayed there, Ted. But you made your choice and I've had to replace you on the investigation.'

By now I'm shouting.

'This is fucked up, Bob. *Fucked up*. It's the pilots, Bob, the pilots. Have you found something on Notonegro? Who is he? Does he have something to do with the passports?'

'No, Ted. We're finished talking about this. Get on the plane. We'll talk when you are back in Sydney.'

And, with that, he hangs up.

I sit there, stunned at Bob's sudden dismissal. But I'm also puzzled. I'm not sure why he's gone off the deep end. Maybe it's the pressure of the situation. Maybe someone is leaning on him from above for reasons beyond my knowledge. Maybe he believes I have let him down in some fashion.

I wait to let the anger fizzle out of my blood. To regain a measure of control. After a couple of minutes, I am calm again, although still annoyed and confused by the thought of returning to Australia. I make my way back to my seat near the front of the plane.

Miller is still there and I wonder how much he has heard. I suspect I became a little loud back there.

'Alright, buddy?' he asks as I take my seat.

'Never better.'

'It's just that I thought I heard a little shouting back there. In fact, it sounded like a lot of shouting. Trouble at home?'

'Have you talked to Bob about me? Maybe when I was sleeping?' I ask Miller.

He looks perplexed. Tilts his chin to the left. 'What? Your boss? No. Why?'

'Nothing. Forget it,' I say, running my left hand through my hair.

This is the point where I should tell him the adventure is over. That as soon as we touch down at LAX I will be packing my bags and making a run for it. But I can't do it. There is no way I am giving this up, not now, to go back to Australia. This is the biggest story in the world. I'm not going home to watch it on CNN.

The biggest problem will be bluffing Miller that I still have status with the investigation. Assuming he is telling the truth about not talking to Bob. But I figure I have at least sixteen hours before Bob twigs that I haven't done as ordered, providing he doesn't check that I have boarded the flight at LAX. But that's a chance I'm willing to take. And to make it that little bit harder to find me, I turn off the location finder on the iPad. No more tracking me around the world on his device.

'Small argument,' I lie. 'My boss tried to order me home. Said I shouldn't be wandering the world with the likes of you. We sorted it out. I convinced him that as I was involved in the cutting edge of the investigation I would be better off staying here as it seems unlikely that the answers would lie at home. He accepted that.'

'Really?'

'Yes. Why?' The paranoia ratchets one mark higher.

'I just figured that he may have been ordering you off the battlefield and that you weren't too happy.'

He is smiling cheerfully. It looks like he is enjoying himself far too much, and, worryingly, that he is not buying my bluff.

'You know how the brass are,' I say. 'Very rigid in their application of the rules. But he saw sense in the end.'

Even to my own ears I don't sound convincing, but there's no way back now. Lies don't have a reverse gear; you just have to keep ploughing forward.

'So you won't mind if we make a call back to Sydney to confirm you are still on active service on this one? We wouldn't want to carry a tourist into action.'

'Nope, that's fine. You go for it.'

Miller stands and wanders to the back of the plane and I wonder if he's serious about contacting Australia. It seems unlikely that he has bought my story and I stare glumly out of the window as the aircraft's nose starts to drop as descent begins. The mad sprawl of LAX soon appears. Los Angeles may be home to the world's biggest dream factory, but it's a horrible metropolis connected by packed freeways stuffed with cars that from the air look as if they are all joined by chains. It's nose to tail as far as the eye can see. To call it a freeway just seems to be mocking everyone.

I struggle in LA. It's a place where it's hard to keep a map of the joint in your head. It seems a city without a centre, in a geographical as well as emotional sense, making it impossible to get your bearings unless you've had the misfortune to live here all your life.

We're nearly on the ground when Miller comes to the front of the plane, striding towards me at an impressively rapid rate. I fear the worst. Has he really called Australia? But he's agitated. All his calm demeanour and ironic cool have been forgotten. He stands in front of me, almost hopping from foot to foot. He is too juiced to even sit down.

'Okay, I don't care what kind of fight you and your boss have had but you can't get off this plane. Neither can I. Change of orders. We are only here for as long as it takes to fill up with gas then we're back in the air. We can't taxi to any terminal to kick you out. Okay?'

'Where are we going?'

'New York. Things are moving.'

I stare at him, aware of my fizzling blood and electric skin as all the wasted hours on this bloody plane start to fade away.

'What do you have?'

123

'Langley has picked up some internet chatter from somewhere. It's vague. New York gets a mention though, as does the name of the pilot on the missing American Airlines flight. Franck Dupree. I've been summoned.'

The captain's voice cuts through the cabin. It's the southern drawl of Connelly, sounding more relaxed than the last time I heard from him.

'Ladies and gentlemen, would you please be so kind as to take your seats. We are on final approach to Los Angeles and will be wheels down in about ten minutes. I will be leaving you there and hope you enjoy the onward leg of the flight to New York. I also do hope you don't hold that bit of turbulence we had at the start of the flight against me. Adios.'

I am left alone with my thoughts. I wonder if this lets me back in. If I can use the time it will take to reach New York to either work on Miller or find some hook into the investigation that will deal me back in. The man himself has disappeared again towards the back of the aircraft. The other seats in the cabin are filling up around me, but so far no one else has been brave enough to sit next to the odd Australian. Perhaps Miller has warned them off talking to me. He is probably still assessing exactly how much to tell me and whether I get to play a part in whatever fun and games await us.

I stare out of the window at the looming airport. Something looks different about it today and it takes me a few seconds to figure out exactly what. It's the lack of planes. Or, at least, the lack of movement of planes. Every time I have been stuck in this shithole of an airport you can't help but notice how slowly everything moves. From traipsing through security and customs to the hours spent sitting on the aircraft waiting to take off. Nothing happens in a hurry, except the rate at which your blood pressure increases. There are always vast queues of both people milling about terminals and planes waiting to get the hell out of LA.

But not today. From above, I can see a lone 747 crawling slowly to the end of a runway and that's about it. I can also see plenty of the buggers parked at gates and many more scattered around the airfield going nowhere. LAX has been turned into a metropolitan version of the famous aircraft graveyard in Nevada. Or, since we are in California, we can mangle that hoary old Eagles song: *'You can check out any time you like, but you can never leave . . .'*

A minute later, we are on the ground.

14

It's a truly impressive turnaround. We have parked a long way away from any terminals, have refuelled and are back on our way in less than twenty minutes. The only people to get off the planes are the pilots. They clearly have a better union than me. I'm starting to feel as if I'm going to spend the rest of my life on this aircraft. I go for a wander to locate Miller and find him hunched up behind a computer, headphones on, not in the mood to be disturbed.

And then we're in the air. Miller stays away and I read through the collective human misery that is the world's new websites on my iPad. The credible publications, like the *Washington Post* and the *New York Times*, are all on the edge of hysteria. The always ridiculous *The Sun* and *Daily Mail* operate way out there anyway and so have relatively little room to move. These rags are torn between predicting the end of the world ('GROUNDED: The day the earth stood still') and blaming the usual suspects ('Islamic terrorists take over our skies').

There is still no indication of who is responsible for the disappearing planes. No claims of glory. Nothing credible, anyway. A couple of the smaller terrorist outfits are having a shot, but no one is taking them seriously.

I continue to read. The process becomes quite hypnotic. Soothing even, despite the chaos and mayhem. And there has to be something here in all this information. Some thread to pull. Some semblance of an idea about who is behind all this. Nothing new occurs. The more I read, the more convinced I am that we are dealing with something new here. Something we haven't seen before. It scares me. I keep reading, sifting, thinking.

Occasionally I shake myself out of this web-induced reverie and try to find Miller. To try to talk to him, work up a theory. Expand on my growing conviction that we have to broaden the net away from the usual suspects in the terrorism game.

It's not until we are on final approach to New York that Miller sits down beside me.

'Sorry, my friend, this is it. I had to make that call and you are out. Your people, my people, all those people have been talking and everyone has decided. And before you jump to any conclusions, no, this wasn't all arranged hours ago when you were sleeping. I stalled them for as long as possible, I stuck up for you, I thought you could be useful in all this. You were an airline pilot yourself—that's an expertise in itself that we could have used on the inside of this thing, but the Australians want you home. There's nothing more I can say. But thanks. I enjoyed your company. There's a ticket in your name at the Qantas counter at JFK.'

He stands and puts out a hand. I take it.

'I suppose I knew it would come to this,' I mutter.

He hands me a card. A plain white business one with only a phone number on it.

'I'm an old-school type of guy. It's more elegant somehow than just giving you a number that you plug into your cell. You know the drill. If you're ever back in these parts, look me up.'

Then he turns and heads back to the other end of the plane.

I am deflated. Angry. Suddenly very tired. I have been on this fucking plane for . . . I don't know how long—and now I'm being dragged all the way back to Sydney. Not for the first time I can't see the logic of those working above me.

But there is nothing I can do. There is no way to buck this system. I grab my backpack and check my beleaguered belongings. I'm about to stuff my iPad away in there with everything else when I suddenly decide I am sick of my every movement being tracked. I did turn off the location finder, but I don't reckon that's worth much. If they wanted to find me, they could without this electronic marvel. I have a quick look around and with nobody paying me any attention I shove the tablet under my seat. It's a tiny act of rebellion, but it makes me feel better.

It's a brisk winter day in New York as I step down from the jet. It's late in the afternoon, the daylight fading. I try to calculate what day it is in this part of the world. Sunday is my best guess. My knees creak and crack as I lower myself down the metal stairs that have been pushed to the side of the jet to allow escape.

The brief flurry of snow that stings my cheeks is a shock: it was summer just a day or so ago in Sydney and Jakarta when I left the southern hemisphere. I delve into my backpack for the old leather jacket.

One of the minions from the plane has been given the job of escorting me to the terminal in a minibus. Maybe they think I will hijack it and try to drive back to Australia. Neither of us says a word, not even a goodbye when I am finally dropped at a pale-green door that brings me to a set of stairs leading inside the airport.

A bulky security guy is waiting for me at the door. Puffy black jacket with a gold logo of some sort of firm, black pants, black shoes, black hat, under which he appears to store a white shaved head. I contemplate making a break for it—just for fun, really, it's not like I have anywhere to go— until I see the gun hanging at his side. This is America. He will shoot me.

At least, being American, he is polite.

'Good morning, sir. Would you like to follow me, please.'

We climb three flights of stairs before he swipes a card through a reader that opens a door and takes us into the public area of the terminal. Here he wishes me luck and disappears before I can even ask him where to find the Qantas desk.

Oh well. On my own again. Naturally.

As I gather my bearings, I become aware of the strangeness of this airport. Not its physical infrastructure, which is as run-down as you expect any large American airport to be, but the atmosphere of the joint. There are remarkably few people milling about. The hustle and bustle that marks these places, of people rushing from one place to another full of the eager anticipation of travel, is gone.

The family groups, the tour groups—all have disappeared. As far as I can see, the place is populated by lone, worried travellers such as myself who are only about to step on a plane because they have no other choice. Everyone else has chosen not to risk it. And who can blame them? This is New York, after all. A city with an experience of terrorism that naturally encourages caution in its citizens.

There is a bank of departure and arrival screens above my head. The most common word up there is 'cancelled'. I search for my flight and sure enough it is still scheduled to leave. If the departure time is to be believed, I have about three hours to kill before jumping on board.

The first thing to do is find the Qantas counter. I wander, ending up in the middle of the usual shops, and after deciding I don't need Armani perfume or a Mont Blanc pen, I spot a sign for airline lounges and decide that's as good an idea as any. There's probably a lovely area set aside for Qantas travellers to rest their weary bodies before setting off for home. Maybe, if I'm lucky, they will even let me have a shower, and at this thought I give myself a surreptitious sniff and decide I am several days past my best in hygiene.

The sign is pointing up some elevators. At the top a little red and white sign with the familiar kangaroo logo gives me further instructions. This leads me to some smoky glass doors. Now, I have been in a couple of these flash airport hideaways before. Not often. Airports were a place of work to me so it was generally considered bad form to pop in for a glass of champagne before take-off. Anytime I did, though, and especially if I was out of my pilot's uniform, I always felt like an imposter. That I would be found out and kicked out at any time. It always felt like a room for the rich, and if not the rich then the self-satisfied. Still, it's possible I was reading too much into it.

With that in mind, I'm now tentative as those glass doors part to allow me entry into this hallowed hall. Behind a long, polished desk—the rest of the airport may be a shithole, but different rules apply in here, clearly—sit two well-manicured, trimly dressed people whose jobs must involve a high level of obsequiousness on a daily basis. As I enter their domain, both heads simultaneously swing to greet me, and I sense them registering in tandem just the faintest whiff of disgust at my approach. You can't really blame them. I'm not exactly looking like a refugee from New York Fashion Week—unless battered, middle-aged Australian has become this season's in thing.

There is one male and one female. I take the female. Decked out in the sharpest uniform Qantas has available, there is a severe angular look to her face, blonde hair pulled tightly back, make-up too perfectly applied.

'Hello, I'm . . . Sean Docherty,' I begin, stuttering suspiciously on the verge of giving the Qantas mannequin my real name. I must be tired. 'I believe you may be holding a ticket for me.'

She looks at me if not disbelievingly then at least disapprovingly.

'Do you have any identification, ah, Mr Docherty, is it?' she asks in a voice that leads me to believe she is auditioning for a role as Queen Elizabeth's long lost Australian sister. I hand over my passport without comment. She scans it, taps a few keys on her computer and hands it back.

'Ah, yes, there does appear to be a ticket here for you. Bear with me a moment and I'll print out your boarding pass.'

As she hands it over to me, I ask: 'Is it okay if I go in there?' gesturing towards the luxurious confines of the club with a flick of my head.

'I'm sorry, Mr Docherty,' the Qantas queen informs me. 'The club is reserved for business-class customers and members only.' She doesn't continue with the rest of that sentence, which no doubt ends with 'and not for economy-class scum like you'.

I turn and walk away, ushered back through those smoky doors with a laugh from the desk behind me for company.

* * *

So I do what everyone in an airport with time to kill does. Find a bookshop, buy the latest John le Carré epic to find out what my life really should be like instead of what it is, pick up a *New York Times* and try to find a vaguely comfortable seat at a café that sells vaguely drinkable coffee. This being America, I don't hold out much hope for the second requirement, but my system is in desperate need of a caffeine top-up and I'm prepared to take my chances. I can't find a regular coffee shop so Starbucks will have to do.

My brain is too frazzled to take in the complexities of the le Carré and I resort to watching the passers-by from my perch on the outer rim of the Starbucks. I have settled into a state of acceptance. The anger is gone, replaced by tiredness and a desire to go home, collapse on my bed and shut out the world. Perhaps by the time I reach Australia the mystery of the missing aircraft will have been solved. I briefly think of Bob and the reception waiting for me at home. It's probably not going to be pretty, but at this point in time, in this morgue-like airport, I don't really care. Fuck them all. If they don't need me, I don't need them.

It's a grim scene. The few passengers wandering about all have haunted, fearful looks. The airport has the atmosphere of one of those ubiquitous zombie films where the last humans are all huddled together waiting for the apocalypse to arrive.

A couple of flight crews walk past. I wonder how many others have called in sick today. It can't have been a wonderful feeling to go to work. Next a cleaner moves slowly by. At least he is safe, I think. A small Hispanic man pushing a large yellow rubbish cart that is almost taller than him. I watch him huff and wheeze for about twenty metres, the story of Sisyphus in my head, when he stops and leans against the wall, exhausted, until he puts a hand on a small ledge to steady himself and pushes on to his next station. The ledge is the kind of small protuberance where a traveller may perch for a moment, looking for a place to rest their still-hot coffee bought next door.

My eyes follow the man, but my attention is soon caught by a small, black rectangular object he appears to have left on the ledge.

'Bugger,' I think. 'The old bloke has left something behind.'

While I'm having the internal debate about whether this is the time to do the right thing and chase the cleaner to return the item or do what most people would normally do (nothing), a tall, upright man dressed in an airline captain's uniform parades down the corridor towards me, and with an easy swing of the hand sweeps up the object. Five seconds later he strolls past my table and, without a glance at me, keeps walking. I am struck by the strange thought that this is the most relaxed man I have seen in the airport all day.

What has he picked up? It looked like it could have been a small tablet. It's about the right size to be a mini iPad. More than a little curious, I dump the le Carré and the *Times* in my trusty backpack and, aiming for a level of calm I'm not feeling, start to trail the pilot.

As in all major airports, the cafés and concessions at JFK are the entry way to the gates where passengers gather to head off to the wild blue yonder. The man in front keeps a steady pace as we pass one gate after another, and he appears to be heading for a gate at the far end of the airport. I drift along behind him, doing my best inconspicuous-spy thing. Trying to channel the le Carré in my bag. There are dribs and drabs of people still around so I don't think I'm being too obvious.

At Gate 41, the pilot lurches left to make his way past the empty chairs in the departure lounge, walks through the doors heading to the airbridge, and enters the tunnel that takes him to the aircraft. I emerge into the still-empty departure area just as he disappears. As casually as I can manage, I walk over to the airbridge entrance, but the doors are now closed. Instead I shuffle to the window at the side of the airbridge overlooking the apron and spot the plane into which the captain has disappeared.

It's a Ukraine International Airlines Boeing 767. My heart sinks. My mind races. *The pilots, the answers must lie with the pilots*, and the thought crowding into my head is: *This is going to be the next plane to disappear.*

I spin around, searching for some idea of when the plane is leaving New York. A departures board tells me a flight numbered PS232 is scheduled to take off in less than two hours, destination Kiev. I have to assume this is the one. The question now is: how do I get on board? The other question, a more serious one: do I want to get on a plane that's possibly heading to oblivion? I push this thought to the back of my mind.

The obvious answer to the riddle about how to get on the flight is to buy a ticket, but I'm cutting it fine. I consider going online to see what I can find, but I've left the iPad on the plane. Instead I decide to head back into the bowels of the airport to find a Ukrainian Airlines counter where I can hopefully just buy one. This comes with the problem of having to leave the relative comfort of being on the right side of the customs and security barrier. The idea of pushing my way out, finding the ticket counter and then dealing again with the good folk at customs, who keep wanting me to undress for them, doesn't fill me with my most optimistic emotions of the day.

Still, on the bright side, what with all this nasty terrorist stuff, it's probably the quietest day this airport has had since it was still called Idlewild. But if I do fail to get on board the flight, my Qantas ride home will have already gone and I'll be stuck in this airport for who knows how long. I start to waver. Maybe I should just forget Ukraine and get on Qantas and head home? A vision of my unmade bed in Sydney pops into my mind and it's undeniably alluring.

Or should I contact Miller and tell him of my suspicions? That would make it his problem. And tell him what exactly? That I saw an airline captain, heading to one of the world's most dangerous regions, possibly pick up something left by a cleaner, that might have been a mini iPad? And even if it was an iPad, what did that mean? There's an ego thing at work here, as well. I haven't covered myself in glory in the last two days, so it would be embarrassing to assemble Miller and the entire US security apparatus for something that turns out to be a false alarm. I need more details.

Bob? Our last conversation didn't end well and I don't fancy calling him to tell him that I'm not coming home. He'll just think I'm finding excuses to avoid heading back to Australia. And maybe he's right.

Anyway, all those fuckers have cut me out of the operation. The Americans don't want me around, Bob thinks it's useless. Yes, it's childish, but part of me just wants to show how wrong they all are.

The adrenalin generated by tailing the pilot is fading and I start to second-guess myself. Maybe my tired, fevered mind is playing tricks on me. But I can't let it go. I've got this far, good and bad, by following my instincts, and the feeling down in my gut tells me something is wrong here.

I decide to play it out, to see where it takes me. I decide not to tell Miller.

* * *

I head back the way I had come. Airports aren't places to run, especially today. Running tends to attract the attention of security guards and they assume the worst: that it's not someone late for a plane or who has left their house keys in a plastic tray at security but someone who has planted a bomb and is about to kill everyone. And today, more than any other day, security is going to be twitchy.

I decide the best I can manage is a brisk walk. Even then it takes me ten minutes to get back to the exit. The cavernous entry hall of the terminal is lit up with the brand names of a dozen airlines in bright neon. Without the usual throng of people, it feels sad and deserted. I check the boards, seeking directions to where Ukraine Airlines might live, and I am finally pointed to a desk at the far end of the hall.

The blue-and-yellow logo of the airline hovers above the single desk open for passengers. The line is short but diverse. An old lady, dressed in black with a long skirt, is being escorted by an equally ancient man in a 1950s brown suit. There are two young men, both wearing jeans and dark T-shirts. They have short hair and a stud each in the left ear. They could be brothers or lovers, but probably brothers; there is a similarity in the jawline that suggests a common genetic inheritance. Both are pushing a luggage trolley that has a large, brown cardboard box sitting on it big enough to accommodate several children in comfort inside it.

Then there is me. Trying to contain my frustration at being held up and nervous about just how difficult it's going to be to extract a ticket from the woman behind the counter.

The oldies finally finish and move on, checking several times that they are going in the right direction, grasping tightly onto their boarding passes. The brothers move up to the counter and there is an animated conversation with much waving of hands and pointing at the large box. It seems the woman from the airline is making the entirely reasonable point that the box is not going to fit on the conveyor belt behind her. She asks the boys to hold the box on the scales so she can measure its weight. More drama. I think I hear the poor woman say something about 'excess baggage' and '$150'. This prompts another round of argument and I wonder if this is the real reason airports won't let us carry guns. In case we shoot the dickheads ahead of us in the queue.

Eventually, after more gesticulating and general unhappiness on all sides, it is my turn. I approach the counter with my best weren't-they-a-bunch-of-morons look. The woman smiles back.

'Hello,' I start. 'I'd like to buy a ticket to Kiev, please.'

The smiling face takes on a look of puzzlement.

'I understand it's a bit last-minute,' I continue, 'but I was already in the airport when I found out that my brother has been in an accident in Kiev and I need to get there as soon as possible. It's quite serious, unfortunately.'

I dig my Qantas boarding pass out of my bag.

'I was just on my way back home to Australia when my parents called me to tell me the terrible news. He was crossing a street and was hit by a bus. It's pretty bad; they're not sure if he'll pull through. But I have to get there.'

The best lies always have a modicum of truth in them: I'm going to Australia and I have the boarding pass to prove it.

The attendant gives me her best sympathetic smile.

'I am very sorry to hear about your brother. That must be a terrible shock. But it may not be as simple as buying a ticket. I don't suppose you have a visa for Ukraine, sir?'

This is a problem I had not contemplated.

'Ah, no . . . This is all so last-minute. As I said, I was just about to jump on the plane and head back to Australia. Do I need a visa? Can I not just get one when I arrive in Kiev?'

'I don't know, sir. I will have to check with my supervisor.'

With that, she picks up the phone. A short conversation later she is back with me.

'Sir, I can sell you the ticket, but there is no guarantee they will let you into the country when you get there. I understand they are quite strict about these things. You are also supposed to have proof of a hotel booking and a departure date. If you are refused entry we can offer no refund, so you take the flight at your own risk. It has been suggested to me, however, that it may be helped if you had a return ticket.'

'Can I fly back from Kiev to Sydney, instead of New York?'

She taps a few more keys.

'Yes, you can. But your flight will be routed through Dubai.'

'That's fine. I'll take my chances.'

I pull out my Sean Docherty credit card and passport and hand them over. It won't take long for Bob to find out I have just bought a ticket to Kiev, but hopefully I will be in the air by then and beyond his reach. I am also not worried about the visa situation. If I'm right, I'm not going to be landing in Kiev, anyway. If I'm wrong, I will be quite happy to leave Kiev as soon as I arrive and go home. Ukraine has never been high on my list of holiday destinations.

'Would you like your ticket to be in coach or first class, sir?'

I decide the closer to the cockpit I am, the better chance I have of spotting anything amiss. Anyway, it's only government money. It's not real, although when Bob gets the bill he may not share my generosity when it comes to the taxpayer coin.

'I think I'll take first,' I say. 'May need to get some proper rest before I get to Kiev to see my brother.' I'm not sure why I needed to add the last little justification. Probably some part of my old working-class brain, inherited from my delivery driver of a father who would be appalled at such extravagance, kicking into action.

'Okay, sir. I can give you seat 2A. Will that be acceptable?'

I graciously agree that it will be and she swipes my card. As I put in my PIN number to complete the transaction I notice the total is $7321.67. In US dollars. Well, that definitely won't make Bob happy. There will be a big, red, flashing light going off in his office right at this moment, probably with a loud metallic voice proclaiming, *'Alert. Agent spending money. Alert!'*

But it's done. I pick up my backpack, take my boarding pass, and head back through to security and customs, wondering if I've just bought a ticket for a suicide mission.

15

Sometimes it's better not to stop for too long to think about what you have done. Momentum has carried me this far: I have to keep running with it. To see where this will take me. A considered, well-executed plan is not what this is. If going to Western Australia had been routine reaction to a developing situation, going to Jakarta had been a whim that turned into a wild goose chase. It was still hard to know whether it meant anything or not. It's not clear if Notonegro is a villain or a victim of both bad timing and forces beyond his control. Running into Miller had been an accident that had seen me shot at, more or less kidnapped, flown halfway across the world and, in the end, had led me to wandering alone through JFK Airport headed to a plane that may or may not be taking me to Kiev. At the very least, it's been an interesting day.

Not for the first time, I thought about contacting somebody—anyone—to let them know what I was about to do. Part of what stopped me again was embarrassment. What if I was wrong? But if it did turn out I was right, I still thought the best way to defeat the bad guys was to creep up on them slowly. To let them think they were safe from detection. If I called in the Americans, or told Bob, there would be an all-out operation, and a high chance that a trigger-happy American would shoot the plane out of the sky and we would be no closer to finding out what happened to the other aircraft and the thousands of missing people. And I'd still be dead.

This, I told myself, was a job for the lone agent. You have to love a bit of unconstrained ego at times.

I had done pretty well. There are still fifteen minutes until boarding. And as the place is running about quarter its normal capacity, getting back through customs shouldn't be the usual tortuous process.

Passport control, however, is shaping as my biggest problem. As soon as my passport is swiped they will realise I am already listed as a passenger on a flight to Sydney. They may also ask questions about the slightly unorthodox situation of me having a seat on an international flight without any sign I had arrived in the US in the first place.

Miller had told me back on the plane that he would arrange something to be inserted onto the government computer network that listed me as having entered the country in LA on a routine commercial flight, but I have my doubts. If I'm forced to tell customs l was brought to America on a US spy aircraft from a Muslim country against my will, it could cause even more trouble. They will think I am either mad or taking the piss, and passport control are not widely known for their sense of humour. I mean, this is a country that likes to scan your eyeball before they let you in.

I approach the heavy-set black man at the counter. He has the non-smiling demeanour of someone who has spent the majority of his life in that chair and is none too pleased about it. With as much deference as I can manage, I hand over my passport. It's like handing up your homework to the scariest teacher at school. He takes it without a word (another classic move to make you feel as uncomfortable as possible), scans it and raises a quizzical eyebrow. Just the one. I take it he's only half-surprised.

'Sir, are you supposed to be here?' he asks in a very New Jersey accent. 'You're down as being on a Qantas flight back to Sydney that departed fifteen minutes ago.'

'Yes, well, I just had some bad news, I'm afraid,' I begin and tell him the story of my recently invented brother—who now has a name, Henry—and his unfortunate collision with the public transport service in Kiev.

The man looks at me sceptically, but as far as I know there is no law that prevents you holding two tickets on the one day and choosing your preferred destination.

He hands me back my passport and boarding pass without another word and waves me through. For a moment, I am miffed he hasn't wished me the best of luck with my brother, until I remember Henry isn't real.

The boarding queue is snaking out of the departure lounge when I arrive. I spot the old couple and the brothers about halfway along and I am just about to join the end of the line and start the slow forward shuffle when I remember today I am holding the magic card that lets me avoid such mundanities. I skip up to the special gate for special people, show them my special first-class boarding pass and head straight onto the plane, trying to ignore the many death stares from those still moving at snail's pace.

Once inside the plane, I turn left instead of the usual right and find myself confronted with an oasis of comfort in the otherwise nasty world of long-haul travel. A tall, blonde, attractive hostie welcomes me on board in a most fetching accent and guides me towards my seat. She informs me that if 'there is anything I can do, please just ask', with a smile that suggests she knows exactly what I'm thinking.

* * *

From my angle, I can't yet see the cockpit door. But as I'm escorted to my seat by my lovely guide, I can see it is closed. Getting into the cockpit in the post-9/11 world is a difficult assignment so I am going to have to bide my time and hopefully come up with a plan. I have to assume my guy is in there, behind the locked door. I haven't seen him since I followed him to the aeroplane, but he is in there now, going through the old routines, the pre-flight safety checks, the weather, the million things a pilot has to do before take-off.

The whole locked cockpit does have some obvious safety advantages over the old-style revolving door approach, but there are a few downsides today. There have been a disturbing number of plane crashes where one of the pilots was locked out as the aircraft deliberately ploughed into the ground, or mountain, or ocean. There was the case of the Germanwings pilot who locked his co-captain out of the cockpit, then drove his plane into a French mountain. One hundred and fifty died in that one. And an EgyptAir first officer who killed more than 200 people by plunging his craft into the Atlantic Ocean not long after taking off from JFK—another act of madness I didn't want to spend too long thinking about. Pilot suicide was, however, an idea that first occurred when the Garuda went missing off Australia. But three pilot suicides was stretching the bounds of plausibility, wasn't it?

I settle into my comfortable seat. I do that thing where you rummage through your backpack even though you know everything that is in there, having already been through it a dozen times. I feel the blurry edges of the le Carré, the soft leather of the jacket, my wallet, and wonder again whether the bigwigs at home have any inkling yet of my recent extravagant purchase.

I take out the le Carré, but I am still too distracted to read. I am looking at everyone, trying to figure out if any of them looks worried or tense or sweaty or nervous. Is anyone showing any telltale signs of imminent death? What are the telltale signs of imminent death, anyway? I can't see anyone praying.

Those at my end of the plane have the calm and assured look of well-moneyed professional travellers. They all know they belong here, deserve to be here, and it strikes me that the most suspicious looking person in this compartment is me.

Maybe this will end with me having to take myself out?

I crane my neck around, stand and stretch, trying to get a glimpse of the remaining passengers filing into the aircraft and heading towards economy. But all I can see are bums, backs and hair. A line of people shuffling and stopping, shuffling and stopping, until they find their allocated seat, shove a bag into the tiny space left in the overhead locker and flop down into the even smaller area they will be confined to for the next nine hours.

The in-flight magazine is as dull as these publications always are. This one has four pages dedicated to the history of basket weaving and points me to Kiev's no doubt fascinating Museum of Ukrainian Folk Art. But it also has a pull-out section showing all the places the airline flies to and plots some rough flight paths. The route to Kiev from New York will take me in a high arc over the North Atlantic before reconnecting with land again over the northern reaches of Scotland, the southern tip of Scandinavia, and settling down over Poland and Belarus before reaching Kiev.

If anything is going to happen, it's likely to be somewhere in the North Atlantic. Once we get a few hundred kilometres off the US coast and are tracking over the North Atlantic, there's no radar and plenty of blackspots—plenty of ways for resourceful, or desperate, pilots to make their plane disappear.

The global aviation system is set up on the understanding that pilots will always want to land their aircraft at the expected point, and that if they do run into trouble they will want to be found. There isn't much built into the system to guard against the whims of the deranged who want their aircraft to disappear. There should be, though. Not that any would ever admit it, but sometimes where you are up there, in that big blue sky, a million miles from home and just as far from anywhere else, your mind can wander. You hold the fate of hundreds of people in your hands. That kind of power can be intoxicating. Sometimes you think you could lean forward on the controls just to see what happens next . . .

Any pilot who tells you they haven't done this is lying. In my more disturbed days of piloting heavy passenger aircraft, these were the kind of thoughts often flying through my head, especially at night when all you could see were the stars above and the twinkling neon of cities below. It was a view that had a magic, translucent effect on my brain and on my soul. Thankfully, while I was probably mad enough for a while there, I was never quite bad enough.

But I know I wasn't alone in thinking such dark thoughts.

I decline the offer of a pre-flight champagne, a decision that takes all the moral courage I can muster. A drink right now seems like the most appealing prospect in the world, but I settle for the orange juice instead.

All seems normal so far. The passengers have settled in, the cabin crew is going through well-practised routines. We reach the point where we start push-back from the airbridge and every passenger on board thinks, 'Well, here we go,' although almost certainly with more fear and apprehension than they have ever experienced before.

As we are taxiing out to the runway, the captain's voice comes over the intercom. He sounds more or less like every other captain I have ever flown with. Smooth, confident, totally in control, with just a hint of the old attitude that screams, 'Yes, we all know I'm doing something you ordinary people couldn't possibly accomplish in your wildest dreams, so just accept my superiority.' A pilot's ego is truly something else, even these days when they're essentially airborne computer programmers who do little of what would be regarded as traditional flying.

His accent is hard to place. Somewhere in the middle of Europe. Maybe German, maybe further east. Educated, possibly from the middle-to-upper reaches of his society's many stratas.

'Ladies and gentlemen, welcome aboard Ukraine International Airlines Flight 232 from New York to Kiev. My name is Captain Stefan Arzu and I will be guiding you towards our destination. Flying time today is nine hours 30 minutes. Conditions, for the most part, are expected to be fine. It's a lovely day for flying. So, please sit back, enjoy your time with us, and thank you for choosing to fly Ukraine International. I'll speak to you again as we approach Kiev.'

And with that he's gone. All very reassuring. No panic in that voice, no nervousness, certainly no reference to the utter chaos that is the world of aviation today. Still, my paranoia kicks in. Did he say 'guiding you towards our destination'? A phrase that doesn't necessarily imply that we will arrive where we expect to be.

I can't be certain that Captain Stefan Arzu is the man in the uniform I saw so nonchalantly swipe the iPad from the ledge in the airport. Trying to make a mental link between the voice and the image suggests it's a possibility, but it could equally be the first officer sitting beside him who is my potential villain.

Soon we are piercing the clouds and leaving New York behind and I wonder if I'll ever set foot on land again. I tell myself not to get too wrapped up in the doomsday scenarios. For a start, I could be wrong. Perhaps the worst thing that will happen to me is that the Ukraine authorities decide to let me into the country and I feel duty-bound to visit their Folk Museum. I tell myself to look on the bright side. If I'm right, I have an advantage that no other passenger on the missing flights has had so far: I know what's coming. The question is whether I'll be able to do anything about it. I just hope that knowledge counts for something and it gives me an edge.

The seat beside me has remained empty so I shuffle across, squeezing myself as far as possible into the edge of the big chair. Now I can see the far side of the cockpit door. I wait. There is nothing else to do. I take up an offer of coffee and tell my favourite hostie to keep bringing me refills. I hold the le Carré up in front of me, occasionally flicking pages to make it look like I am reading the thing in case anyone else is observing me, but I have my eyes fixed on the reinforced, bulletproof dull-grey door that leads to the pilots' chamber.

But that door doesn't move. No one comes in or out. No toilet visits. Not so much as a crew member taking in the captain a cup of tea and biscuit.

Then it happens. Just a lot slower than what I had expected. We are a now more than two hours into the flight and almost as far over the Atlantic as it's possible to be before heading towards land again. By now we are well out of radar range and from any other prying eyes that could be tracking our progress.

But when I say it's happening, I don't mean there is a great moment of terror. No armed men in masks are charging down the aisle. No bombs are exploding. The aircraft is not suddenly screaming vertically towards the ocean, or heading higher at a terrifying angle.

I look around. All seems normal. Most of the passengers I can see behind me are sleeping, others are involved in laughter-filled conversations. I look for the crew, but they seem to have disappeared, until I catch a glimpse of one seated in a crew chair. She looks extremely pale. Is she sick? What is going on?

I try to focus, but I feel a little light-headed myself despite the four coffees and my monastic refusal of the many offers of wine and beer. A little snooze suddenly seems like a fine idea. But it's my fingernails that attract my attention. They had turned a peculiar shade of blue. I have seen this before; I know what it means. My body is not getting the oxygen it should be. I'm running out of the stuff and my system is shutting down.

My head feels like it's underwater. I can't think straight and now every movement is a huge effort. I'm aware the cabin behind me has gone a deathly quiet. Those high-spirited conversations have ended and with a great effort I turn around and see everyone is asleep. Even the pale crew member has her eyes closed and is still in her seat. And, more than anything else, I want to join them. The power of sleep is calling, it's overwhelming, but I have to hold on.

I look above me. If we are running out of oxygen, why haven't the masks been released? What are the pilots doing? Have they noticed the cabin is depressurising? Or have they overridden the automatic drop-down facility of the oxygen masks?

I reach up and with what feels like my last conscious action I scrabble to unlock the compartment where the oxygen mask lives. It drops down and I grab it, push it onto my face and breathe like I have just finished running a marathon.

My senses return and I try to figure out what is happening. The other passengers seem peaceful, happily asleep, but as I look closer it seems that no one is breathing. I drop my mask for a second and approach the woman nearest to me. She has her eyes closed and is perfectly still. I touch her on the arm. Nothing. I give her a more vigorous shake. Her head swings back and forth. No indication of life. Perhaps if I can get a mask to her I can bring her back. I reach above me, release the oxygen mask and attach it to her face, and for a minute I stand there trying to will this woman back to life. Nothing. I'm too late. She is gone.

But that's as far as I can get. I want to check others, despite my rational self knowing it's futile. That everybody here is now beyond my help. I'm starting to feel lightheaded again. Without my own mask, I can feel the oxygen seeping out of my body, so I return to my seat. I try to control my breathing. To stop taking in huge, deep breaths. I feel close to panic and need to take control of my body.

I tell myself the quickest way to death for me now is to lose my head. The thought strikes me that I'm trapped inside a metallic coffin. That there are close to 200 dead bodies behind me on this plane. Women, men, children, babies. All gone.

I still can't see into the main cabin. The curtains that separate first class from the rest of the aircraft are drawn, shielding me from that vision of hell. I think of the old couple heading home and those brothers and a deep rage builds inside me directed towards whoever is still in that cockpit flying the plane. What kind of person must they be?

The fact that it would have been a peaceful end for these travellers, an end they would have been entirely unaware of, brings no comfort. Flying at more than 40,000 feet in an unpressurised cabin brings a life expectancy that can be measured in minutes.

I know there are oxygen bottles somewhere in this cabin. Every plane carries them as the supply into the masks only lasts fifteen minutes. They keep them in case of emergency—I think this qualifies.

With everything silent, all that remains is the flicker of a dozen TV screens at the backs of seats. The programs run on regardless of the situation.

I can't give in to despair, but I can't fall into the anger trap either. If I'm going to stop whoever is behind this evil and figure out what the fuck is happening, I have to remain calm. As hard as that may be.

I can sense my own oxygen starting to run dry. I'm still thinking about finding the bottles when the plane starts to dive. Fast. Faster than a Boeing 767 should. It feels like it's going down almost vertically. If I hadn't been strapped into my seat I would have been flung to the back of the aircraft. As it is, the g-force of the dive has pinned me right back. The sensation is of a very large man planting his knee in the middle of my chest and not letting up.

The dive seems to go for hours. The level of chaos in the aircraft cabin has risen by several notches. Everything not tied down is crashing its way to the back of the cabin. This includes people. I hear bodies collide with bulkheads, with the roof, with each other. Above the noise I am sure I hear limbs snap and heads crack. It's sickening. Overhead lockers have been forced open and bags and clothes are flying through the air. I can hear a smash of a food trolley banging into something solid. Bottles are cracking into walls, into people. Carnage.

Above all else comes the whine of the engines and the creaking of an old aeroplane being asked to do things it's not supposed to. I start to think I'm going to die.

Perhaps the rest of this crazy plan is to ditch the plane into the dark, grey ocean. If we hit the surface at a steep enough angle, will the plane just cut through the water and head straight to the bottom? Is that why no debris has been found from the other planes?

I cling onto one last, hopeful thought. If the plan from the start was to drive the plane into the ocean, why bother killing everyone first?

My brain is bursting. My lungs are collapsing. I long to look out my window to figure out how long I have to live, but I can't move my head. I can't even seem to swivel my eyeballs.

Unwelcome thoughts flood my mind. If this is the end, how will I be remembered? As a good man? Unlikely. As a bad man? Hopefully not. Will I be remembered at all? I doubt that a government that has never officially acknowledged my existence will admit that I am no longer around. A state funeral is probably too much to hope for. Will they at least say I died trying to do some good? That I was making an effort to save other people's lives?

I think of my daughter and how I failed her so many times. I think of my wife and all the things I did to let her down. I even start a conversation with a God I haven't spoken to in so long he'll have to look up my file on a celestial computer to remember who I am.

Before I make promises I have no chance of fulfilling, the nose of the plane starts to lift. The force against the aircraft is still enormous and I can sense the pilot's struggle to pull out of this death dive, but little by little he is winning the battle and the 767 starts to straighten itself out.

But it's a close-run thing. I can now move my head enough to see out the window and I think of being in a paddleboat as a kid. That if I could reach out of the window I could trail my fingers through the water. I have never been this close to water in an aircraft before. It's unnerving, and I am overtaken by the fear that if the waves get too high we could be wiped out. But I soon realise I can breathe again. The bloke flying the aeroplane is a mass killer, but he certainly knows his way around the controls. The dive was planned, well executed. A manoeuvre designed to make us even more invisible.

Now that the threat of imminent death has passed, I start to think of the man in the cockpit. Who is he? I have to assume he is the man I saw so casually making his way through the New York airport. But it's hard to equate the image of that relaxed and outwardly professional pilot with the killer in the cockpit.

What drives a man to such a lunatic action? This is a man with education, with training, with enough skill to force a Boeing 767 to do all sorts of things it wasn't designed to do, including flying this beast 50 metres above the waves where the smallest error of judgement will send us into the drink.

Yet despite all that, something or someone has so comprehensively corrupted his moral compass he has killed all his passengers. All except one.

I wonder if he has stopped to think about all the dead bodies he is now towing through the skies. And what of the co-pilot? Is he in on this plot or is he another victim? On the balance of probabilities, I have to assume the pilot is the lone wolf and has taken out his colleague. It seems unlikely to me that two such like-minded crazies could be found knocking around together in the same airline. What can I do about it is the next question to come crashing through my skull.

There is no way for me to get into the cockpit. It's an armed, locked steel door and nothing this side of a large axe and a shotgun will get me in there. Anyway, if I start banging away at the door there is a fair chance I will give away the element of surprise, the one thing that does give me a genuine edge over the nutter flying the plane.

He doesn't know I'm alive. He doesn't know I'm here. He must think everyone is dead and he can go about whatever his business is unhindered. Hopefully, there is something I can do about that. But the *what* remains the burning question.

I don't know where we are going and I don't know how long it will take to get there. I don't know what will be waiting for me when I arrive either, apart from more fruit loops carrying heavy weaponry. And, I think we can be certain, they will not be happy to see me. But I can't just sit here waiting for death. I need to do something.

We are flying on an even keel, possibly just edging higher, so I decide it's safe enough for an exploratory walk. I know I'm going to be walking into a death chamber, but if there is any chance someone has been left alive back there then I have to go and take a look. To see if I can help them, to see if they can help me.

* * *

With an eye on the cockpit, I gingerly raise myself out of my seat. Another glance out my window confirms we are flying perilously close to the waves, although not quite as close as before. Still, it's a terrifying sight that nearly persuades me to stay where I am. It seems crazy to be trying to walk through the aircraft when any small rogue pocket of air could send the plane crashing into the drink. But it's no worse, I tell myself, than sitting here waiting for my end.

I get a proper look at the first-class end of the plane. Our rapid dive towards the waves has caused chaos. The overhead lockers are all hanging open and hand luggage, clothes, books, phones, food and drink have been flung all over the place. Cracked and broken laptops and tablets lie in the aisles. One seat has lost a couple of the bolts that pin it to the floor and it now hangs at a 45-degree angle. Even the bloody oxygen masks have dropped down, too late to save anyone.

Some of the passengers who were not strapped in have been flung with great violence into the bulkhead that separates this part of the plane from the rest. There is a great smear of blood on one wall. By the galley, two bodies lie on top of each other in a grotesque tableau, arms and legs sticking out at broken angles. If the depressurisation of the cabin hadn't killed them, the high-speed collision with the interior of the aircraft would have.

Yet others appear no more damaged than me. Some are still strapped to their seats. They could be contentedly dozing after finishing dinner with a glass of wine. I shake a couple of bodies, more in hope than expectation, but there are no signs of life.

I pick my way through the debris. I am trying to be as careful and quiet as possible, even though it's highly unlikely my friend at the front of the plane will be able to hear anything. Parting the curtains that have so far been shielding me from the back of the plane reveals even more horrors.

Possessions are strewn all over and broken bodies lie everywhere. It is gruesome. There is a man with several large chunks of glass, probably from a smashed wine bottle, embedded in his face. I find a leg severed below the knee just resting by itself on one seat. There are dead babies and children; I am barely in control of my emotions. The anger, the sadness, the grief are overwhelming, but I stumble on, trying to find a flicker of life. I need someone to share the horror with because I am not sure I can cope on my own. Surely someone else has survived. Please.

When you read about plane crashes, you think, 'How awful, poor people,' but you block out the mental images of the brutal reality of vulnerable bodies being smashed to pieces inside a flying tin can. It's self-preservation. If you did let your mind wander down that alleyway, you would never set foot inside a plane again.

I walk slowly all the way down one aisle to the rear of the 767. Or as close as I can manage. The back galley and toilet area resemble an old-style scrapyard, with food trolleys, bags, plates, cups, blankets, pillows and people stacked up all the way to the ceiling.

I don't know how long it has taken me to reach the back of the plane. How long does it take to travel through hell? It could have been ten minutes or two hours. All the while, the altitude of the plane hasn't changed. We are still wave-hopping at something close to 800 kilometres per hour.

With the back section of the plane blocked by all the mess, I squeeze myself through the fourth row of seats from the back, picking my way on tiptoes from armrest to armrest, trying my best not to tread on the departed while avoiding bashing my head on the low-slung ceiling.

I find my way through to the parallel aisle that will take me back to my seat. It's more of the same over here. Dead and mutilated bodies. It's clear there is no life except for mine and the black heart at the front who made all this happen. The curtains are drawn to keep the prying eyes of the economy-class passengers away from their betters in first. I stop there for a moment, just surveying the field ahead, but there is no sign of the pilot. That door is still shut, nothing seems to have changed in the cabin to indicate he has left the cockpit while I have been away.

I slide back into my seat, traumatised. No idea what to do next. No idea if I will have the opportunity to do anything. What my body is telling me it wants to do is sleep. It must be something to do with my brain's fight-or-flight response. It can't figure out a way to fight—there is nowhere to run. It may as well just switch itself off.

It's a dark sleep. Almost the sleep of the dead. No light penetrates. No dreams to be recalled. Which is a shame because a good old-fashioned nightmare could have provided some relief from my present reality. But my little holiday from that reality leaves me even more disoriented. When I wake, I don't know how long I have been out, and it takes me a second or two to put my situation back together in my head.

The plane is still burrowing its way through the sky. I try to find a flicker of hope. Surely every spy device in the world is looking for this fucking 767? Satellites, radar, reconnaissance aircraft, weather fucking balloons. The earth is being scoured at this very second for this very aircraft. Someone has to spot us.

Yet here I am, in the hands of people who in the space of two days have made four pieces of the some of the most highly sophisticated engineering on the planet disappear without trace. So much for the surveillance state. And they have managed to find at least four exceptionally trained, well-educated pilots to do their bidding. To kill hundreds of people and disappear with their plane. At some level, it's impossible not to be impressed by the sheer chutzpah of the enterprise. Which brings me back to the question: who the fuck is behind this and why?

The obvious suspects are the usual ones. Some flavour of out-there Islamic extremism. If you are playing the odds, this is usually the best place to start. Their form guide is impeccable when it comes to organising these kinds of mass-murder events. Your Christian terrorists don't tend to have the skills or the track record to pull something like this off. Sure, they can blow up an office block in Oklahoma with a fertiliser bomb and kill hundreds, but that is pretty basic compared to purloining planes.

During this reverie I stare out of the window. I used to enjoy looking at the ocean; I used to find it very soothing. Not so much anymore. But as I'm taking in the nearby sea view, it becomes clear that the ocean is slowly moving further away. We are rising again. Not swiftly, but gently. We float up to what I would guess is about 3000 feet before we level off again.

Then there is movement. The cockpit door is opening.

16

I move into my best dead man's repose. I slump over, nose just above my knees, arms down either side of my legs. I decide it's best to hide my face in case it betrays any signs of life. I'm not sure what the fuck I'm going to do next, but surprise is the only friend I have right now. I try to restrict my breathing. Making it irregular and as shallow as possible. Eyes closed.

It's impossible to see or hear if my bloke has left the safe confines of his cockpit. More than anything I want to open my eyes to check, but it seems too risky. I hang forward in my position and hope for the best.

Then footsteps. Definitely footsteps. They must be close or I wouldn't hear them. Then they stop. It feels as if he is standing beside me. Looking directly at me. I wait for a shout, a touch. The cold barrel of a gun pressed against my ear. But . . . nothing. I hold my breath and order my body to be as still as possible. This would be a bad time for a nervous fart.

I can't really tell if he is looking at me or just surveying the destruction. I'm not sure how much longer I can keep this up. Then footsteps again and I sense him moving away, stepping his way through the debris as he heads further up the aisle.

Now I open my eyes. I don't move my head or my body. I'm just looking at my shoes. They could do with a polish. I'm concentrating hard on whether I can still hear the pilot, trying to place him in the cabin without having to look for him. But all I can discern is the white noise of the aircraft—that relentless hum of the jet engine is washing away all other sounds. I give it two minutes, then three. Surely, I reason, if he thought I was still alive, he would have said or done something by now.

I risk a glance to my right and see nothing. Ever so quietly, I unbuckle my seatbelt, moving only one hand to do so. I continue to hang forward in my dead man's pose until I decide it's time to move. This could be my only chance to confront the lunatic. Maybe even gain control of the aircraft.

I roll to my right. Doing my best to keep my head below the top line of the seats, I slither over the armrest from my seat by the window into the one by the aisle. I peek around the big, well-padded chair and, meerkat-like, extend my neck without moving the rest of my body.

As far as I can tell he is no longer in my part of the plane. I stand, it's time to go. My first move is towards the cockpit door. If I can get in there, I can take control of the plane, get on the radio and find some place to put it down. But as I carefully make my way to the aisle, I see with frustration that door is closed. Arzu, like all good pilots, has done the right thing and pulled it shut behind him as he left. It also means he is the only one who will be able to open the door again, using the secret access code that needs to be punched into a keypad to allow pilots back onto the flight deck.

I still have a crack, go up to it and give it a push then a kick in an act of unbridled optimism, but it remains firmly closed. Nothing short of a grenade will open a cockpit door. I turn and face the rest of the aircraft. I need to see the fucker who caused this mayhem. I need to get information from him about who and what is behind this day. I need to find out if there are more like him out there. And something else. I want to hurt this fucker. Really badly.

The possibility that he is armed has not escaped me. It's likely I will only get one chance at this. If I get it wrong I will be joining all the other corpses in the back of the plane.

Outside the cockpit, I pick my way as quickly as I can through the chaos and reach the dividing curtain standing sentry before the rest of the plane. I pull it back, enough to give me a look inside the main economy cabin. Still nothing.

Next I slide through the flimsy barrier, trying hard to disturb as little as possible along the way. This time I see him. He's about twenty metres away, his back to me as he meanders past the first galley and toilet area, about halfway down the plane, heading deeper into the main cabin. I can't see his face; he's still wearing his pilot's cap, which strikes me as absurd in the circumstances. But it's the same man I saw pick up the iPad in New York, I'd recognise him anywhere. The same bloke I followed to the aircraft. Captain Stefan Arzu.

Then I see he does have a gun. It's hanging low in his right hand, barrel pointed at the floor. It would seem he is not expecting any company, but still needs the feel of the weapon to give him a measure of comfort.

I wonder what is going through his head as he walks into that back chamber of horror. Does he retain enough sense of his own humanity to feel remorse for what he has done? Or is he enjoying all this death and destruction? From behind I can't read his body language. He looks right and left. He steps gingerly round a few bodies, but doesn't touch them or even seem to look too closely at them, and the thought strikes me that he is on a victory lap, proud of his work today.

I'm still hiding by the curtains separating the different part of the cabins. The aircraft has all its interior lights on and it's light outside as well. All this makes the job of creeping up on the bloke more difficult. No shadows to hide in, no black spots to cover my presence. He's nearly at the back of the plane and is bound to soon turn around and head back my way.

I decide I'm best off where I am. Any movement is risky. I could easily be spotted and the jig would be up. If I keep an eye on him, and which aisle he comes back down, I can wait behind the curtain. Trusting he won't see me there. I look around for something to use as a weapon. Something heavy that can do real damage.

Under a seat nearby, I spot a full-size bottle of champagne. It's empty, but still heavy. Another benefit of flying first class: they use proper-sized bottles when serving passengers. I pick it up. It has a nice heft in my hand and if I can manage a decent swing I'm confident I can do enough damage to bring him down swiftly.

I risk another look through the curtain. Where has the fucker gone? Then I spot him. Unlike me, he has managed to find a way through the debris and crossed through the passage where the toilets are right at the back of the plane and is now heading towards me along the other aisle.

I could be imagining things, but I fancy I can hear the fucker whistling as he picks his way through the mayhem. And unless I am going completely nuts, the tune that is floating towards me is 'The Star-Spangled Banner'. I'm not a big fan of the Yanks, but even that strikes me as a bit much.

I reckon he will be with me in less than a minute. There is nothing to do but wait. As soon as he emerges through that curtain I'm going to cave his skull in. I'll stand on the chair nearest the entry point. I figure it will give me more momentum on that downward arc. It will also eliminate any possibility he will spot my feet under the curtain.

The tension is killing me. I get one shot at this. But he seems to be in no hurry; he's enjoying his stroll and doesn't want his moment of triumph to end. His whistling jukebox has changed disc to 'God Save the Queen'. He seems to be working his way through the national anthems of all the Western imperialists, although if he manages to get to 'Advance Australia Fair' I will be impressed.

His hand comes through the curtain, pushing it aside. I take the champagne bottle back and, with elbow cocked, I have it hovering above my head, waiting for the rest of my captor's body to appear. When he comes through the curtain and I bring the bottle down as hard as I can. But as my arm comes down, he reacts to the movement above him, and his left arm shoots up and protects enough of his head to deflect my blow.

I still hit him, and hard, but instead of making contact with the top of the head I take some arm and hit him around the earhole. He makes a grunting sound and staggers, reaching for the nearest seat to steady himself, but he doesn't go down as I had hoped.

He still has his gun and he's soon bringing it up as he swings around to find me. I can't give him the time to aim his weapon or I'm finished. I launch myself at him, again swinging my bottle as I go. I think I get at least one good hit in before we both tumble to the floor.

However hard I have hit him, though, it doesn't seem to have made much difference. We bang from side to side in the aisle. My head makes painful contact with the sharp edge of a chair leg. He's is trying to manoeuvre his gun to get a good shot at me, but I grab his hand with both of mine and force it away from my face.

There is a startlingly loud noise. The gun has gone off. My ears start to ring, but I don't feel any pain. I haven't a clue where the bullet has gone, but at least with the aircraft still flying at such a low altitude I won't have to try to survive sudden decompression all over again.

The shot though has given me a surge of adrenalin. This is a battle I need to win. I am bigger than my opponent, but he is strong and wiry, and I can't see how I can end this with sheer force. His face comes close to mine. I bite his nose and don't let go. The surprise and pain causes him to drop the gun and I swiftly bring my knee up with such force that his testicles have soon introduced themselves to his throat.

The gun has skittered away under a seat. I stop the biting and he rears back, both hands going immediately for his nose, before he realises the greater pain is further south and his brain sends them there instead. I take the opportunity to smash the heel of my hand into his bleeding nose and he falls off me. I grab the gun and spring to my feet. I have the weapon in both hands. Bent over. Aggression pouring through my body. I kick the fucker in the head, again and then again. I hear myself screaming, 'You sick fuck, you sick fuck.' I'm on the verge of losing it here; I have to pull back. There is information I need to get from this bloke.

He's cowering on the floor. Arms up, trying to protect his head. The blood is flowing freely from his nose, which is now at an angle it wasn't 30 seconds ago. It must be broken.

I order him to sit up and move to the nearest chair. I even tell him to put his seatbelt on. It's not much, but if he makes another run for me it will hold him up at least momentarily.

'Are you Arzu?' I ask him.

Dark eyes stare back at me with hatred. Up close, I see he is in his early forties, dark hair, dark moustache, olive skin. Just a little under six feet tall. A newly crooked nose spoils what may have been considered a handsome face. But he hasn't answered my question.

'I know you are Stefan Arzu,' I tell him. 'You introduced yourself a few hours back to all those people you were about to murder.'

Still nothing.

'If you won't speak to me, I guess I'll have to make up my own name for you. How does mass murderer fit? Or madman? Or lunatic? Child killer, perhaps? How about something grander—Slayer of the Innocents?' Thinking perhaps some quasi-religious, medieval term may prick his ego.

He remains quiet, but the intensity of the stare has ratcheted up a few notches.

'Okay, brave Slayer. Where is this plane going? How long till we reach the destination?'

When the same hard look comes back at me, I put the gun up his broken nose. I move it around. I can feel the bits of cartilage moving and grinding against each other, but I can't hear much as the screams are too loud.

I stop and look at him.

'Again, two questions. Where are we going? How long till we get there?'

'Fuck you,' comes out as a twisted, strangled cry.

'Words at last. He can speak. Not much, but it's a start. Tell me, Slayer, where are we going?'

'Stop calling me that,' he says in an accent that I had started off thinking had German overtones but am now not so sure. The busted nose may not be helping but I fancy it's from somewhere in the far reaches of Eastern Europe.

'Sorry, did I hurt your feelings there? My apologies. It's just I've never met someone who has murdered as many people as you have today. I'm not sure what the appropriate form of address is. Or are you upset I didn't address by you rank on what is, after all, still your aircraft? Okay, *captain*, last time. Where the fuck are we going? How long till we get there?'

The gun is still pointed at the centre of his forehead. He looks me in the eye.

'There are always sacrifices to be made in war,' he says.

I feel my anger rising again.

'You dumb shit. This is not a war. These are just people. Kids, parents, grandparents, brothers, sisters. Going home, going on holiday. You need two sides for there to be a war. The other side needs to know there is a war on so they can fight back. But I don't see too many soldiers here. This . . . this is just slaughter.'

I calm myself. Take a deep breath. Lower the tone of my voice, regain a measure of control. 'Let's make this the last dance, Arzu. Where are we going? How long till we get there?'

Nothing. Another idea comes to me. I ask Arzu a question. 'How are you going to land this aircraft?'

'What do you mean?'

'Let me be clearer. How do you see yourself landing this plane with a bullet hole in the centre of your forehead?'

For the first time he looks worried. It appears this is a problem that has not occurred to him.

He stutters: 'If you shoot me, you will die as well.'

'Yes, Arzu, but to be honest that's a price I'm willing to pay at this stage. I feel like I'm ahead anyway. Like everybody else here I should already be dead. So, if I can take you with me, at least I've accomplished something today.'

I stare at him. I'm gambling, he's thinking. It's likely Arzu is on a suicide mission and may not be that perturbed by the thought of death. But there is more to this plan than just killing the passengers and disappearing the plane into the ocean, never to be heard from again. As a plan that doesn't make sense. Whoever is behind this madness must have a second stage in mind. Part one was stealing and disappearing the planes. But that's not the endgame here. Something else is coming. Something even more terrifying and Arzu is not going to want to let his boss down.

He breaks.

'Okay, okay. We land soon. Maybe half an hour. We are going to Africa. An abandoned airfield on the west coast. But you let me land the plane, they will shoot you anyway.'

'Let me worry about that,' I mutter. 'Get up.'

He wobbles to his feet. Putting hands on armrests to help pull himself up, then to steady himself to stop himself from falling to the floor.

He steps in front of me and I put the gun in his back.

'Cockpit,' I order.

We walk back through the carnage. I avoid looking closely, my eyes fixed on the back of my captive's head. We reach the cockpit and he punches in the code that opens the door. It slowly swings open and I crack him on the back of the skull.

The unconscious Arzu's a dead weight and I struggle to drag him back to the economy section. I find a spare seat in the middle of the third row. I look around for something to tie him up with and amid all the debris I find a couple of seatbelts that have been shaken loose from their moorings. I tie them together and then as firmly as possible attach Arzu to his seat. It won't take him long to escape these bounds when he wakes up, but it's the best I can do for the moment. To prolong his current state of unconsciousness I give him another whack on the scone.

* * *

It's been a while since I was in charge of a large passenger aircraft. The last time I was in one it ended badly. No deaths—not unless you count the end of my career. The thing never got off the ground. But the sight of a worse-for-wear captain being escorted off the flight deck probably didn't do much for the nervous flyers on board.

Still, I'd flown 767s before so everything was familiar. As long as I didn't take into account the dead first officer sitting in the right-hand seat. What had killed the man isn't immediately obvious. There are no wounds that I can see and it strikes me as unlikely to have been caused by the depressurisation that had killed everyone else. Unlike the passengers, a first officer would have quickly figured out what was going on, especially given my friend the captain would have needed to reach for the oxygen himself to stay alive.

But that is a mystery for later. For the moment, I have to figure out what is happening on this plane. I slide into the captain's seat, moving a clear plastic Tupperware container that has been wedged down the side, leaving the dead guy where he is. I've flown with worse first officers, I figure. And anyway, I don't have the time or energy to drag him out of the cockpit.

My first glance tells me we were flying at 3000 feet, heading south of due west, but dropping. The latitude and longitude readings tell me I am 25 degrees north of the equator and 15 degrees to the west of the prime meridian, the imaginary line running through Greenwich in London. This puts me somewhere off the west coast of Africa, just as Arzu had said.

I reach for the flight-management computer. It has a setting that tells me the nearest five airports to my current location. The only trick is that the airline needs to load the codes into the computer first, meaning it only picks the ones that are generally relevant to its needs. I'm not optimistic that an airline from Ukraine will have thought it was necessary to program African airports into its database.

Only one code is displayed—GSLG. It's a jumble of meaningless letters. It doesn't tell me where I am going.

The blue sea sits below me. The sun is low on the horizon, but coming up rather than going down, so wherever I am it's early in the morning. I am heading more or less straight at the sun, so every time I look out the window I am squinting into that spinning orange orb. I have the impression there may be land ahead.

I search for the fuel gauge and find more bad news. It's hovering around 1.4 to 1.5 tonnes. I pluck a figure from the back of my old airline captain's brain. A 767 burns through about four and a half tonnes of fuel an hour. Conclusion? I am not going to be airborne for much longer.

One thought is crowding my mind: should I contact someone, anyone, on the radio to tell them I am out here?

The radio is operated through the pilot headset. But when I put on the set I hear nothing. No static, none of the normal radio hiss. The radio has been turned off too and I don't know how to switch it back on. These blokes took no chances. And without the radio through to traffic control, the aircraft is harder to track.

But that gives rise to another thought. How did the captain know where he was going? He must have been awfully confident of reaching his destination without once having to speak to anyone to guide him in. The only conclusion is that he has entered the coordinates into the aircraft's automatic pilot and left the whole flying business to the computer. The landing, though, could be another matter entirely. If we're headed towards some bum-fuck airport in the middle of nowhere, we're unlikely to discover there the necessary equipment to guide in something as big as a 767.

Maybe the pilot didn't know where he was going to end up? My mind returns to the iPad he picked up in the airport. It must have carried the coordinates and flight instructions for the automatic pilot. Was he given a code to an airport— the GSLG sitting in the flight computer?

The 767 is heading steadily and without complaint to whatever bastard destination it has been told to head for. I now have less than twenty minutes of fuel left in the tanks before they start to run dry and we drop out of the sky.

But if this thing has been planned as well as it seems to have been, that's not going to happen. What is more likely is that this plane is supposed to land somewhere—and land soon. But where? And where does that leave me?

The fuel situation means I can't take control of the plane and fly my way out of trouble. The odds are that if I change course now my next stop will be somewhere in the ocean.

As unhappy as it makes me, I have to place my trust in the madman who has brought me this far. Then something else from my piloting days kicks in, an old memory of how things should be done when you are flying 767s and landing is not too far away. I check a dial above my head. It's the one that tells the automatic pilot it's time to begin the descent. It's been set at 500 feet per minute. Even my poor mathematics tells me I have only fifteen minutes until I am back on the ground.

17

The nose of the 767 dips forward. The steady note of the engine changes down a gear. Well, here we go. It's landing time. And decision time for me. What next? Do I stay in the cockpit and give myself up, try to reason with whoever is in charge down there and find a way to keep myself alive for as long as possible? Or do I land this thing, retreat to the back of the plane, play dead until I've figured out if I can get myself out of this mess?

The first option strikes me as silly. To voluntarily place myself in the hands of murderers is suicide. What's one more body to these people? They'll shoot me between the eyeballs as soon as they see me. My only hope lies among the dead. I need to find somewhere to hide.

Then I realise what my bigger problem is going to be: the pilot. Somehow, in all the excitement of the last few minutes, I had forgotten about him.

I jump out of the seat and head back into the cabin.

A definite sour note has crept into the airless compartment. Nature is doing what it does to 200 dead people trapped inside an elongated tube and the results are overwhelming my senses. You can see it, you can smell it, you can taste it.

Arzu is still unconscious. The plan, such as it is, is to keep him that way. I briefly consider just shooting him, but I can't quite bring myself to be that brutal. Still, I'm no Mother Teresa. I give him another belt with the blunt end of the gun to prolong his sleep. I make some effort to make him as difficult as possible to find. I force him as far forward as possible, then find a couple of blankets to throw over him, then add some bags that have fallen from the overhead bins. It's not much, but any little time it buys me could help.

I can only assume there will be some kind of reception crew waiting on the ground, all keen to meet their new hero. When they discover their pilot is missing, they will go through the place rapidly, and probably angrily, to find their missing comrade. Somewhere, in all that confusion, I am hoping to find a way out of here.

The plane continues to drop gently towards the earth. We are at about 2000 feet now. Through the window, I can see the horizon coming up to meet us. I make a quick dash back to the cockpit to see if I can spot land. And now I can. It's still a couple of kilometres away and with no distinguishable features. Flat, barren, sandy. I can't make out anything that resembles civilisation, but the lights of a landing strip are visible.

Here is where things get risky. I have to land this fucker. The automatic pilot has got me this far, but it can't land this thing itself. If I did leave things to the automatic pilot, we would drone on until we ran out of fuel and then we'd take the quickest route to the ground. It wouldn't be pretty.

It's been a few years since I've tried to land a heavy passenger jet. I'm hoping it's like riding a bike, but that would be too simple. A pilot's life is defined by repetition. It has to be to eliminate the prospect of mistakes, which when you're flying a big fucking plane can mean death for a lot of people. So, it's training, training, training—then repeat. The advantage is that all the steps, all the manoeuvres I need to complete to land this thing, are buried somewhere deep in my subconscious. My skills may be rusty, but they are still there. I just need to find them.

There is only about five minutes until we touch down. Automatic pilot has been disengaged. I have control of the plane. It lurches down fast and steep and the computer display in front of me immediately flashes three red angry lines instructing me I'm too low to land. That I won't make the runway. I pull back on the wheel and overdo it. Now three white lines tell me I'm too high.

I don't have much time to get this right. A macabre thought occurs: at least if I do stuff it up, the passengers are already dead . . . The readout flashes between white and red, but I feel I'm slowly getting the hang of this caper again, although anyone watching from the ground will want to breathalyse me as soon as I touch down. *If* I touch down.

Ahead of me I finally see the field. The runway comes up quickly and I fly right over it. I see a collection of drab buildings: perhaps a hangar and what looks like some barracks. I can't see anything resembling a city or even a small town. The airfield is close to the coast, but all I make out are sand dunes, which then gives way to scrubby vegetation, stunted trees growing at odd angles from the prevailing winds, and a whole big heap of nothingness.

At the edge of the runway is a collection of four-wheel drives. The welcoming committee. I drag the 767 round in a big circle and line up for my final descent. Slowly, slowly, the earth is coming up to meet me. The bright, fluorescent landing lights that frame the runway are clearly visible and I am aim somewhere in the middle.

Fifteen hundred feet, one thousand . . . The runway comes up at a terrifying speed. Then we bounce hard as the massive 767 lurches back up, wings clawing at the air, looking for lift, but gravity prevails and we settle back to earth, skittering along the runway until finally the plane brings itself to a stop.

I feel myself breathe out. But now what? The prospect of just quietly taxiing over to the welcoming committee seems daft, so I decide to buy myself a little more space by parking the aircraft at the end of the runway and having them come to me. I flick the switches to turn off the two giant engines and a sudden peacefulness fills the air as the whine of the jet power plants fades away.

As I landed, I had the brief impression of another collection of low-set buildings, grey and unprepossessing, about halfway along the runway. Presumably that's where the rest of the bad guys are waiting for their prize.

Well, if they want it, they can come and get it.

I head back into the body of the beast, trying to determine the cleverest way to hide myself long enough to fashion an escape. I try to push away the thought of 'escape to what?'. The little I could see from the cockpit window showed only a long, empty desert. One step at a time, I tell myself. Get out first, figure out where to hide next.

I decide to adopt the hide-in-plain-sight philosophy. I figure the bad guys won't know what's wrong or what they are looking for until they are well inside the aircraft. Logically they will come in through the main entry point and head towards the cockpit. That moment may provide me with my best chance of escape, although, again, to where? A vision of 30 well-armed lunatics waiting outside the aircraft fills my brain, all staring at me along the barrel of machine guns as I climb down the stairs. That makes me feel a tad vulnerable; 'sitting target' comes to mind.

I come to the main cabin door. It opens into the area between first class and economy. There are not enough bodies, not enough chaos to hide here, so I head further back. There I do something I know I will spend the rest of my life trying not to think about.

I find a row with three dead people spread across four seats. Two of them, a man and a woman, must have been in their sixties. The man has a bald pate, with neat white hair around the back of his head. Wearing a long-sleeved shirt and tan trousers, he strikes me as a mid-level manager type. Probably American, heading to Ukraine because he and his wife were adventurous souls, looking for some-where different to go on holiday. He has his arm around the woman next to him. A red-headed woman, hair tied back. She looks younger than her husband by five or ten years. For no sensible reason, I am suddenly sad that I never met them in life. Beside them, with the spare seat in between, is another woman, around 30. Long, black hair framing a round, friendly face, with a nose she likely spent most of her life telling herself was too big.

The anger at the wasted lives strikes me again. I try to take a deep breath to calm myself, but the pungent tang of death in the air almost overwhelms me and it's all I can do to stop chucking up everywhere.

Trying not to breathe, I slip into the seat between the couple and the woman. It's a profoundly disturbing experience to sit yourself among the dead. I treat them like they are still alive: I have to stop myself saying 'excuse me' as I brush past, trying to avoid treading on any toes. I move the man's arm as I sit down. It's cold. The skin stiff, the elasticity and electricity of life gone.

Through the nearest window, I strain to catch a glimpse of anything happening outside, but it's hard to see anything. I fancy now, though, that I can hear engines approaching. At a rapid rate. It sounds like multiple vehicles. I imagine they all stop in skids and clouds of dust, piling out of the vehicles with big, ugly guns at the ready. I try to concentrate on the numbers. How many engines? Maybe three or four. Probably Toyota Land Cruisers or something similar. Perhaps six to eight passengers in each.

Then voices. Too indistinct to understand what is being said or even in what language, but there is an intimation of anger in the tone and pitch.

Several minutes pass and nothing more happens than loud shouting of one word again and again:

'*Arzu, Arzu, Arzu.*'

They are calling for the captain. Happily, he has not yet rejoined the land of the living. But the delay puzzles me. I expected an immediate assault on the aircraft. What are they waiting for? Then I feel a gentle bump on the side of the plane and I understand they have been waiting for a truck with ladders to reach the door of the aircraft.

Then I hear footsteps running upstairs, a battering of fists on the side of the plane. More shouts of 'Arzu' and angry words in a language I can't understand, but could be Arabic.

The hardest thing is trying to control my breathing. Look, I have been in all sorts of situations before that would seem far from normal. Situations of violence and guns, of threats and intimidation, of life and death. But nothing like this.

For the first time I can remember, I feel scared. Before now, it has all been theoretical. I didn't know what I was getting into. I was pursuing a destination I wasn't sure I would ever reach. Now I am here.

These are people who have murdered extensively today. They are brutal, but they are also smart, calculated and cruel. They have made at least four aircraft disappear—and the last time I checked no one had a clue where any of them had gone.

The boys outside the 767 have given up on attracting the attention of the still-slumbering Arzu. I can hear them scratching about at the door handle, trying to work out how to open it from the outside. Obviously none of them have any aviation experience as they haven't figured it out, but it's only a matter of time before they find the small switch just under the external handle that will grant them access to the craft.

They continue to bang away at the door. Someone with either a sledgehammer or the blunt edge of a gun is doing nothing for the plane's resale value. I hear someone yell 'shoot, shoot' in English.

And then, with a sound like the final gasp of a dying man and a sudden release of air, the door is open.

I figure that since my dead-man's pose worked well enough last time to fool Captain Arzu I will try it again now. I place my head between my knees, imagining myself looking as dead as humanly possible. It's method acting taken to its illogical conclusion. I figure that, if nothing else, I need to hide my face and disguise that I am still capable of breathing.

My plan, such as it is, now centres on remaining as still and lifeless as possible until these fuckers get off the aircraft again. Perhaps then I can sneak out and see what my options are.

A great noise of men enters the cabin. I'm still head down, eyes closed, but in the space of 30 seconds the aircraft is full of at least twenty others. Great clumping boots are smashing their way up and down the aisles. I can hear dead bodies being kicked and others being roughly cast aside. A voice continues to shout for Arzu. If they are conducting a body-by-body search to find the captain then I could be in some trouble here. I hope I haven't disguised him as well as I thought I had. I also hope he isn't quite ready to wake up and give me away.

They soon find him. I can't look up or move, but I sense a bundle of activity near the spot where I dumped him.

Now multiple voices are shouting. But nothing happens to indicate my friend has regained consciousness. Perhaps I hit him harder than I thought? Maybe I killed the man? I don't feel any remorse if I have. I'm sitting among his dead. I can touch them, feel them beside me. I can generate no pity if he is gone. If he's dead, the world is a better place.

My most immediate thought is one of self-preservation: if he has expired, his mates will seriously rip the place apart looking for whoever did it. In the current situation, they can only arrive at one logical conclusion. Something has gone wrong with their plan. They will know a passenger has survived and somehow managed to overpower the man they trusted to carry out their work. I suspect they will be rather keen to find that person.

The boots are on the move again. Two sets, maybe three, are heading slowly back down the aisle towards the main door. There is a lot of grunting. I have the impression they are carrying something heavy. The captain. They're taking him off the plane, but it's still not clear whether he is alive or dead.

My back is aching. I reckon it's been about ten minutes so far and this is not a natural position to hold for any length of time. My legs are going numb. The hamstrings feel like they will either snap or cramp. The urge to move, to stand, to at least rub my legs is almost overwhelming.

The search of the plane has started again. From behind I can hear bodies being shoved aside. The dead are being asked to prove they are not alive. Just another indignity.

Then there is a man at the end of my row. Out of the corner of my eye I can see dusty, beaten-up black boots. He grabs the old man in the aisle chair and gives him a shake. When there is no response he moves roughly past the old bloke to get closer to his next targets. He grabs the woman next to me. Same result.

Then a hand lands on my shoulder. I am shoved back towards a sitting position, my hamstrings screaming in relief, then just as violently I am flung forward. I'm not that good an actor, there is no way I can hide it. I am still a living, breathing human. Although I don't fancy my chances of hanging onto that status for too much longer . . .

It takes a moment for my new friend to compute that I'm not just another corpse. He shakes me again. As my head travels back towards my knees for the second time in rapid succession, the genius starts shouting. It's definitely Arabic. Something about its rhythms and sharp edges. I don't know what he's saying, but it's loud and urgent, and I guess something along the lines of 'I've got him, I've got him'.

I look up. There is no way out of this mess. The bloke is still holding me by the shoulder. It's a firm grip. He's big. Dressed in some kind of black army fatigues, AK-47 draped over the shoulder. I can see the open door, but I can't see a way out. Not alive, anyway.

I smile at my assailant and give a wink. The last thing I remember is the butt of that AK-47 swinging towards my head.

18

I wake in darkness. Head thumping. I put my hand up in a futile gesture to stem the pain. I feel sticky hair and manoeuvre my fingers around to find the source of what I know is blood. And there it is. A deep furrow just above my right ear. It feels enormous, like I could run one of those Matchbox cars I used to play with as a kid along its grooves. I just hope it feels a lot worse than it is.

As my eyes adjust to the gloom, I start to get a sense of my situation. Not that there is much to see. I have woken on a floor of hard compacted sand. I am the only thing in the room, which is about three metres by three metres. No windows. A door of some kind of heavy-looking wood. And that's my lot. There is light leaking in from under the door, but no other form of illumination.

I have no idea how long I have been unconscious or what time of day it is. I stand up, unsteadily, head still pounding. The first instinct of my knees is to buckle and for a moment

I stagger like a drunk who is trying to remember where the next bar is. It's stiflingly hot and the smell in here suggests the last time this room was used was as a hotel for goats. I have just enough energy to stand and wait for the swaying, spinning room to come to its senses. A deep breath, then another, and I start to feel like my mind and body are reconnecting.

I pace in the square room. Into my head jumps the image of a boxer marking his territory before a big fight. But how much fighting I am capable of at the moment is another question.

I stop at the door. It's not as sturdy as I initially thought. There are cracks and warping and a dryness to the wood. Not that I'm banking on knocking it down with a shoulder charge or a well-aimed kick anytime soon. As far as I can tell by squinting through the gap between door and frame, there are at least three locks holding it closed. Also, while it's impossible to see anyone through the crack, I get the definite sense of a presence nearby. It would be foolhardy to assume that this is only one unarmed person.

I bang on the door just to see if I can get some sort of reaction. As loudly as I can, I shout, 'Hello, hello, I'm here!' Not a sound is delivered back. Not even a 'fuck off'. The entire place is covered in a blanket of silence.

I retreat from the door, wondering if there is anything I can do next. I could fake illness, then take the guard by surprise. But surely that only works in the movies. A tunnel? Christ, I hope I'm not here that long . . . And if I again use the movies as a reference point, tunnels only lead to death. I have seen *The Great Escape* at last 35 times. It never ends well, although I suppose most of those guys did die on a nice, peaceful green hill in Europe and not inside a stinking prison in an unknown African desert.

I slump against the wall furthest from the door, sliding down until my arse hits the earth. I ponder how I managed to find myself here and what could have been done differently. Nothing springs to mind. Well, nothing that would have worked. In hindsight, perhaps I should have turned down the offer of Miller's lift, but it didn't feel like I had too many choices at that point. Being stuck in an Indonesian prison, though, might be preferable to my current situation . . .

So, I did what I always do. Followed instincts rather than carefully thought-out plans. You could say this is not the best way to approach this job and you know what? You may well be right. But here we are. The question is—what's next? I feel calm. It's not resignation to my fate, it's a desire to find a solution to this problem. I'm not going to let these fuckers beat me, beat all of us. Now I just want to know how they did it.

* * *

Even temporary isolation can do funny things to your brain. Time slips by, sometimes slow, sometimes fast. Slow, when you are paying attention to your surroundings and figuring out what, if anything, you can do about it. Fast when you slip into a half-sleep and forget where you are.

The Longines sits on my left wrist. A big metal thing. More dials than it needs. But it does shine in the dark.

According to the watch, it's about ten to three on the eighteenth. Which is of less help than you would think. All it means it's ten to three in Jakarta which is the last time I remember adjusting it. What it does tell me, however, is that it has been four hours since I regained consciousness.

In that time, I have been given no food, no water. No acknowledgement in any form that I am here at all. It seems unlikely they have forgotten about me. More probable is they are arguing about what they are going to do with me next. Deciding what form of torture will take the longest to kill me.

The simplest, easiest most expedient thing to do would be to just shoot me through the head and dump me somewhere in the desert. That's what I would do in their situation. It avoids complications later. No one is ever going to find my body. No one has a clue where I am, including myself.

Maybe I would have some value as a hostage. But what kind of hostage? The type where the bad guys demand a ransom of $10 billion and a ready-fuelled jet to take them to Brazil. As they already have at least four jets, that seems unlikely . . .

There is the other type. One that fills me with even more fear than the relatively simple and painless bullet between the eyes. The use of the hostage to send a message. A tool to inspire terror.

Into my mind jumps images I've seen all too often on TV and in newspapers of those poor souls in orange jumpsuits, on their knees, hands bound behind their backs, while they wait for the barbarian in the black pyjamas to cut off their head. And then, just to add to the indignity, the video is uploaded to YouTube.

That is not the way I want to go out. I vow to fight with everything I have to avoid that ending. I'd rather run and be shot in the back; I'd rather take a bullet than end my life meekly on my knees in surrender. I will not read out propaganda condemning the West while pleading for my life. But I also know all those poor sods before me probably made the same promise—and look how they ended up.

The wait goes on. Perhaps this is part of the process. To wear me down. To beat me psychologically. To prepare me to acquiesce to the indignities to come. I try to shake my mind free from the overwhelming negativity, focusing instead on ways of escape and forming a plan to get out of this hole. But, again, reality strikes. Even if I did by some miracle get out, then what? Where do I run? How would I survive? They are going to know the terrain around these parts an awful lot better than me. It all seems so futile.

It's seven hours in now and still no contact. Not so much as a glass of water. My throat has turned a sandpaper texture that makes swallowing painful. I don't like to think of exactly what I would give up just to be given a glass of water right now.

At eight hours, the door finally creaks open. I am curled up on the floor. Some kind of weird dream had been running through my head when the light from the open door flooded the room and at first I thought it was part of the strange scenario in my head involving a steam train ploughing across the Sydney Harbour Bridge.

Reality is imposed by a swift and painful kick to my ribs. Then words. Harsh and loud, but this time unmistakably in English.

'Up, get up' is the instruction.

Slowly, I rise. A job not made any easier by the fire in my ribs. It's possible they are cracked or broken. This day continues to improve.

'Faster' comes the next order.

By now, I am more or less bent double. I swing my head towards the voice and fix him with what I hope is my best steely gaze while holding my hand up in an attempt to ward off further blows.

'Okay, okay,' I say. 'I'm doing my best.'

'Do better,' the man says.

My new friend is wearing the same dust-covered black boots and green camouflage outfit as my acquaintance with the AK-47 back on the plane. But where that bloke wore his uniform like an old sack recently released from potato-holding duties, this man has a different bearing altogether. One of clear authority.

I stand straight to my full six feet four. I am only marginally taller than him, although with his sharp black military beret set at a jaunty angle, it's possible he shades it. There's a straight aquiline nose, dark eyes set back in his head, skin a shade of light brown. He's not looking at me with any sympathy. I have the impression that he's only just restraining himself from kicking me again.

It may be best not to provoke this guy. He's not armed, but behind him in this small cell are two heavily armed goons who will happily follow any instructions to kill me.

So I try for what I hope is a nonchalant look, doing my best to suppress the sensation of fear and intimidation flooding through me. This, I tell myself, is a bad time for any show of weakness and decide to put my own imprint on proceedings.

'Who are you? Where are we?' I demand, using my best commanding voice. 'And who the fuck are you lunatics?'

Nothing. My captor looks me straight in the eye, betraying no emotion, and turns to leave. His two accomplices step forward. One grabs me by the left arm and shoves it high up my back; the other repeats the trick with my right arm and half-carries, half-drags me out of my prison. As the saying goes, 'resistance is futile'.

We emerge into a corridor. It has the feel of an army barracks. The kind with all colour and character leached out in favour of form and functionality. The overhead fluorescent light is white and harsh. There are still no windows, but there are four or five doors on each side of the aisle, which runs about 30 metres in length. It's a large building.

At the end of the corridor, we turn right then left, then I am marched through some double doors and into a bigger space with tables and chairs. This must be a dining room. It is deserted. We press on to the other side of the room to a door that leads to the outside world.

The pain from my ribs could still be there, but I can't feel anything apart from the screaming agony from my shoulders as the two thugs keep a firm grip on my arms, taking delight in keeping them pinned against my back at an unnatural angle. The man in front continues to march on.

Then we're outside. The first impression is one of heat. Heat is not something new to me. I grew up in Australia.

But this is hot. Stinking hot. The sun, big, bold and yellow, is still retreating from the highest point of the day. I judge it to be around five in the afternoon.

There is a strong wind blowing in from what I assume is the interior of the continent. It's picking up particles of sand and grit and throwing them into my face. I try to keep my mouth shut, but the stuff is penetrating my eyes and mouth, and I spit out any debris that comes my way.

As the march continues, I look around, trying to make some sense of my surroundings. We're headed down the side of the building where I had been kept. It's about 50 metres long and dull green in colour. Windows are small, far apart and high up. There are more buildings beyond the edge of this one—we are clearly heading towards one of those.

This is definitely a military base. Maybe army, maybe air force. It's not a civilian field and it's not new. It makes me think we are either in a country with no legitimate government worth the name or these guys are operating with the blessing of whoever is in charge. Either way, it doesn't fill me with confidence that a rescue party will arrive anytime soon.

More buildings appear, though smaller in scale. Offices and small supply sheds. Further afield are other larger buildings—taller, wider, bulkier. Probably aircraft hangars, but as the doors have been pulled down it's difficult to know for certain.

If I lifted my head, I fancy I could see the ocean I flew over to reach this blighted spot. To my right is the runway. Dusty, grey. I may have been the first to land here in a long time. The plane still standing where I had left it, about half a kilometre away. Mad plans to make a run for it and take off enter my head and just as quickly disappear. The thought of being shot in the back isn't so attractive and I remember that the plane was more or less operating on fumes by the time we reached the tarmac.

But it's also the only aircraft I can see. If there are other planes, they are hidden. I suppose there is a chance they have been stored away in the hangars.

The man in charge is still about three paces in front. He hasn't so much as glanced over his shoulder at me since we started moving. His two helpers are not great conversationalists, either. I stumble along in grim silence, battling the sand, trying to ignore the heat and wondering where this is all leading.

At the end of the long building we make a sharp right turn away from the runway towards another small cluster of buildings. I am dragged up three steps and we are standing on a porch. Even after only a couple of minutes in the brutal sun, it's a relief to be under some shade.

We've stopped at the door and my man in charge raps on it. Almost immediately it is opened by another man in the same drab uniform. He doesn't say a word, just steps out of the way to make room for our party to pass. There is a small entry chamber, a hallway and more closed doors. We pass them all and arrive in a bigger room at the back where there is a desk with a black leather chair. Against the back wall is a bookcase, empty, except for a Dan Brown novel sitting on the bottom shelf.

There is an attempt at a little more luxury in here. Under an aluminium window frame sits a brown couch, possibly leather. The room is air-conditioned, which is a blessed relief. A unit on the wall is blowing refrigerated air into my face and I try to clear my mind for whatever challenge comes next. Near the bookshelf is a small table with chairs and on the wall a large world map with a bundle of red lines scrawled on it. Some I recognise as plotting the route of the disappeared aircrafts.

I look for the red line out of New York. As expected, it's heading towards Africa, although a sudden quick shock to the back of the head with a rifle and the order 'eyes front' stops me from picking a precise location. Somewhere in the northwest, perhaps. Morocco, Algeria, or even Libya. Libya wouldn't be good. It would be very bad.

The four of us are standing quietly now in the room. I'm wondering why I've been brought here, but I also have to assume that whatever happens in here is going to define my chances of staying alive for much longer. My mind is racing. Examining opportunities for escape, calculating odds of fleeing intact. Nothing is encouraging. Every escape needs at least three elements to succeed: a workable plan, surprise and at least a few minutes' head start.

Of course, weapons, backup and some fucking idea what lies immediately beyond this base would also help, but you can't have everything. So far, I'm stuck on 'workable plan'. I can't see a way around the guns pointed at the back of my head and the knowledge these blokes wouldn't give a second thought to disconnecting my head from the rest of my body. But there may still be time and opportunity.

And then we are joined by another man. The boss. Not for him are battered military fatigues and dust-covered boots. He's wearing a crisp white *thawb*. The long garment is covering his body all the way to his wrists and ankles, and he sports the *agal*, a twin black rope holding the *keffiyeh* head covering onto his head. He has a heavy but well-trimmed beard, and he is wearing aviator glasses, meaning all I can really see of him is his nose, mouth, chin and hands. Everything else is covered, although I fancy I can see an expensive-looking gold watch peeping out from under the thawb.

But some things can't be hidden. He is not a tall man; in fact he is the shortest in the room by a decent stretch. And he is pale—much paler than the other men in the room. He's even paler than me. Like he has spent a whole lifetime indoors trying to avoid the sun. Is he a Westerner?

He doesn't acknowledge my presence as he walks in, heading straight to the black chair behind the desk where he sits down. The goons push me forward and position me in front of the desk. Still, the man does not raise his eyes to meet mine. In front of him are several pieces of paper. They appear to be computer print outs. Perhaps from news websites. I imagine I can see the words *aircraft* and *terror* in a couple of headlines. Others are written in different languages. There is nothing else on the desk.

He quietly sifts through the material for a minute or so. Then, raising his head, he takes off the sunglasses and stares at me with startling blue eyes. Not what I expected.

'What is your name?' he asks. No preamble.

Not knowing what they know about me, or whether they found my backpack on the plane, I decide to stick with the name in the false passport. I can't see any harm in giving up a made-up name.

'Docherty,' I say. 'Sean Docherty.'

'Where are you from, Mr Docherty?'

'Australia.'

'And why would an Australian be going to Ukraine?'

'It wasn't my original idea. I had a ticket to go home to Sydney. That's why I was at the airport. But I received some bad news. My brother had been in an accident in Kiev. A traffic accident. He lives there, an engineer in the gas industry,' I say, giving my fictitious brother a little more of a back story.

He gives me a small smile, but it seems unlikely he believes me.

'That is very sad,' he says. 'Very sad indeed. I do hope he recovers.' He rises from his position at the desk. He walks past me and does a circuit of the room.

'You are something of a nuisance, Mr Docherty,' he continues.

His voice is odd; I can't quite place the accent. All I can determine is that it doesn't match the clothes. There is nothing Middle Eastern about his vocal stylings. I can detect a hint of something English, maybe also a hint of west coast America. As I said, odd. It doesn't fit our surroundings, and it doesn't fit with my assumption that this whole enterprise is being run by Islamic terrorists. I wonder who this guy really is.

'What can I say,' I replied. 'I didn't set out to be a nuisance. It kind of overcame me when I found myself on a plane taken over by mass murderers. I guess I felt a kind of civic duty to do something about it.'

'Noble of you, I'm sure. But I suspect you are not telling me the whole story, Mr Docherty. Today I have run perhaps the most audacious strike against Western imperialists the world has ever seen. Including bin Laden. I snatched four aircraft out of the sky. I have hidden these planes in different places around the world. Everyone is looking for them. Our world—sorry, *your* world—is teetering on the edge of chaos. I am the one who will now give it that final, gentle push it needs to descend into anarchy.'

He is now standing behind the desk. With a flourish he opens his arms wide, like an actor taking the acclaim of the crowd. There is certainly an ego at work here. He lowers them again and fixes me with a dead-eye stare.

'Yet I now have to worry about you. The only survivor from my, if I do say so myself, masterful plan, I ask myself: why has he survived when a thousand others are dead? What makes him so special?'

I shrug. 'I'm just a bloke on a plane.'

'Don't fuck with me,' he says in a sudden burst of fury. 'Today you saw what I am capable of. Do you really think you can match me?'

'I'd have to sink a long way to match you, you evil bastard,' I reply calmly.

When you have nothing more to lose—I can't see myself getting out of this one intact—it gives you a little more freedom to push the boundaries. I figure this bloke is probably operating on the unsafe ground between sanity, insanity and ego. Perhaps if I push a few more buttons he will make a mistake. All I know is that if I'm passive and accepting, I will soon be taken from this room, into the desert and shot. But instead of reacting, he sinks back into his chair and again fixes me with those blue eyes. I search for any sense of humanity lurking in there, but in this case they're only windows to the soulless.

'Evil is such a Western word,' he murmurs in such a low voice that I struggle to catch the words. 'Your corrupt politicians love to use it, your immoral newspapers think it's clever. You think it's a way to judge us. To shame us, even. You call us evil while bombing our children. You call us evil while letting your own people starve to death in the street. One day, perhaps soon, we will all be dead and then Allah can judge who is truly evil. I look forward to that meeting, Mr Docherty—do you?'

I stare flatly back at him.

'Mate, there is no god. There is only the here and now. As far as I can tell, it's a crying shame someone like you has spent a lifetime chasing ghosts and fairy stories made up by some other nutter who was also stuck in the desert and given to delusions. Think of all you've missed out on.'

This time I got a reaction. But not the one I wanted. As my new friend laughs at me, the tall commander in the crisp uniform grabs a rifle from one of his soldiers and smashes me across the back of the head. Down I go. Not unconscious, but dizzy. In a crouch, I put a hand on the floor to steady myself. It feels like I have tried to grab hold of a roundabout going at full speed. I topple over.

Everybody laughs this time. For half a minute I lie on the warm floor. Then, trying to regain a small measure of dignity, I force myself up. The room is still spinning and my head is still thumping, but I am standing again. Doing my best to look unruffled.

'Mr Docherty, surely you know how unwise it is to taunt the Prophet, blessed be his name. After all, look how it turned out for those unfortunate cartoonists in Paris.'

This time I say nothing.

He smiles again. 'Mr Docherty, it's possible I may have overrated your skills. Looking at you now, I see a man who got lucky. For whatever reason, you were spared today. If I were you, though, I'd enjoy the next few hours. They will be the last you ever know. Although, on the bright side, at least you will have a front-row seat to enjoy the full beauty of my plan.'

I must have looked confused.

'Mr Docherty, you can't be thinking I have finished with you just yet? No, no. Are you a sporting man?'

I nod.

'Consider this the half-time break, then.' The man turns to the guards. 'Take him away.'

19

We take the same route back to my cell, my arms jacked up behind my back by the two goons. It's not getting any less painful, although the ligaments in my shoulders have been nicely stretched by now. Again, I see the aircraft sitting quietly in the distance and wonder about my chances of making a run for it. It doesn't seem any more likely than it did twenty minutes ago. But I'm also intrigued by those last comments from the man who never bothered to introduce himself. It feels like I am creeping closer to understanding what all this is really about.

'This the half-time break . . .'

What else does he have planned? I had been assuming I was looking at a straight terrorist operation. The act itself was enough. Hijacking four large passenger planes and making them disappear in full view of the world is a hell of a trick, no doubt about that.

Another of his phrases pops into my head. The one about a final, gentle push into anarchy. What does *that* mean? In the old days of simple hijacks, he would have demanded a ridiculous sum of money or the release of some brother freedom fighters from jail in Israel, America or Britain. This feels different. There is some grand scheme in the back of that malevolent head if he thinks he will outstrip bin Laden. He isn't going to be asking for $100 million to return the planes and the bodies.

The same worry thrums away—who is he?

Head throbbing, shoulders screaming, I am finally thrown back into my cell. I stumble and fall, but pick myself up in time to see the door close. I shout out.

'Food! Water!'

But there is no answer. After all the talking and the exposure to the heat, I am parched. I don't like to think of how many hours it has been since I last had a sip of water or something to eat. I park myself back in my corner where, tired to an extreme I can't remember ever experiencing, I fall asleep.

But not for long. The door soon opens letting light into the darkness and a soldier walks in with a tray. On it sits a glass of water, a jar with steam rising off the top, perhaps tea, and plate with some flat bread and assorted straggly bits of meat. Another soldier walks behind his colleague, light bulb in hand. My exhausted brain immediately leaps to the wrong conclusion. I'm going to somehow be plugged into an electrical socket and charged up. The man must have registered the terror on my face and understood because he smiles, reaches above his head and attaches the bulb to a sad-looking electrical cord I had not noticed hanging from the ceiling. It's only a light.

'Who are you guys?' I ask. 'Who's in charge?'

Nothing.

The tray is placed on the floor in front of me. The light left on. And they leave without a word.

The water goes down first. One gulp. Gone. It nearly comes straight back up, but I manage to hold onto it. It was warm, somewhat dusty, but up there with the best I've ever drunk. Immediately I feel better, more human.

My hunger dictates I have a crack at whatever meat is in front of me. Probably camel. But I'm not in a situation to be picky. All I know is I should take whatever nourishment is on offer, the fuel tank is hovering well below the E mark. I wrap the meat up in the flat bread, which is still warm, and force it down. Thankfully I don't taste too much, but there is a satisfaction in feeling the warm glow of food making its way towards my stomach.

The dim light from the bulb doesn't reveal much. The only addition to the cell are the bare wooden beams in the high ceiling. I walk slowly around the cell, neck craned upwards, but I can't see a way out. Even if I did find a chink in the armour I'm not sure how I would climb the four metres of smooth concrete towards that freedom.

The walking combined with the food and the water brings on what nature demands your body do and I'm seized by a sudden pain in the gut. My immediate thought is the bastards have just poisoned me. Doubled over, I sink to my knees. The initial surge passes and I stumble to the door, banging on in and shout for a bit of help.

The door opens a crack.

'Toilet,' I gasp.

The door closes. Another wave of pain grips me. Is it poison or just the effects of my body kicking back into gear after not eating or drinking for more than a day?

Two minutes later a wooden bucket is thrown into the room. Trailing it is a white ribbon of toilet paper. Not in a position to be choosy, I squat inelegantly over the bucket and just let it all go. The relief is instant. The smell something else. But at least I'm functioning again. I take the bucket and place it as far away as possible. I bang again on the door and shout for someone to take my mess away, but this time no one answers, so I return to waiting.

* * *

Again I sleep. Again I am rudely awakened. Groggy and sleep-sick, I check the luminous dials on my watch. The journey back to consciousness seems to involve a long climb from the bottom of a deep, dark well. As far as I can tell I've probably nodded off for about three hours.

The source of my return to consciousness is the same trio who fetched me from this cell last time. The sharply dressed officer type, who shows no signs of rank, stands back once more while the other two pull me roughly to my feet. They look uncomfortable this time, though.

'Enjoying the smell, boys?' I ask.

We retrace our steps. I'm now getting a fair idea of how the compound works and I start to see small rays of hope. Possible escape routes, possible hiding places. Beyond the hangars, the land starts to rise, but it's flat in every other direction. If I ran west, I would end up at the sea, which wouldn't help much. The view south and east is unremittingly barren. No cover, nowhere to hide. But north, beyond the two main hangars, the land slopes upwards. It's probably sand dunes. They appear to be heavily vegetated. If I get the chance to run, that's the direction. It's clear my chances of escape are still on the anorexic side of slim and there is no indication of what is beyond that first dune, but at least the scrub will provide an element of cover, a chance to hide.

I'm dragged back to the room that houses the man in charge. This time he's already sitting behind his desk as I enter the room. He greets me with a disturbingly friendly smile.

'Mr Docherty, it occurs to me I was a little rude to you earlier,' he begins in that strange off-putting voice. 'I didn't introduce myself properly. My name is Khalid Mustafa Al-Arabi. But you may call me "Your excellency". Welcome to my caliphate.'

'Congratulations, I'm sure,' I reply. 'Break out the champagne.'

A chuckle. 'Ah, yes, the usual Western response to good news. Drink. Get married. Get drunk. Have a baby. Get drunk. Die. Get drunk.'

'Well, can I at least have one? I'll toast your imminent death.'

'Mr Docherty, I think we both know my prospects for a long life are significantly greater than yours.'

'Another one of your delusions, Khalid, my old pal. There's only so long you and your desert rats can remain hidden.

This may be a big world, but it's being watched by a million eyes, and one of them is about to look your way.'

'Really? Perhaps I should just give up now? Lend you a phone and let you call the cavalry?'

'That certainly sounds like the best plan you have come up with in a while.'

The smile fades as if he is tired of this conversation.

'No, Mr Docherty, I have much better, much grander plans for you. I'd hate for you to miss them. Trust me, it will be spectacular.'

The self-appointed caliph stands and gestures to the soldiers. A dismissive wave of the hand and they disappear from the room, leaving just the two of us for company. I am intrigued. What is he up to? It seems a high-risk manoeuvre. I scan the room for an escape route. There is a window, locked by the looks, but by no means unbreakable if, say, a chair is thrown at it. A quick jump through and a bolt to the sand dunes suddenly seems a possibility.

Khalid senses my intentions.

'Don't get too excited. There is no escape. You may well be able to overpower me, but then what? Outside that window I see you look so longingly at are two soldiers carrying machine guns. You won't get far that way. And my recently departed colleagues stand on just the other side of this door. They are similarly armed. So put aside any hopes of a daring break-out. It is futile. Instead, sit down, and I'll outline to you exactly how you will die. I can only give you one promise. It will be more impressive than getting shot in the back by some illiterate Arab who believes he is doing Allah's work.'

I hesitate, puzzled by the insult he has directed at his own men, but pull out the seat and do as I am told.

'I am sorry to be the bearer of bad news,' he continues, 'but your death is inevitable. It will be memorable, however. That I can promise you.'

'Well, we all want to be remembered, I guess.'

It strikes me his voice has changed. That uncomfortable mix of geographic improbabilities has fallen away. What remains would appear to be an accent I associate with the south of England. Not exactly Prince Charles and his ilk of inbred class warriors, but definitely something from that universe. Plummy, rounded vowels that speak of a public-school education, black tie for dinner and ritual floggings.

'I won't pretend that your presence here has not been an annoyance to me,' Khalid is saying. 'You're the one loose end in my otherwise perfect plan. And I don't like loose ends. They need to be chopped off or tied up and made into something useful. As it happens, I am going to do both to you.'

'Who are you?' I ask.

'I have already told you. I am Khalid Mustafa Al-Arabi.'

'That's who you are now, but who were you before? What's your real name? Alfred? Algernon? Percy? Peregrine? You're not from around these parts, are you, old bean?'

A smile.

'What matters, Mr Docherty, is not my past but your future. That is what we are here to discuss. Would you like to hear about it?'

I'm not so sure that I do. But being here and trying to figure out this deranged lunatic is preferable to being dragged back to my cell and locked up again. Anyway, this is a bit like going to the world's maddest fortune teller. He is going to predict how I will die. Who wouldn't want such vital information?

'Certainly, Lord Algernon. Do continue. I'm all ears.'

'The good news for you is you will be getting back on that plane and getting out of this hellhole. Most likely within the hour. Refuelling has just started. The even better news is that you will be flown back to the US.'

I admit I'm starting to get optimistic, even though common sense would dictate that's foolish.

'The not-so-good news is that while there will be a take-off, there will be no landing.'

My optimism comes crashing back down.

'Not in any recognisable sense of the word, anyway,' Khalid continues. 'Mr Docherty, you would be aware of One World Trade Center in New York. I think the Americans call it Freedom Tower or some such nonsense in their usual simplistic fashion. They built it near the spot the Twin Towers stood before that old ratbag bin Laden started up his city demolition business in 2001. Now, being the predictable morons they are, the Americans have constructed an even taller building on that site. I suppose they think they are really showing the world how big and strong they are. How they will never be defeated by terrorism.'

I am starting to get nervous.

'So, Mr Docherty, that plane you're about to get on will fly back to America. And straight into Freedom Tower. Let's see if we can make history repeat, shall we?'

There is a long silence after this.

'You'll never get away with that,' I blurt out, immediately embarrassed by this cliché. 'I mean, seriously. They'll shoot the plane down before you get anywhere near the place. The Yanks may have been taken by surprise by bin Laden the first time around, but they are hardly going to fall for the same trick again.'

Khalid relaxes into his chair. He steeples his fingers in front of his face, which is holding a look of quiet contentment.

'Under ordinary circumstances, you may be right. But would you regard these as ordinary circumstances? Four planes have gone missing. I would suggest that almost every military aircraft in the world is out looking for the dear departed. Wouldn't you say? Do you think anyone has given any thought to the possibility of one of those planes flying back to the US? Much less into the heart of New York City?'

It pains me to admit, but he may have a point.

'As you have seen, I have already made four planes disappear. Who says I can't make them reappear as well?'

'Hold on,' I start. 'What do you mean about the four planes reappearing?'

'Simple, Mr Docherty. Around the same time that your 767 is slicing through the New York skyline, another will be ploughing its way into the Sydney Opera House, the third will be aimed at the Eiffel Tower, and the fourth will touch down at the Maracanã football stadium in Rio de Janeiro while 80,000 people are watching Flamengo play Fluminense. Magnificent. No?'

I am stunned. Shaking. All I can manage is a repeat of my feeble 'you'll never get away with it', but I'm not so certain I believe that anymore. The audacity and scale of the plan is breathtaking. He doesn't even have to succeed in hitting all four targets. Even if he strikes one the world will be in uproar.

I'm imagining the horror. The carnage. Hundreds of thousands of people will be killed. And killed by missing jet planes themselves still carrying hundreds of dead bodies.

Khalid must see the fear in my eyes as he chuckles to himself. Quite taken by his own mad brilliance.

'If this is all so well planned, what do you need me for?' I ask in a voice that I'm struggling to keep the emotion out of.

'Oh, just for my amusement really. And perhaps a bit of misdirection. You will be strapped into the first officer's seat—that front row seat I promised you. Your last earthly memory will be an extreme close-up of Freedom Tower. Afterwards, we will announce you as one of the glorious martyred heroes who gave their life for this noble cause. That should cause some angst in Australia, I should think. Although they may have to take our word for it, as I imagine your DNA will be difficult to locate given it will have been atomised and spread across most of the five boroughs. How about a picture, then? Of course, we will take a nice colour shot of you in the cockpit just before take-off.'

I feel ill at the thought of becoming a poster boy for terrorism.

'But who is flying these planes?' I ask. 'And how have you found four pilots crazy enough to offer up their lives for, if you'll excuse the expression, a deranged psychopath?'

'Always with the insults, Mr Docherty. Really, I thought we were past that. But the answer to your question is they're not doing it for me. I have promised a lot of money to the

family of one pilot, another is about to be charged with some
quite unpleasant crimes against children and wants a final
'fuck you' to society, while the third, to use your own words,
may actually be deranged. They also think their deaths will
please Allah and usher them to the mystical kingdom where
70-odd virgins will be waiting to service them on an hourly
basis. Mad, I tell you.'

He pauses for a moment.

'But it's not all bad news. You will have company on your
last flight. The fourth pilot. An old friend, in fact. Happily,
the unfortunate pilot whom you treated so unpleasantly on
the way here has made a full recovery, although his head is
still a little sore and his nose is no longer straight . . . Still,
he's looking forward to flying you back to New York. He
thinks he is flying that plane all the way to heaven. Can't get
much madder than that.'

This is the second time he has insulted Muslims. It's
puzzling. Up until now, I assumed I was dealing with just
another insane Islamic bomber. Full of hatred of the West,
ridiculous plans for world domination, a casual attitude
to the worth of a human life. But without his soldiers his
attitude has shifted. Like his voice. I am starting to think
I am dealing with two different people, or at least someone
with many different agendas.

'What am I not seeing here?' I ask. 'Among your goons, it's
all the usual, bog-standard Muslim terrorist stuff. Western
evil this, Islamic supremacy that. Now you are making fun
of the blokes you're sending to their deaths? I am wondering
what is going on.'

The maddening chuckle again.

'Ah, Mr Docherty, such cynicism. What happened to you as a child to make you such a doubting Thomas?'

He looks happy with his use of this Christian reference. But I remain silent, and he moves to fill the void.

'This is not one of those situations where I now let down my guard and you discover my most intimate secrets. I've watched James Bond movies. Very instructive.'

The smile fades from his face. A face devoid of basic human empathy and emotion. It is replaced by a look of cold calculation. 'Let me leave you with this thought. It is possible to walk both sides of the street at the same time. And think about this: Iraq, Syria, Yemen. Hundreds of thousands of square kilometres, tens of millions of people, billions of barrels of oil. Who controls them? If the West goes into a terrorism-inspired downward spiral, a bit like after September 11, what happens next?'

With that he dismisses me. 'But perhaps I have said too much. No discipline. That's always been my problem. Can't ever stick to the rules I set for myself.'

He summons the guards. As they enter, he speaks again, his voice returning to that strange mix of accents and inflections.

'Please take Mr Docherty back to his cell. And, Mr Docherty, in case we don't meet again, fly well. I won't say happy landings.'

We all know the routine by now so my friendly guards don't bother with the arm-wrenching this time. Instead they content themselves with poking me in the back with the muzzle of a machine gun and trusting I get the general idea.

I start the walk back to my dusty cell. My mind is ablaze, trying to figure out what Khalid's ultimate intention is. His grand plan seems not to be an end in itself, but the start of something bigger and even more frightening. This is stage one. What has he got planned for stage two? Although if the first part of the plan succeeds I won't be around to worry about what happens next.

As we round the corner nearest to the runway, I spot the 767. A low sun is rebounding off the yellow, blue and white livery of the Ukrainian jet, partially blinding me, but there is no mistaking the sight of a tanker pumping aviation fuel into the big machine. It seems I am running out of time if I want to find a way out of this mess.

I squint for a better view and hold my hands over my eyes. On the ground near the front of the plane a mound has been built. At first I can't tell what it is, but then the sun reflects off something silver as it arcs from the plane to the top of the pile and I understand what I am looking at. They are emptying the plane of all its luggage. And I know why. They are making the aircraft as light as possible. They will be filling the fuel tanks to the brim to get as much distance as possible out of this aircraft. If we really are heading back to New York, we will need to do so as close to the ground as possible to avoid being detected by radar. And flying low burns up fuel at a far higher rate that when you're high in the sky at cruising altitude.

I look for bodies to see if they are being similarly thrown out of the plane, but I can't see any. I assume Khalid thinks the horror of the attack will be amplified further when people learn that the plane was full of the dead.

I turn to the guards. Maybe if I can make them believe Khalid, or whatever his real name is, is a fraud, then they will turn against him. Perhaps even help me out. Clearly, I am becoming desperate. It's hard to unwash the brainwashed.

Looking straight ahead, I talk loudly.

'Khalid doesn't give a fuck about you guys. I don't know what he's up to, but it's nothing to do with building a caliphate. He told me anyone who believes in Islam is deranged. His words—'

And with that I am administered a short, sharp whack to the back of the head, courtesy of the blunt end of that machine gun. You could probably build a papier mâché copy of my head from the indents that must have by now been preserved on the end of that weapon.

As I sink to my knees on the hot sand, regretting my familiar recklessness, the soldier in charge leans over to whisper in my ear.

'You are wasting your time, my friend. These two don't speak any English and I have no interest in anything you say.'

Another grand plan bites the dust. Along with my face.

Head ringing, I slowly rise. The two grunts meet my gaze with a dead stare. It would take a hammer and a chisel to make any impact on those hard heads. We shuffle off together. My feet dragging, bringing more dust into the air. My captors behind me, letting me take my time, guns ever at the ready.

I'm soon back in my cell. I assume this will be the last time. When I'm next taken from here I will be strapped into a plane with a suicidal madman. A madman, it must be remembered, that I knocked unconscious while spreading his nose across his face the last time we met. It's unlikely to be a happy reunion.

But somehow this is possibly the best outcome I could have hoped for. It beats the swift execution in the desert that seemed the most likely way of me ending my days. Now at least I have some extra hours to figure a way out of this. Khalid knows I will do anything in my power to find a solution, which makes me again wonder about his motives. Why would he leave me with any hope at all? Is it just my propaganda value?

I haven't been captured on film so far, but perhaps I don't need to be. If I am filmed, no matter what I say, I will look like the unwilling captor that I am. But if they pull this off, I can be included in the subsequent honour roll as a glorious martyr. I can't see anyone who knows me believing it, but it's a big, scared, cynical world and there will be plenty who will. Plenty looking for someone to blame for this horrible day. My name will be up in lights.

It's a profoundly depressing idea. I think of my daughter. In her own unhappiness with me, will she be all too willing to believe the worst of her father?

I find myself at the cell door. The pain in my head has just about subsided. The kaleidoscope of colours that were dancing in front of my eyes has dimmed as what's left of my brain stops jiggling in my skull. The familiar push in the back propels me into the cell, the door closes, the key turns and I'm left on my own again.

20

Time passes slowly. The heat builds. I am as still as I can be, hunched over, head in my hands, but the sweat drops from my forehead onto my stomach. In my absence, a jug of water had been left. Some flat bread as well, although no meat this time. Even better, the toilet bucket has been removed.

As I sip the water and tear at the bread, the conundrum of who Khalid is and what his real intentions are eat away at me. Trying to unpick the mind of a madman is not easy. What passes for logic and reason in Khalid's brain is likely to be so far removed from my own version of reality that finding any path to understanding is beyond me.

But if not religion then what? Revenge? For what? This has surely gone beyond being upset because he was picked on at school, or was dumped by his first love at university. This has been a hell of a fuck you to the rest of the world, but it must be driven by something more than emotion.

The only answer is money. Nothing drives the world like money. Or, to be more precise, nothing drives the world like the pursuit of money. But what is to be found out here in the middle of nowhere—I still don't where I am—that makes all this worthwhile? He talked of oil, he talked of control of land and people. Does he really believe he can build a caliphate out of all the misery and dispossession felt by so many in the Middle East? Does he think it's a way of controlling all the oil in the region? It's certainly a big carrot.

I drift. Thoughts come back to me of family and friends. Good decisions and bad. It occurs to me that I may not have much longer to think about the life I have lived and the people I have loved.

If I thought there was an afterlife I could look forward to seeing my wife again. Apologise for my neglect and self-ishness. And while making promises to myself, I tell myself I'll find Eliza as well. There is still time to make it right between us. I just have to make sure I survive.

I'm veering into dangerous territory now. Self-pity and sentimentality are two of my less endearing traits. But if you can't be a little morose when facing certain death at the hands of some of the world's most deranged people, when can you be?

As my emotions lurch from the sentimental to the silly, the door opens. In strides Khalid. Again, it's just him and me. He looks agitated, more so than before. I wonder where this is going. Perhaps I have managed to crawl under his skin.

'Just so you know,' he begins, 'the same rules apply as before. No funny business. Out there sit some psychopaths with guns, all extremely eager to shoot you through the head. Apparently you fit several categories in the Koran that justify the killing of infidels, or whatever the fuck chaps like you are called. So be careful.'

He is striding around the perimeter of the room. I try to follow him, but it just makes me dizzy, so I stop on one spot and he circles around me like a shark sizing up its prey.

'Maybe I would rather die now,' I say, 'and instantly, in a hail of bullets, than be strapped into that 767 with only a maniac for company and sent back to the US just so I can fly into that tower in New York. Maybe I'd like my death to be simpler. I can't see how overpowering you would be a problem, either. I could probably do some real damage to you before your goons came in the door.'

He laughs at me. Still pacing.

'No doubt you could, Mr Docherty. No doubt you could. But I like to believe I am good at reading people and my reading of you is that you will try to postpone the moment of death as long as possible. Not only because you enjoy life but because your ego tells you there is still a way out of this. That you have hope. Mr Docherty, your ego is wrong.'

I remain silent. He may be nuts but it doesn't mean he is always wrong. Khalid continues to pace. Another two laps of the room. Three. It's as if he's deciding something, working it out in his head with each length of the cell. Finally, he stops. He has come to his decision. He wheels around to face me.

'This really is our last meeting. In ten minutes you will be taken from this room and back to the aircraft. You will be strapped in tight. Very tight. No prospect of breaking your bonds. So, if I were you, I'd spend the last few hours of your life making peace with the world, and your god, if that is your wish. It will be easier for you that way. Better, I think, than struggling and plotting and sweating to achieve something that can only end in failure. I wouldn't like to think of you as having your last moments on earth defined by failure.'

This is just getting weird.

'Your life advice is fascinating, Khalid,' I say. 'And timely. I'm touched by your concern for my wellbeing. Have you thought about writing a self-help book? What could you call it? *The Seven Habits of Highly Deranged People? How To Shoot Friends and Influence No One? Who Moved the Bomb?*'

Khalid steps towards me. For a moment, I think he is going to throw a punch, but he gathers himself and stops in his tracks. Staring at me with baleful eyes. He almost looks disappointed.

'Not crazy, Mr Docherty. No. A crazy person couldn't pull off what I have. There are other adjectives I grant you that may work better. Greedy, perhaps? Ruthless? Without doubt. There may also be a little self-aggrandisement and narcissism in the mix somewhere as well. I don't think there is a lot of self-delusion.'

'Who are you?' I ask again.

'What does the Muslim world lack, Mr Docherty?'

I'm not sure what he means. 'Lack? Certainly a lot of people live in parts of the world that are defined by poverty and violence. But I don't see you as some kind of rescuing angel, to be honest.'

'You are half-right, Mr Docherty. Excellent. You are improving.'

He stops and smiles at me. Wonderful. Now I am being subjected to a little psychopathic stand-up.

'A little joke,' he offers. 'Even in these uncertain times we must leave some room for humour.'

'That may be easier for you than me, given the circumstances.'

'Yes, perhaps you are right.' He sighs, looking a little sad. I almost get the impression he wants us to be friends.

'My point is the Muslim world lacks leadership,' he goes on. 'The US president is referred to as the leader of the free world. The Catholics have their Pope, some Buddhists look to the Dalai Lama, even the Anglicans have the Archbishop of Canterbury. But who leads the rest? Who do the world's nearly two billion Muslims turn to for guidance? Did you know, Mr Docherty, that by 2050 there will be more Muslims on this planet than Christians? What an opportunity for the right man.'

There is a small silence as I try to process this latest thought bubble.

'I would have thought there were plenty of self-styled Islamic nutters out there claiming to be the leaders of their people. There was quite a nasty stoush around Iraq and Syria there for a while, I seem to recall. Every city, every country, every region has someone or other claiming to speak for all Muslims.'

'Maybe so. But think about it. Most of these guys are either too small to be noticed beyond their immediate enclave, are hiding in caves in the backblocks of Afghanistan or Pakistan, or, as you noted yourself, are too busy fighting each other to really notice what is going on anywhere else.'

'Okay,' I say, scratching my head. 'But even if you are right, and that is a big if, are you suggesting they'll all set aside their differences and come and work for you? How can you possibly make that happen?'

'In the usual way, Mr Docherty. By bringing the West to its knees. Not physical ruin, you understand. What I figured out is that you can't do it with bombs alone, or using cars and trucks to run down people in the street. The West will be brought undone by economic and emotional ruin.'

'And how are you going to do that?' I ask before realising the stupidity of my own question.

'I have already done it. Of course, you have been out of touch with the rest of the world for the last few days. Let me summarise for you. Wall Street is down 40 per cent. The US dollar has fallen 35 per cent. The oil price is up 35 per cent. As of today, there is not a single airline flying anywhere in the world. In the last 24 hours, the US president has made an unprecedented three live addresses to the nation. There are riots in the streets from New York to London to Moscow. The world is teetering. *Your* world is teetering. It only needs one more push from me.'

'Sending the planes back,' I say, my voice a monotone.

'Sending the planes back,' he echoes. 'Who knew the West was only four planes away from falling to pieces?'

'Where are the other three planes?'

'That's not information I feel the need to share. But they are safely hidden away. Being refuelled as we speak. Ready for their last flight to glory.'

I feel like I have just run a marathon. My legs struggle to hold me upright, my lungs are burning, my guts sweltering.

It's a mad plan, but there is an inherent logic to it that could see it work.

Khalid waits for me to say something, but I'm all out of words. He mistakes my hesitancy for confusion.

'Let me be clearer for you, Mr Docherty. Who was the big Muslim baddie before me?'

'Bin Laden.'

'Correct. And what was his biggest triumph?'

'Knocking down the Twin Towers.'

'Indeed, Mr Docherty, indeed. And that single emblematic act placed old Osama right at the top of the pile. He was seen by the West, and by many others with likeminded tendencies, to be spiritual and actual leader of a fair few of the world's Muslims. But, Mr Docherty, what was bin Laden's biggest mistake?'

'Getting shot by the Yanks?'

'I concede that may also be a contender, but, no, that's not what I am referring to. Bin Laden's biggest weakness, which then made his biggest mistake inevitable, was his refusal to countenance compromise. That ridiculous Stone Age philosophy of his made it impossible for him to come out of that cave and engage the world beyond some silly videos. I have no such impediments.'

I can't stand still any longer. I move in a circle with Khalid at the centre. He follows me, turning his body to track my movements, but doesn't try to stop my movement or even tell me to stop.

'I have to ask something. Are you actually Muslim? Do you believe in, I don't know, the Prophet Mohammed jotting down the word of Allah for the purpose of informing the world of His will?'

A chuckle.

'I was brought up within the faith,' Khalid says. 'The faith of my fathers, you might say, but I no more believe in the fairytale propagated by that chap Mohammed than the balderdash you had to listen to during endless Christian sermons at school.'

'But how . . . how did you do this?' I stammer.

The animation leaves his face. The light leaves his eyes. It seems I have tripped some internal switch.

'That, Mr Docherty, you don't need to know. Be a clever boy and spend the rest of your life trying to figure it out. Farewell, Mr Docherty. It's been fun. Give my regards to the Big Apple.'

And, with that, he turns and leaves.

21

The door has been closed for less than a minute before it opens again. It's my favourite threesome come to escort me to one last dance. A strange thought strikes me. What if these were the only three soldiers Khalid possessed? Then I remember the couple of dozen thugs who searched the plane after I landed.

As I'm marched down that bare corridor for the last time, I start to fantasise about there being an outside chance I could take these three and scarper. All I would need do is to grab one gun, a quick fight, then I could fuck off in whatever direction seemed least likely to get me shot in the back. Back towards those sand dunes, I reckon.

The door of the barracks opens and I see it is night. In the gloom, partially lit by fires in scattered, empty fuel drums, I become aware of hundreds of watching faces. My escape fantasy quickly dies. Khalid, it appears, really does have his army.

I walk out towards them, my compadres still at my back. Everyone is turned towards me. Then, as I approach, they take a step back in unison. In the half-dark, with the shadows cast by the fires, it's an eerie experience. A brief glimpse of hell. Or, to stick with the biblical analogies, it's like Moses parting the Red Sea. I walk along a tunnel of hate with the guns behind to steer me in the right direction.

The Ukraine International 767 has been moved since I last saw it. Strangely, I hadn't heard a thing, an indication of my mental state, perhaps, that I had somehow missed the not unquiet roar of two enormous Rolls Royce engines as they had fired up and rolled the aircraft nearer to the camp. The captain, as Khalid had said, had clearly recovered.

Feeling a bit like the Christian being fed to the lions, I aim for a look of studied nonchalance as I make my way to the aircraft. Like taking a stroll through a crowd of people who would all happily tear me to pieces was an everyday experience.

After the parting of the ways, there was an initial silence from the assembled mass. But as I make my way through the crowd, a low moan from hundreds of men builds to a rumble, which in turn rises to a crescendo. It is a full-throated expression of loathing. For a moment, I become the embodiment of everything these blokes think they are fighting against.

It's not much fun being the object of hate from hundreds of heavily armed, deranged men. There is a sense you are the only still point in a sea of fury. There is also, unsurprisingly, fear. When you read or watch stories about terrorism, detailing some atrocity in a faraway land, like

'Car bomb kills 50 in Baghdad' or 'Suicide bomber kills 30 in Kabul', there is an intellectual understanding that something terrible has occurred but no real emotional connection. You may feel some pity for the victims, but it doesn't seem possible to get inside the mind of whatever drives these people to such violence. So you move on. Don't dwell on that darkness. I mean, what can you do?

But to see the raw ugliness up close is terrifying. To see the embrace of violence, while at the same time understanding these are people who believe they are on a mission from God, bends the mind.

As I shuffle through the sand, making my way through those last few metres of hate towards the aircraft, I'm torn between searching the faces of those around me to find some understanding of what was happening in their heads and the terror that if I catch the wrong eye I'll start a riot. A riot that will end with me being torn limb from limb in some sort of medieval re-enactment.

But as I finally reach the 767's stairs, the only damage I suffer is inflicted by the scores of blokes who managed to get close enough to me to spit in my face. Disgusting, but not deadly. Not immediately, anyway.

I move on from one horror to the next. As I climb the stairs back into the aircraft the smell reaches down to grab me. It's the tang of several hundred dead bodies that have been left to rot in an aluminium tube that has been sitting in the hot sun all day.

Halfway up the stairs, I stop and chuck up what little is left in my guts. Tears prick my eyes. I put my hand in front of my mouth and nose in a futile attempt to ward off the stench that seems to be taking on a solid form and invading my guts, my lungs, my eyes, my bones. I know I will never lose the sense of that smell whether my life span is another eight hours or another 80 years.

I move from the light into the dark. It's a literal and metaphorical journey. I pause as I enter the cabin, looking to my right and taking in the sight of the dead. It's unnerving to see all those people just sitting in their chairs as though waiting for the aircraft to take off. The noise from outside the plane has stilled to be replaced by the buzzing of flies attracted to the corpses, but as I stare at the departed the phrase 'quiet as the grave' comes to mind. But I don't linger.

At the not-so-gentle urgings of my escorts, I continue to move into the aircraft. I take a left turn towards the cockpit and head back through the first-class section. I walk past my original seat. To my surprise, tucked away under the spot where I had spent most of my journey to this place is my backpack. It had never been picked up. When these blokes found me they obviously didn't make any effort to figure out where I had been sitting. At least my jacket is safe is my first thought.

The cockpit door is open. My old friend Captain Arzu stands up to greet me with a smack across the face with the gun in his hand. It stings, a lot, and my moist eyes fill again with tears. He connected just above the bridge of the nose and I can feel blood trickling down the back of my throat. Still, I take some satisfaction in the state of his head. A big plaster across a nose, which really isn't as straight as it once was, and two big, beautiful black eyes. I can see why he is not happy with me.

I stare at him through my watery eyes, determined to give him no satisfaction in thinking he has cowed me. 'Ah, Captain Slayer, still picking on those who can't defend themselves? What a brave man you are.'

He lunges for another crack, but by now the man in charge of our detail has come up beside me, put his hand on the captain's chest and quietly warned him: 'Enough.' This makes me relax, until he adds, 'You will have eight hours to do whatever you want with this man, but right now you have more important duties. We will tie him to the chair, you get this plane ready to leave.'

Arzu gives me one more hard stare, but acquiesces and returns to the captain's seat. There's not a lot of room in a cockpit; most of the space is taken up with a million switches, dials, displays, levers. Even though I had landed this thing only a day ago, it momentarily amazes me that there was a time I knew what they were all for.

The order comes from behind me: 'Get in the seat.'

I do as I'm told and take my position in the right-hand chair. As promised, it looks like I am going to have a wonderful view of our journey. And then, before I am aware of what is going on, the man in charge says, 'Docherty.' I look around and find myself starting into a shiny new iPhone. He takes my picture.

With a grin, he holds the phone's screen in front of my face to show me his work. I look tired, somewhat beaten-up, beard emerging, but it's identifiably me. And I can see how it will be used to make me look like a participant in this evil day.

The guards step forward to pin me more firmly to my seat. After a little pushing and shoving between them, it becomes clear they both can't reach me at the same time to do the job. In other circumstances it might have been funny. A bit like getting tied up by Dumb and Dumber. Eventually the boss man gets sick of the charade and orders them out of the way.

'Fucking idiots,' he calls them. Proving that, in some ways, we do all speak the same language.

He squeezes between me and the cockpit window. After asking the others to hand over the industrial-strength gaffer tape they are carrying, he sets to work.

'Hands,' he orders, motioning with his own hands in front of him, wrists facing in towards each other. I comply and he binds my hands so tightly I can feel the blood flow instantly slow to my fingers.

Then he puts a knee on my right thigh and pushes me right back in the chair. With my head pressed against the cushion, he wraps the tape across my forehead and around the back of the seat. He swirls the roll around three times before breaking it off with his teeth. He then proceeds to do the same with the bottom half of my face, covering my mouth and nose. I start to panic. I can't breathe. I look up at him in a mute horror. Surely this is not the way I'm going to die? He gives me a terrible, evil smile and then swiftly brings out a dangerous-looking flick-knife from his pocket. He snaps it open, brings it towards my face. I'm trying to push even further back in my seat, as if a few extra millimetres will spare me from the blade. Then he slices open the tape around my mouth. I feel the tip briefly sting my upper lip as it does its job, but I'm more grateful to be swallowing air again.

He moves to the floor and ties my legs together, then to the chair's steel supports. I know it won't take long for my thighs to be screaming and for my legs to become numb.

The final flourish is to bind me from neck to hip with the same tape, going back around the chair in taut loops. This last move also pins my hands and arms right into my torso. I imagine I must look like a giant, shiny, grey mummy. If my bits are found in a few hours on the streets of New York, it may take the experts a little while to piece it all together—in a metaphorical as well as, unfortunately, a biological sense.

Job done. My guardians leave the cockpit. My companion, the captain, follows them, leaving me trussed up in the seat. I strain and wriggle, but I can't move as much as a millimetre. It feels like I have been trapped under a slab of concrete. I can swivel my eyes, but that's it. Feeling a rising sense of claustrophobia, I bite back my urge to panic.

Looking out of the cockpit window I can see nothing but the dark night sky. Clouds have blown over, blotting out stars and moon. It's a good night if you want to make an unobserved flight.

Somewhere behind me I feel a small change of air pressure and conclude the captain has closed the cabin door and take-off is imminent. Thirty seconds later he has returned to the cockpit, takes his seat, pausing only to deliver another blow to the side of my head. The whack makes my vision explode in a starburst of greens, reds and blues. But I also hear my man exclaim in pain, and through my multicoloured visual display I fancy I see him wringing his hand. Given my head is so tightly bound to the chair, it would have felt like punching a rock.

With any luck the shock will stop him hitting me again for a while, although there are many other, softer parts of my body he can inflict damage on without doing himself too much harm. Sitting down, he runs through his pre-flight checklist, says something unintelligible into a walkie-talkie he has by his side; they are clearly taking no chances with broader radio communication. It does, however, seem to me that the aircraft's radio is in working order. The headset is at least plugged back in. Next Arzu puts his right hand on the throttle between us and gently pushes it forward to begin our taxi to the runway.

We bump along the ancient, pockmarked tarmac until we reach the end of the runway. I see its faded grey and white markings spreading out for a couple of kilometres ahead of us. And then we're away. Because I am already taped as tightly as possible to the bloody chair I miss the usual g-force pinning me back in the seat. But we accelerate quicker than normal and are in the air in a matter of moments. Then I remember the only cargo on this plane is me, Arzu and all those dead bodies behind us.

We blast off into the sky and climb at what feels like almost a vertical ascent. Given how light the aircraft now is we rise at a phenomenal rate, clearly trying to gain as much altitude in as little time as possible. It's a long jag to New York. We will take a more direct route than the one that brought us down here, but I reckon it will still take somewhere between seven and eight hours to reach our destination.

Arzu is going for the extra height given the radar coverage out here is still pretty much non-existent, but I expect the closer we get to New York, the lower we will be flying. Finally, we level off. Arzu engages the autopilot but stays where he is, staring fixedly ahead through the cockpit window. I can't see the altimeter, though I think we must be at about 30,000 feet. The altitude will help us arrive in New York sooner and preserve fuel for the low-level flying Arzu will need to do if he is going to approach his destination unimpeded. The desert has already given way to the ocean. We are flying north.

22

For a while all is quiet. The captain is concentrating on his job rather than on inflicting further violence on me. I take this in with a swivel of my eyes. My vision is just about clear again. Arzu's head is constantly on the move. Left, right, up, down. He's nervous. Scanning the sky for other aircraft, for anything that may spot him and give his position away. All it will take for this plot to be rumbled is one stray aircraft to ask questions about why a Ukrainian Airlines 767 is ploughing through the dark night sky when every airline in the world has been grounded.

This, of course, is something of a long shot. Given that at any point in time there are probably around 5000 commercial flights crisscrossing the globe, there's a whole lot of empty sky right now. No doubt there are military aircraft up here somewhere, satellites as well, but it's at times like these you realise what a big world we live in and the chances of spotting one rogue plane are infinitesimally small.

I don't put much hope in the idea of being spotted by satellite. No doubt all the transponders, which identify this aircraft, have been switched off. Radio communications won't happen. It would truly be a miracle if anyone or anything was to locate us.

Is there any possible way out of the shit? Is there an option where my life doesn't end by flying into a large building in downtown Manhattan?

I try to shift in my seat. Try to find a little wriggle room. I struggle and strain. But no luck. They have done a thorough job of strapping me in. But my exertions attract the attention of my companion, who, in time-honoured fashion, whacks me in the side of the head, although this time with an open hand. I mark this down as a small victory.

Physically, I am incapacitated. This leaves my verbal and intellectual skills. A thought that doesn't raise my spirits. I can't see myself appealing to Arzu's better nature. Or of talking him out of this mad path of destruction. I mean, how do you appeal to the better nature of a bloke who has volunteered to fly a 767 into the side of a building? He clearly has no regard for his own life, or anyone else's, so how do I make a bargain in such a situation?

On the other hand, I can't just sit here quietly for the next seven and a bit hours, calmly awaiting death. It's time to give something, anything, a shot.

I start small. I ask for a name, wanting to confirm it's the same one I heard being shouted just before I was captured after the plane landed. The same one I heard announced before I embarked on that last, mad flight.

'Look, as we are now stuck together for the rest of our lives, can we talk?'

Nothing. Given all the tape around my face, it's hard to form words. I sound like one of those pricks from the upper classes who barely move their mouths when they talk just in case they are forced to breathe in poor people's air. I persist.

'Come on, there is no point in not talking to me. The least you can do as you are transporting me to my death is tell me why I am about to die. You must have your reasons.'

I even try a little flattery.

'There is no way I can agree with what you are about to do. I have probably already made that clear. But at some level I do admire your commitment to the cause. I wish I felt that committed to anything in my life. And I admire your bravery. I may have fought for my country at one point, but what I was mainly fighting for was myself. Fighting to save my own life.'

More silence. I was just about out of words when he finally spoke.

'Please, Docherty, no more talking. I am under orders not to speak to you.'

I give a bitter laugh. 'Mate,' I say as I continue with what can only be considered a charm offensive, 'who's going to know? This is a one-way ticket. If you need quiet to contemplate what's going to happen next and to make peace with your God, then fine, I'll shut up. But the time may pass a little easier if we talk.'

'What do you want?' he says.

A chink. The first. Every escape tunnel starts with the first strike on a seemingly impenetrable surface. I hope this is mine.

'Okay, captain. Let's forget what happened before. My anger is gone. Don't get me wrong, I'm not happy about it, but I have accepted it. The one thing I would like to know, though, is why I have to die. Can you explain that to me?'

'Because, Docherty, you were chosen.'

'What do you mean chosen? By who?'

'By yourself when you got on my plane and decided not to die with the others. Then maybe by Khalid when he thought you would be a useful propaganda tool.'

His English is heavily accented, but it's not the German I first thought it was. It seems now to come from somewhere in the far eastern edges of Europe, but it's also educated. Wherever he grew up, someone did a fine job in teaching him English.

'You have put yourself in this position. Why would you go to a shithole like Ukraine? What were you doing there anyway?'

I toy with the idea of telling him my real name and job, just to see if it elicits any reaction, just to see if it unsettles him at all. But I decide against it. There may still be some advantage to keeping my identity secret, although I don't know what it could be. My caution may just be habit. In this line of work, no information, no matter how small, is ever offered up willingly. I decide to keep with the 'brother' cover story.

'Like I told Khalid, I was on my way there to see my brother. I hadn't planned it. He was injured in a traffic accident. I wanted to go and check he was okay.'

He gives no reaction. I don't know if he believes me or not.

I worry he's about to close down on me again. I have to keep him talking, Silence is not going to help me here. If I have any shot at building that metaphorical escape tunnel, I have to keep chipping away.

'But you're a pilot. You must have seen a lot of the world. You must have been born with a certain curiosity about this big planet of ours. Why else would you do this job?'

I am still rigid in my seat. Head pinned back and eyes pointed straight ahead. But I fancy out of the corner of my eye I can see Arzu turn his head and look at me. There is a silence for a while as he perhaps considers whether he wants to answer me or not.

'My father was a general in the Soviet air force. Sometimes the choices you make are not made by you.'

'You followed in your father's footsteps?'

'Yes.'

'From what I'm hearing and seeing, you are a highly qualified, highly competent air force pilot. You had a good education. You come from a family that I imagine had certain privileges. You were doing well in your life. So how did you end up here? Help me, I don't understand.'

More silence. Then anger. White-hot anger. But from a completely different direction than I expected.

'Docherty,' he screams, 'don't you presume anything about me. Don't ever talk about my family. Don't ever assume you know why I am here. You don't know, you couldn't understand! You talk of privilege. You stupid Western fuck. Your Western arrogance makes you believe you know everything about everybody. You want to analyse me? You know nothing about me. You know nothing

237

about family. You know nothing about loyalty and you know nothing about revenge.'

Not knowing how to reply, I say nothing and let the hurricane blow itself out. The flight continues in silence. The words loyalty and revenge are still echoing through my brain. It occurs to me Arzu has not used any words common to your usual fanatic. No Allah, no jihad, no *Allahu Akbar*. None of the religious idolatry we have been trained to expect from the terrorist world.

It makes me wonder if there is something else going on with Arzu that I haven't figured out. I search back to the conversation with Khalid as well. He made it quite clear that whatever his motivations were they weren't religious. This makes things trickier. When you can define the opponent, it's easier to fight them. It makes them more predictable, more understandable.

But there is something about these blokes I can't define. I don't have a proper handle on what either Khalid or Arzu are chasing. It's more than just terror, religion and fear. Khalid spoke of building some kind of power structure, his caliphate; Arzu of loyalty and revenge.

I let Arzu be. I figure we have another six hours of flying time left before we come up on New York with a rush. I don't want to equate flying time with life span, but it's a hard conclusion to avoid.

My view out the cockpit window hasn't changed much. It's still dark. The clouds are breaking up a little. I can see the odd twinkle of a star filtering through the gaps, but nothing much else. We drone on into the emptiness, the only difference being I fancy we've lost some altitude. This could end up being a real skimming-the-waves operation. I didn't enjoy it too much last time.

Flying that low also gives you a much better idea of the terrifying speed you're travelling at. When you are high in the sky, it always feels so serene, like you are hardly making any progress at all. But when you are metaphorically bouncing along the waves, the full power of those two enormous engines hanging off the wings is readily apparent. I'm trying not to think of them driving me into an enormous, unmoving concrete and steel structure, but I'm not having a lot of success.

* * *

As surreptitiously as possible, I try to stretch the bonds that hold me tight. It isn't easy. The tape is so constricting I'm struggling to even fill my lungs with enough oxygen to breathe. For half an hour, I concentrate on nothing apart from flexing all my muscles. If nothing else, I need to keep some blood flow going so if by some chance I break free I won't fall flat on my face the moment I try to stand up.

I develop a routine. Try to move right foot, wiggle toes, then contract and expand calf muscle, then do the same with the thigh muscle. Then start all over again on the left leg. Then I work a little higher. Stomach muscles, in and out, take as deep a breath as possible to expand my chest cavity, try to roll my shoulders, then neck, back and forth and side to side.

At first I can feel my muscles contracting and relaxing, but nothing much else. But, gradually, I believe I detect a slight give in the tape. It's only a millimetre here and there, if that, but it's a start.

As I do all this, I keep swivelling my eyeballs, trying to get a handle on what Arzu is up to. He seems perfectly still, looking straight out the cockpit window, occasionally adjusting a control here, a control there. It's hard to tell if he is ignoring me or has temporarily forgotten me as he struggles with the situation he now finds himself in.

In the silence, I allow myself to imagine that Arzu is battling with himself. That there is some chance he sees the madness and carnage that lies in front of him and will change his mind. That he will find something to live for—a wife, a lover, children, sister, brother, parents. That he will pull up a map, find the closest airport and gently bring us back to safety.

The longer he is quiet, the more I allow myself to indulge in this preposterous fantasy. I must have allowed myself the luxury of forgetting that we are travelling with a cargo that already includes 290 dead people.

Rationally, I know there's no incentive for Arzu to land the plane in the orthodox fashion of my dreams. If he did, all he would be looking forward to were 290 murder charges, global hatred as the face of terrorism and his own death once the Americans get hold of him.

After an hour, he breaks the silence just to confirm my worst fears.

'Not so long to go now, Docherty. Are you ready to die?'

'No,' I mutter. 'It wasn't in my schedule today, I have other things to do. Can we do it another day?'

A small laugh. A noise of contempt.

'No, Docherty. This is your day. It's time to make your preparations. There is no going back. Today, you are going to die.'

There's a dryness in my mouth, like I have been swallowing sand, and it takes extreme mental discipline not to collapse into myself, give up and start begging for a mercy I know will never be granted.

Instead I say, 'Arzu. Water. I need a drink.'

'Open your mouth,' he says.

I do so, the little as I can manage. Then a water bottle is swinging towards my slit of a mouth. It's in Arzu's right hand. He hasn't left his seat, but has manoeuvred it backhand-style. I feel like a baby receiving its bottle from its mother and I wonder if the day's indignities will ever end. Then I remember there's a definite end point for all my indignities and I decide being force-fed some water is probably not the worst thing that will happen to me today.

I take the water gratefully. The precious liquid washes around my mouth and slides down my throat, and instantly I feel a lot better. Stronger. Better able to deal with this mad situation. The panic subsides. I put it back in its box and close the lid. Arzu takes the bottle away.

'Thanks,' I splutter as the water spills down my chin.

We relapse into silence as the aircraft continues to slice its way through the air.

23

I continue my exercises. Working up and down my body. A mantra in my head: 'Keep the blood flowing.' I picture it moving around my toes and calves, thighs and chest, neck and brain. It gives me an odd sense of comfort that my body, while inert, hasn't stopped working just yet.

I fancy I have also made progress with all that tape holding me in place. Not a great deal, though; not enough to think I'm going to spring free at any time. But enough to give me encouragement to keep going.

I can feel more give in the tape around my right ankle. Just a little elasticity. It's only millimetres, really, but it's something to keep working on. It's what I need—the challenge not to give up. Not yet. There is nothing in my head that would qualify as a well thought out plan, but I just need to persist in the belief that at some point an opportunity will arrive. I just need to be ready to take it.

It's also time to work on Arzu again. The silence really

isn't helping me; it's letting him off the hook. I need to get inside his head, spark something from him, even anger. I need to shake him out of this soporific détente we have settled into.

'Arzu, we are going to die,' I begin. 'And we're going to die together. That's about as big an eternal bond as I can imagine. But I want to know why you're doing this. It's not going to change anything, but I need to understand. Can you grasp that?'

For a while, nothing. Then:

'Okay, Docherty. But first you tell me something. Who are you?'

'You know who I am.'

'No, I don't. We have friends. Friends with access to information all over the world. They checked your story and we think it doesn't work. We ask, "Who is this Docherty who leaves New York for Ukraine?" We find he only books the flight to Ukraine at the very last moment. That he was supposed to be on a plane home, to Sydney. That it looks like your name was entered into the system in some unusual way. It almost looks like you didn't enter the US on a regular commercial flight. So, tell me, Docherty. Who are you?'

This is a bit of a shock. I had been happy in my arrogance that I was hiding behind my assumed name. It was a shell I had built around myself, hoping it would protect me. I contemplate sticking to the 'fake brother' story. It explains some of what he already knows, but not everything. I give a deep sigh and decide to tell the truth.

'How long have you known?' I ask.

'We had suspicions early on, but some of our friends in America only got back to us a couple of hours before take-off.'

I think back to my penultimate chat with Khalid. When he outlined what lay ahead of me. Perhaps that was when the message had been delivered. 'Docherty isn't who he says he is.'

'You know, you were lucky,' Arzu says.

'How's that?'

'You weren't meant to be on this plane.'

'Oh.'

'You were to be shot between the eyes and dragged out into the desert and left for the animals. There was some argument about cutting your head off.'

'That sounds pleasant.'

'But when Khalid found out that your story didn't make sense, he thought he'd stick you on the aircraft instead. You see, we may not know who you are, but someone does. It's likely you are a spy of some sort. After we crash into the tower, perhaps we'll find out your true identity. Perhaps that's good for us. To have a Western spy on the plane at the moment the tower topples—for the second time. It shows you can't stop us. Or maybe we can convince people that you were one of us all along.'

I give up the pretence.

'My name is not Docherty,' I concede. 'It's Ted Anderson. I work for an arm of the Australian intelligence services.'

'So, what are you doing here, Australian? This is a long way from home. This is not even your fight.'

I laugh. 'Mate, you don't know Australians very well, do you? My country has been getting into fights that don't concern us for a long time now.'

'It is true you are the first Australian I have met. But I think this was a bad fight for you to pick. You can't win.'

Arzu goes quiet, but I need to keep talking. What else can I do? It's a small distraction from this situation. Perhaps I can even distract him long enough find my way out of this.

'I was following the planes,' I continue. 'The first one went missing off Australia. I was called in to help find it. We thought it was an accident at first. You know, a rivet had broken or something and brought the plane down. One thing led to another. As you know, I finally found my way to New York. Was actually waiting for my flight to take me back to Australia when I saw you pick up the iPad left by the cleaner at JFK. I followed you to the aircraft, then doubled back to buy the ticket to Kiev. Why did you need that iPad, anyway?'

Silence. Just for a moment. I am hoping now that I have told him a secret he feels some sort of duty to start telling me some of his. I need him to believe there is some sort of link between us. That as enemies we can still be friends.

He begins to speak. Decision made.

'I didn't know where I was going. I knew what I was doing, I understood all my actions, but my destination was a secret until I switched that iPad on.'

'There was a map on the iPad?'

'Yes.'

'So, where were we? I couldn't quite figure it out beyond somewhere on the west coast of Africa'

'Western Sahara. An old, abandoned airstrip.'

'You didn't know the destination. But you knew what the mission was? You knew what you were going to do? You knew you were going to kill all those people and you knew that eventually you would be getting back on that plane and taking it to New York?'

There is a quiet 'Yes' in reply.

I knew what the answers would be to all those questions, yet part of me is still overwhelmed by the neurosis contained in them. But more than the madness is the fanaticism and commitment to a cause that persuades you that killing thousands by the end of this day is a righteous, justifiable course of action. I struggle to contain my emotions. I can feel the anger trying to escape from every pore. I feel the restrictions of my captivity more than ever. I want to get up, I want to breathe properly, I want to walk away from this confinement, this death sentence. I want to escape from this tin coffin.

The panic is rising, and the fear, the loathing washes over me. It's an act of enormous will not to scream, not to show this sad killer how much he fills me with revulsion.

Another moment passes. Then another. And, eventually, I regain a sense of my calmer self. The blood that I can feel and hear rushing around my body slows just a little.

Arzu remains silent. The plane drones on into the unending dark.

'Tell me,' I begin softly. 'Why are you doing this? You can stop this if you want to. Why are you giving your life away like this? What is this vengeance you are chasing?'

A harsh, guttural sound escapes his lips. Neither laugh nor sneer. A bark, full of disgust and contempt.

'Docherty, sorry . . . *Anderson*. Some habits are hard to break. Before I said revenge. I misspoke. What I am after is justice.'

'Arzu, this is not justice, this is mass murder.'

'Your mistake is to believe all lives are equal. That simplification is an indulgence of your corrupt Western world view. The truth, Anderson, is that some lives are worth much more than others.'

'Do you mean Islamic lives? Do you think they are worth more than the rest of us? Do you think your God will thank you for this barbarity?'

'You are not listening. I go to my death willingly, yes, but I'm not expecting to be rewarded for it like those fools who carry a bomb in a backpack and walk into a café. They are going to the same place that I am—hell.'

This is perplexing. I am struggling to follow his logic.

'Sorry, Arzu. I'm lost here. Whose life are we talking about, then?'

'My older brother.'

Now we are starting to get somewhere.

'Your brother? What happened to him?'

'He's dead. Killed by Americans in Iraq, in that filthy shithole Abu Ghraib. Murdered, tortured, humiliated. After they killed him, they burned him, and after they burned him, they threw him away.'

There is not much you can say to that. I have no doubt he is telling me the truth. Why would he lie? If he had reeled out the standard *Allahu Akbar* nonsense I would no doubt have swallowed the cliché easily enough. I couldn't see any point in Arzu making up some complicated lie to justify the unjustifiable.

And, secondly, everyone with a television and access to the internet for the last fifteen years knows the Americans perpetrated some true horrors on people they judged as enemies in places like Abu Ghraib and Guantanamo Bay. They were places that where whatever innocence and moral authority the US held in the days after 9/11 had gone to die. The pictures of cruel and stupid soldiers perched atop the bodies of naked Muslims spoke of a terrible depravity deep within American culture that had been released by the fury of that awful day when the Towers crashed. And Arzu's brother had been one of them. Maybe even one in that photograph of the pile of bodies that had been seen around the world.

I could understand his anger, his hatred of the US and even its allies such as Australia. But surely this vengeance, this retribution, was too much?

'What happened?' I ask. 'I mean, how did he get there?'

'I loved my brother. He was seven years older than me. He was clever. He was strong. He was kind. All I knew growing up was that I wanted to be just like him. He was religious. He grew up dreaming of being an iman at our mosque.'

'Where did you grow up?'

'I'm a Chechen. From Grozny.'

Chechnya. Another fucked-up place in a fucked-up world. Home to gangsters and terrorists, royally rooted over many centuries by the Imperial Russians, then by the Soviets, then by the current Federation. Repressed and smashed as they may have been, the Chechens hung onto their identity, fought for it, killed others to prove it as well.

'My brother was not a radical, not what you might call a terrorist. But he watched the US invade Afghanistan, destroy Iraq, wage war on the world's Muslims and he could take no more. He left one night. Leaving behind a note that my parents wouldn't show me. But I knew. I knew he hated injustice, and in this world all he could see was injustice.'

I remained quiet. I still couldn't see Arzu as he spoke. But I could sense his stillness and distractedness as he told his story. He wasn't paying me any attention and I continued to wiggle and struggle, and, bit by bit, my chains were loosening. Now I could move my feet back and forth a few centimetres. There was some play in my wrists and I could move my neck again.

'Arzu, you speak of justice. But this is not justice. You must be able to see that? If your brother was the kind and gentle man you say, he would not want this.'

The flash of anger returns.

'Don't tell me what justice is, Anderson. You have no right. You and your Western arrogance. Was there justice in destroying Iraq and killing tens of thousands of innocent Muslims? Who stood up for justice when you were killing women and children in Afghanistan? What about Guantanamo? Abu Ghraib? Are they your idea of justice? You despise me because you say I have killed innocents. But there are no innocents anymore. You changed the rules. You with your "them and us" view of the world. Well now the "them" are fighting back. You should not be surprised. Oppressed peoples always rise up, eventually. And we are only just beginning.'

As he speaks, my right foot comes free. I'd managed to work against the metal edge at the bottom of the seat until it finally weakened and frayed enough for me to break the tape.

Arzu hasn't noticed. But while I am bursting to move my aching leg to restore the circulation in the mostly dead limb, I remain as motionless as possible and go back to work on my left leg. Meanwhile, time to keep prodding.

'How did you kill the crew?' I ask casually. 'That was a neat trick. They didn't die of asphyxiation like everybody else, did they?'

'Do you know your French history?' he returns with a strangled laugh.

'It's not my strong point,' I concede.

'It was Marie Antoinette who said, "Let them eat cake." That's what I did, Anderson. Arzu, in his wonderful kindness, brought in some cake for the crew. We shared it around. They thanked me for my consideration. No one noticed I didn't have any to eat myself. Shall we say the cake had a magic ingredient?'

'You poisoned them?'

'Yes, a nice slow-acting formula that allowed them to continue with their normal duties right up until the point where they couldn't.'

Don't ask me the logic, but of everything I've heard today this is the most sickening. I thought I could just about get my head around the depravity of everything else, even all the dead bodies. But there was something more personal, more intimate, in coming to work with your colleagues, some of whom you have flown with all over the world, and poisoning them with a cake.

In my head I could see the happy faces of the crew. The women who had shown me to my seat, brought me coffee. Their delight that their captain was so considerate, so generous as to bring a treat that they could all share. It seemed such a violation of trust.

'That's a low act, Arzu,' I say quietly. 'The act of a coward.'

In a flash, he's out of his seat and beating me around the head with his fists. It's an attack of pure rage. He wants to kill me. He's crashing blows on my face, chest and stomach with his fists, arms, elbows, knees. I am being pummelled to death and there is nothing I can do. Pinned to the seat, he climbs on top of me like a lover, straddles my legs to get even closer and inflict more damage.

I feel my nose cracked sideways, and the blood flows out down my face and drains down the back of my throat. The harsh, sour metallic taste fills my mouth, tears are streaming down my face.

Among the fury, I realise the nose of the plane has tipped downwards. I wonder if Arzu has switched the plane to manual. Probably not. But in his haste to punch the living shit out of me, he has probably whacked the controls with some part of his body and disengaged the automatic pilot.

'Arzu, Arzu,' I gasp. 'The plane, the plane. We're crashing.'

The words penetrate his blood lust and rage. He jumps off me and back to the pilot's seat, grabbing the controls. By now we're on an awkward descent. The nose is down and swinging from side to side, and we're falling quickly. I can see the dull grey sea below me, whitecaps rolling into one another. My immediate thought is that it looks cold.

Arzu is wrestling the yoke. Various warnings are blasting through the cockpit telling us we are in imminent danger of flying into something that we shouldn't. As if we need the advice. I watch the altimeter in front of me spinning downwards. Through 4000 feet, then 3000, 2000 . . . I glance at Arzu, who is holding on tight, doing everything he can to save the aircraft.

The view of the ocean is filling the cockpit window. But just as I am about to give up hope, the nose of the aircraft starts to rise. Just a fraction at first, then by increasing amounts, and finally we are flying straight and level once again.

I look at the altimeter. It says 750 feet. Another two seconds would have seen us slicing through the water, never to be found again.

'Nice flying,' I say. But there is no response from the bloke who is both my saviour and my murderer.

24

I close my eyes. Bloody, bruised, busted. Tired beyond life itself. I just want all this to stop. I don't know how long my eyes have been closed. I may have just blacked out. My body looking for respite, a small moment to heal.

When I come around from that brief spell of unconsciousness, I immediately see something is different. I can move my head, for starters. On instinct I swing it towards Arzu. He doesn't notice. He is back concentrating on flying. Back to manual, this will at least take his concentration off me for a while. I notice the knuckles on his right hand. Red and bloody.

It's not until I move my head back that I understand the significance of my situation. Arzu beating me up has loosened the tape holding my head to the seat. A sudden, hopeful stab of adrenalin washes through my body as I quietly try to determine whether any other body parts have sprung free. My right hand is now loose. I look at it like it's an old friend that I lost touch with many years ago. I try to wiggle my fingers, but there is no response. I'll have to be patient, waiting for the blood to flow and my limbs to wake from their long slumber.

There is only a small thread of tape still holding my left hand down. One sharp tug will free it. Both ankles are now untied and the tape around my chest has more or less given away.

I have no doubt that once I have recovered my full faculties I can break these chains and escape from the chair. Things, I decide, have just got interesting.

But I stay still as I can. I have a new advantage, but that only lasts as long as Arzu doesn't clock to it. I also need to work out what my plan of attack is beyond the basic aim of trying to kill him—or at least incapacitate this fucker long enough to take control of the 767 and find somewhere safe to land it.

Jumping him will be difficult. Not just because clearing away the last of my ties to attack him will give him plenty of notice of what is happening, but because since our last engagement Arzu has made no real effort to take the aircraft back to an altitude that gives any kind of safety net. The altimeter is registering 1000 feet. That is not a lot of room to move. Another prolonged struggle will see us both heading back towards that welcoming sea. Not a great idea.

I risk another quick glance. Still nothing. I close my eyes. Concentrate on staying outwardly immobile, but doing what I can to get my circulation pumping. Soon, very soon, I'll need this body to be working at as close to capacity as possible. My life is going to depend on it. How long do I have to find an answer? Maybe an hour, maybe a touch longer. The end is coming, one way or another.

We continue to skim the waves. It's not a pleasant sensation. One small error here and we are done for. Logically, I know this would be the best solution. If we ditch here, only he and I die. There is no glorious finale in New York.

But I don't want that. It may be pure selfishness. It may just be that the desire to stay alive overrules all other emotions. Of course, I rationalise it by telling myself that I can still find a way out of this madness. That I can find a way to take the plane away from Arzu. That it will be better if I can get the plane down on the ground, where I can tell people what is going on, help them find Khalid, and maybe have time to do something about the other planes—the ones heading to Sydney, Rio de Janeiro and Paris—before they inflict even more chaos and misery on an already terrified world.

But I know I'm probably kidding myself.

There is a long period of quiet until Arzu finally speaks.

'Not long now, Anderson.'

Head pointed straight ahead, I reply, 'What do you mean?'

'New York, my friend. New York. My kind of town. So good they named it twice. The Bronx is up and the Battery down.'

I can't help myself. I turn my head to look at him. He doesn't seem to notice. What I see is a man in the grip of a mad fever. There is a greyness to his skin, a sheen of sweat covering his face and hair, and though he has both hands on the controls they are jumpy, uncontrolled, like a man in the latter stages of Parkinson's. He is rambling.

'Yes, Anderson. "New York, New York." One of my favourite songs. Frank Sinatra. Maybe he will write a new verse just for me,' he says, ending with a laugh.

'I wouldn't be too hopeful,' I tell him. 'Frank's been dead for quite a while now. And, anyway, he didn't write it.'

'Dead? Just like all those other New Yorkers are just about to be then, Anderson?'

'Sinatra was from New Jersey, fuckwit,' I say, not really sure why I'm arguing the finer points of the Sinatra biography.

'Oh, okay. Never mind. Lots of dead *Americans*, then. It's all the same to me.'

Whatever grip on reality Arzu once had has clearly now drifted free of its moorings. I realise it's futile to try to talk him around. He wants to die. And he wants to kill.

'How long?' I ask.

'About 30 minutes. Enjoy the last moments of your life.'

I immediately start to scan the skies. If we are only half an hour out of New York, I can't believe the US Air Force is not on full alert. But I see nothing. No jets, military or otherwise. It's still dark as well. Travelling west to east the whole journey has been in darkness. It's an inky black night. No moon, no stars. The only light anywhere is the dull illumination coming from the electronic dials in front of me. All the 767's outside lights are off too, making it even harder for anyone to spot us.

The instruments tell me we are still flying straight and level, altitude 1050 feet, well below radar capability, speed 850 kilometres per hour.

There is nothing above us. Nothing ahead of us. Except New York. Waiting again for the madness to arrive.

25

I watch the minutes tick by. Tick. Tick. Tick. It's becoming a worry that my life span can be now counted by numbering off my fingers and toes. Thirty minutes is now twenty. There has been no further conversation. As yet no sign of New York, or anything else on the American coast. Still no sign of a waiting military response, either.

For the first time I think I believe Arzu is going to make his destination. I think I somehow felt that there would be some sort of reception committee, a safety net that would catch us, and probably kill us, before we made it anywhere near the US coast.

Now there seems to be nothing to stop us. We are just going to fly straight into New York as had always been planned. I wonder if right now the three other planes piloted by the other madmen are sneaking up into Sydney, Rio and Paris similarly undetected. The thought makes me sick.

I'm only going to get one chance at this. One chance to stop him. And it has to be now. If the plane ditches in the water, it ditches in the water. So be it. But it can't go any further.

I test the bindings on my left and right legs. I am confident that if I stand up with enough force they will fall away. I am not so confident that my legs will respond in the way I want them to after all this confinement, but that's a chance I am going to have to take.

Right arm. Left arm. All good. As I lean ever-so-slightly forward, I can feel the tape come with me. Okay, this is the moment. Time to move. This isn't going to be a complicated plan: I'm going to take him by surprise, jump him, somehow kill him or knock him out, and take control of the plane. Simple.

I steal a quick glance at my captor. Nothing seems to have changed. Hands on the yoke, staring fixedly ahead at his date with death, although I catch what seems to be the hint of a smile on his face. I bring my gaze back to the front. A couple of deep breaths to compose myself. I give myself a count of ten. I am counting down. Six, five, four, three. Click.

Click? In a reflex, I turn my head. Arzu has a gun pointed at my skull. It's a gun I hadn't seen before, that I didn't know he possessed, but on reflection I shouldn't be too surprised. I am mesmerised, staring down the long, black tunnel of the dark blue gun.

'Don't move, Anderson. Did you take me for a fool? That I didn't notice all your movements? That I didn't know the tape had come loose? It is you who are the fool. Please, try and take the gun away. I will enjoy putting a hole in that skull of yours.'

I turn in my seat to properly look at him. Nothing to say. He has his left hand on the controls, the right has the gun pointing at me. He has shifted around in his seat to keep an eye on me. It's a difficult way to control an aircraft as large as a Boeing 767 and I reckon he can't keep this up for long. Either that gun hand slips down a bit or he will start to lose control of the plane.

We are still flying at about 1000 feet. There is no room for error from his point of view. Or mine, come to think of it.

But he might not have much longer to hold on. For the first time, I can see the lights of the United States of America. Not many, but there is a dull glow on the horizon where only a few seconds earlier there had been nothing but darkness. As every moment passes, this vision becomes clearer. Out of the left-hand side of the plane I can see the lights of what I assume to be New Jersey. We're now only minutes from New York itself.

We have also started a slight climb. Freedom Tower is 1776 feet high. The number always stuck in my head because it was built to that exact dimension to commemorate the founding year of the United States. I guess they thought it was a big, clever fuck you to all the world's terrorists, but at this moment all I see it as is a fucking big magnet for the maniacally deranged. They have essentially painted a big bullseye on themselves and invited the world's most dangerous nutters back for another crack. I just hope, despite any evidence to the contrary, that their defences have improved a bit since 2001.

New York City is starting to take shape through the cockpit window. I put together the pieces of the famous skyline. I can see the Empire State Building and perhaps that strangely shiny reflection a little to the right of it is the Chrysler Building.

And there, standing like a beacon at the bottom of Manhattan, is the tallest thing on the world's most densely populated island. Freedom Tower. One World Trade Center. Whatever you want to call it. It's 104 storeys of glass and chrome stretching from my vantage point into the night like an eighteenth-century lighthouse. And we're headed straight for it.

Out of options and out of time, I perform the last manoeuvre I can think of and with any luck it's the last thing Arzu is expecting me to do.

With as much speed as I can muster, I throw myself violently forward onto the control column in front of me. Arzu still has just his left hand on the controls. An enormous noise immediately fills the cockpit, followed by a smell of cordite and smoke. He has fired the gun. The world goes dull, it feels like my head is underwater, but there is no pain, no immediate sensation of being hit.

But everything has gone colder. Maybe he has hit me. Then I understand. The bullet has missed me and taken out the cockpit window. The chill air outside is the cold I feel. I have my hands on the controls trying to drive the plane down into the black sea below.

I wait for the next bullet to end the argument. But instead I feel the aircraft starting to pull out of the dive I have tried to put it into. I look across at Arzu, who has placed the gun between his legs and is using both hands to regain control of the aircraft. And he is winning.

It's just as well we are so low in altitude because the sudden decompression caused by the window exploding would have otherwise killed us. As it is, the plane's defence mechanisms have kicked in and the oxygen masks have fallen from the cockpit's roof, though we don't really need them at this height.

In desperation, I flick the catch on my seatbelt and in the same movement start to stand, the tape ripping off the seat. I feel the pain in my legs from the sudden effort after hours of immobility, but I try my best to ignore the agony as I surge towards Arzu. I tackle him in his seat like a football player. Arms around his chest and arms. I feel the plane suddenly lurch sideways. The gun. Where is the gun? I reach for it between his legs, the last place I saw it. It's not there. Arzu has freed a hand and is raising the gun to shoot at me. I try to grab it. Too late. I don't see how he can miss at this range, but he hasn't been able to get his arm around far enough. He fires. The noise this time isn't as overwhelming, perhaps absorbed by the sound of rushing air from the broken window.

But he has hit me. A sharp, hot needle of pain erupts somewhere in my upper left arm. I don't think the bullet stuck. It's passed through the fleshy part of the back of my arm and continued its trajectory to somewhere in the cockpit. Being winged somehow gives me an adrenalin shot and one last surge of anger, mixed with fear, mixed with a desire to end this fucker once and for all. I am still on top of him, still in the tackle hold. I can see the gun waving around in his hand. Arzu is torn between trying to shoot me again and regaining control of the plane, which is lurching all over the place. In the fight, I have lost track of how close we are to arriving at our target.

Where is that fucking gun? Arzu is trying to free it up for the coup de grâce. Again, I surge at him. I take the gun in both hands and wrench it from his grasp. I hear the crack of bone, a cry of pain. It's still in his hand, but I've forced his useless fingers to point back at him. Pressure his finger on the trigger. The gun explodes for a third time.

Arzu stops struggling. I stop struggling. I look at him. The bullet has taken away most of his jaw. He is dead. At last.

26

I take a deep breath. I need to get my bearings back in a hurry. Need to regain control of the plane. I jump back into the co-pilot's seat and look out the window.

Fucking hell. Directly in my line of sight, not 500 metres away across the water, is Freedom Tower. Arzu may still get to complete his mission after all. A quick glance at the instruments tells me we are flying at 900 feet, travelling 750 kilometres per hour and heading straight towards the middle of that glass building. I fancy I see the lit-up Statue of Liberty below me as I approach from the south towards Manhattan.

With everything I have, I pull the control stick to the left. The left wing dips down almost 90 degrees as the right one goes up almost 90 degrees. The plane is just about vertical to the ground below it as I sweep past the 104 storeys of the tower. I have no idea how close I am to the building, but I have the impression the belly of the plane is just about scraping the enormous thing and I can see the reflection of the 767 rippling in all that glass and steel as I sweep past. I still have the yoke at 90 degrees and I wait for the sound of impact, the terrifying collision between immovable object and aircraft. But nothing comes. Then I realise I am past it.

But this is Manhattan. There's always another skyscraper just around the corner.

I don't see what it is. Only that it's big and in my flight path. I try to fling the plane to the right and simultaneously gain some altitude to take me above the skyline. But I am not a slalom skier who can weave in and out of the posts at great speed while traversing down a slope. I am trying to guide a cumbersome 767 through Manhattan, preferably without hitting anything. I am pretty sure this has never been attempted before.

I skim past another building, find a little clear air, and the nose of the plane starts to edge upwards. For the first time in some minutes I take a breath, feel a wave of optimism wash over me. I'm going to get out of this, going to survive and tell the world my story. I just need to find somewhere to put this bird down and all will be well.

But nothing is ever that simple.

As I slowly climb out of the Manhattan street level and into clear air, leaving the billion lights of New York City behind me, I am looking around, trying to get my bearings. I know JFK and La Guardia are only a few minutes away. I just need to get my head straight and figure out which way to go. And if I can gain enough altitude, I should just about be able to see at least one of the fields.

Instead, what I see—and I have no idea where they have come from—is about half a dozen extremely scary-looking aircraft, probably flown by highly jumpy pilots.

Oh good. The cavalry has arrived.

As far as I can tell, I'm now surrounded by a bunch of F-22s. One of the US Air Force's more advanced and capable killing machines. Of course, as I am flying an unarmed 767, I could be shot down by a World War II Spitfire, never mind the most expensive hardware the US government has on offer. My only surprise is that they haven't blown me out of the sky yet.

But then I look down. I'm still flying over Manhattan. I can see the dark outline of Central Park directly below me. It's more than likely my new friends are waiting for me to head out over less populated terrain before shooting their expensive missiles at me: a crashing 767 in the middle of Manhattan would be something of a PR disaster for the US government, even in these particularly strange circumstances.

They may think, which also works in my favour, that the plane is still full of live captive passengers instead of 300 dead ones, and that is staying those itchy trigger fingers for the moment as well. But I can't know that for sure; I don't know what has happened in Sydney, Rio or Paris. The whole show may have been revealed in all its depravity by now. If the other hijacked planes have already been used as terrible weapons then the boys in the F-22s are not going to cut me a great deal of slack.

I keep heading north up the great island. It's the safest route I can think of. My other concern is fuel. This thing has been in the air a long time. The fuel gauges are bumping along the bottom looks like fewer than two tonnes, so if I have half an hour's worth of gas left I will be surprised. All the low-level flying has sucked just about all the juice out of the tanks.

In the meantime, out of my left cockpit window I see two F-22s, seemingly hovering, motionless, as I continue my regular 700-kilometre-per-hour speed. Out of the right window are two more. They are doing nothing overtly aggressive at this point, but I feel like a sheep surrounded by dogs who are trying to herd me into the pen. These planes are trying to guide me away from Manhattan and I have to keep correcting my course to stay straight and level.

I've lost track of where I am. There's still a lot of people and buildings down there, but I may have wandered off into the Bronx by now, so I start a big, lazy left-hand turn and aim the 767 back down over Manhattan. I know this is going to scare the bejesus out of my escorts, but this is my last chance of survival and I'm going to cling onto it as long as I can. I tell myself that if the whole thing becomes untenable I will just have to ditch the plane into the Hudson River. It's been done before.

I have this sudden mental image that the footage of this plane flying over Manhattan is probably on every TV screen, tablet and phone on the globe as people all over the world watch in terrified fascination and wait for the inevitable conflagration. I wonder if they know anything about me by now. Whether they know my name, and, if they do, what they are saying about me. The rogue Australian who somehow managed to become involved with this evil terrorism plot. What is Bob thinking? What is my daughter thinking?

The idea scares me and I realise I need to communicate to people that what they think is happening is not actually happening. In all the tension of the last twenty minutes, it hasn't occurred to me to switch the aircraft's radio system back on. That the continuing silence isn't helping me.

I reach for the switches. I turn the radio back on, all the navigation instruments, the transponders. I want the message to go out. I am here, I am not hiding.

The radio erupts back into life. I rip the headset from Arzu's ruined head. Someone is speaking. I seem to be joining a conversation that is already underway; the Raptors had probably been trying to talk to me from the moment they flew up to meet me.

'Follow us,' the clipped, military American voice is saying, 'and you won't be harmed. If you don't, we will shoot you out of the sky. Your time is running out.'

I have completed my turn, the Raptors as my shadow, and am heading right back down the middle of Manhattan. Ahead of me is Central Park again, further afield I spot the Empire State, and I mentally trace the grid of streets that define the island. The straight lines of Fifth Avenue, Madison Avenue, Park Avenue, the slash that is Broadway cutting across all of them. In the far distance, I can make out Freedom Tower, happily still upright.

I speak into my headset: 'Hello, my name is Anderson, Ted Anderson. I am flying this 767. Don't shoot. Don't fucking shoot. I am on your side. I'm an Australian, for fuck's sake.'

A pause.

'Mr Anderson, my name is Captain Granville Grapple. I can assure you, sir, that unless you do exactly as you're told

I will be shooting you out of the sky as soon as I fucking can. We are not fucking around here anymore.'

I can't say I was expecting a welcoming committee, but this bloke is clearly so close to the edge that it won't take a great deal to push him all the way over.

'Captain Grapple, I hear you and understand your concern. I know this doesn't look good for me, but I'm not going anywhere until I receive some guarantees of my own.'

Basically, I don't trust these fuckers. They are nervous. They want to shoot someone and it may as well be me. But as soon as I have uttered the word, I know 'guarantee' is a little inflammatory given the situation.

'Anderson, you listen to me, you murderous little fuckwit. You will do as you are told or I will blow you up right here, right now.'

Time to play bluff.

'Well, you won't, Grapple, for two very good reasons. One, there are still 300 people on this plane and you don't want to distribute their earthly remains all over Central Park. Second, a 767 crashing into somewhere like Times Square is going to create an awful lot of damage. A lot of dead Americans. Another 9/11. I'm not sure your bosses are going to congratulate you and award you another pointless tin medal if that happens. Do you?'

'Don't worry about your landing spot, Anderson. We can handle that. What the fuck difference does it make, anyway? You are going to put that thing down wherever the fuck it does most damage. I am going to stop you doing that. And, Anderson, I know you're the last living soul on that plane. I saw what your friends did in Sydney.'

Dear God. They made Sydney. I instantly grieve for my home town. What carnage has been wrought on my favourite place in the world? I want to ask Grapple what happened, how many have been killed, what damage has been done, but that's going to have to wait. An idea has formed.

'Grapple, Grapple. Wait. Just wait. I can prove I am who I say I am. I can prove I'm not a terrorist. I just killed the fucking terrorist. I blew his head off. Call Alan Miller. He can prove I am who I say I am. He's the one that got me out of Jakarta. Got me into New York, actually.'

'Who the fuck is Alan Miller, Anderson?'

'CIA. I have his business card. You can check for yourself. Do it.'

'You don't give the orders here, Anderson.' But then he goes quiet.

I continue my glide down the spine of Manhattan. The island is only about 21 kilometres long, so soon enough I am going to be forced into another steep turn to head north again. I know as soon as I wander off the island and over the water that I'm toast. I don't think they will hesitate for a second to shoot me if they have the chance.

Looking down, I see that even though it's late at night there are thousands of people on the streets, cars are jammed everywhere doing a slow-motion crawl. I get the impression the entire island has come to a stop. That hundreds of thousands of necks are stretching back, pointing all those faces up to the stars, looking for me, looking for where the terror is coming from and praying that today they won't be an unlucky one.

Now I see the vivid neon circus of Times Square. I imagine myself on one of those famous outsized video screens. Ahead, again, I spot Freedom Tower. It's as good a navigation point as any, so I adjust course marginally and head towards it, although this time I am hoping I don't get quite so up close and personal.

The radio has been silent for more than a minute. I begin to worry as I prepare to loop around the Tower. I scrub off some speed, veer, then bank left into what is supposed to be a graceful arc. But I've either taken the F-22 closest to me by surprise or he is trying to pen me in to stop me flying where I want to go.

From the cockpit I shout a very loud 'fuck' as I wrench the controls back left to avoid a collision. Too late. I hear a terrible grinding on my right-hand side. A shudder runs the entire length of the plane. It lurches back left. I struggle for control; I've lost more speed in the collision and the thing is heading for a stall. I put the nose down to gain some more speed, but the response seems slow and soft. Out of the window, the F-22 seems to have disappeared, but I can't see where to. I wonder if I've knocked it out the sky and think this must be the only time a boring old 767 has taken out the newest fighter jet on the market. I wouldn't fancy being that pilot when he gets back to base. Presuming he has survived.

My more pressing concern, though, is that my limping, non-responsive aircraft is again now on a direct line with the Trade Center.

'Eventually I'm going to hit that fucking thing,' I think as it again fills my cockpit window.

I try to find more speed. In the end, I do what all pilots do when faced with looming catastrophe: talk to the aircraft.

'Come on, baby. A little more, just a little more, please. I promise I'll get you down soon. We just need to miss that giant fucking building. Come on, come on.'

Slowly, the plane seems to shake itself out of its torpor. The controls start to respond better, I find the speed I'm looking for, and as I tug the yoke hard left, for the second time in my life I see a large plane I am flying miss one of the world's most iconic buildings by a whisker.

I breathe. I check on the whereabouts of the Raptor but see nothing. I take it as a good sign that there's no smoke, no fireball rising up towards me from the Manhattan pavement. I try to have a quick look at the wing to see what damage has been done, but from where I'm sitting it's impossible to tell. So I concentrate on taking the 767 back up the island.

The fuel situation is critical now. This will have to be my last loop. The radio springs back to life.

It's Miller.

'Hey, Ted, how's it hanging, old pal? You enjoying your tour of Manhattan?'

I can't remember when I have ever been more grateful to hear a voice in my life.

'Miller! Fuck me, they found you. I can't believe it. I thought they were going to shoot me out of the air.'

'Well, don't get your hopes up yet. There are still some very nervous military types around here who'd be only too happy to make that happen. I'm in New York, old friend. Just watching you tootling up and down the island. It's quite a sight. I'd say there are about twenty million fucking terrified people down here at the moment.'

'I bet. Tell me what I need to do. Let's finish this madness. I'm just about out of gas. Can you find somewhere where I can put this bugger down on tarmac?'

Hoping to put at least some minds on the ground at ease, I veer gently over to my right so I am flying over the East River.

'Have you enough fuel to make it to JFK? It's about ten miles from your present position. Just a couple of minutes flying time.'

'Yep. Fine. The low fuel indicator has been on for quite a while, but there still seems to be a dribble in the tanks. Where is JFK from here?'

'Hold on, Ted, I'll put you on to the nice man from air traffic control. He can talk to you like a pilot. See you on the ground, buddy.'

'Okay. Control?'

'Yes,' comes back the answer from a new voice.

'What's my course? What's my frequency?' I say, amazed I am using phrases I thought I had long forgotten. It's remarkable what can sit in the back of your brain just waiting for the right moment to be useful again.

'Your course is 135, frequency 111.5 for runway 13L,' says the faceless man, giving me the numbers I need to plug into the plane so it will take me to JFK.

I find the right dials, make the changes and hit the approach button. The plane slowly yaws around and heads to the airport. Miller is soon back in my ears.

'Doing fine, buddy, just bring her home.'

'I will, mate, just as long as there is enough gas in the tank.'

Miller must detect the fear in my voice. He replies soothingly.

'Okay, Ted. Okay. That's not a problem. You can bring this bird down without any trouble at all.'

'You know how long it's been since I landed one of these in a big city airport?'

'Prefer not to know, if it's all the same with you, buddy. But don't worry, the airport is all yours. There is nothing in the air except for you and your friends beside you. Nothing has left or arrived at JFK for the last 24 hours. Just get it down. All other landing lights have been turned off apart from those on your runway.'

'Okay. Okay.'

I am looking for the lights of the airport. Nothing yet. I have a ridiculous flashback to the movie *Flying High* when poor demented Striker is trying to land: 'I may bend your precious aeroplane, but I'll get it down . . .'

From here on in, it's my motto as well.

Then I see them. Twin rows of green and white lights stretching into infinity. I adjust my course to line up. Altitude is 1000 feet, speed a little more than 450 kilometres per hour. The runway looks to be about three miles away. Maybe I can make this, after all.

The low fuel warning that has been blazing away for a while suddenly turns up a notch. An alarm sounds, but it seems quieter in the cockpit. The port side engine has stopped. The fuel has finally given out.

'Miller, Miller,' I yell into the headset. 'I've lost an engine. Repeat. I've lost an engine.'

I glance out the cockpit window to see what is below me. Nothing but the lights of a million New York homes. I look for an unpopulated black spot where I could perhaps crash-land, but the airport still seems to be my best bet.

Miller comes back on the radio.

'Ted, Ted, calm. Don't lose it now. You can still do this thing. You can still get it down. You have enough height and enough speed. Just keep it together.'

I take a deep breath. Momentarily close my eyes and try to regain some element of composure.

'Okay. Leave it with me. I'll do this.'

I gather myself. Concentrate on the task at hand. I can get down with one engine. These things are designed to fly with one donk operating. I trained for this many, many times.

What I don't recall training for is flying with *no* engines.

'Miller, the second engine has cut out as well. I'm gliding now. Gliding.'

The sudden quiet is unnerving. I hear the wind whistling through the cockpit window. But there is less than a mile to go.

Without the power from the engines, the controls feel that much heavier. It takes an extreme effort to keep the nose up. It also occurs to me that it's going to be awfully difficult to stop this plane once it's on the ground. No reverse thrust from the engines, no hydraulics to work the flaps. But one problem at a time. I'd better try to land first.

The lights are edging closer. Everything feels as if it's moving in slow motion. Like running in the ocean. But I'm making ground on the airport. New York is slipping past. The runway lights are dazzling me and I can now determine the outline of the terminal. But it's at that moment I realise I am not going to make the runway.

Another yell into the headset. 'I'm not going to make it, I'm not going to make it. I'm short. I'm short.'

Miller. By now also shouting. 'Just hang in there.'

The airport is now coming up in a rush. The landing gear. Oh fuck. No hydraulics. There is a handle for the dreaded gravity drop. I find it. Pull it. And hope to God the gear falls into place on its own. Unfortunately, the only way I will find out is when the plane hits the ground . . .

Down, down. Suddenly, it feels like I am dropping like a rock. The earth is coming up to meet me at an almighty speed. I am skimming rooftops. This is just far too close for comfort. There is what looks like a large hangar on the edge of the airport. I hope there's no one in there.

If the wheels are down I am, at the very best, going to mightily scare quite a few people. I have visions of wheels scraping roofs. I don't want to think about the worst.

The plane keeps lingering in the air. By now I am shouting at it.

'Come on, you fucker. Come on. You can do this. *Come on.*'

I see the airport's perimeter fence. Nearly there. Nearly there. Just a few more metres. I somehow maintain enough height to creep over that hangar. But that's where my luck runs out.

There is a crash that sounds like the end of the world. The plane wrenches itself to the right. The right wing hits the ground before the rest of the plane does. It digs into the earth. Breaks off. We are cannoning through all the green landing lights. The body of the aircraft thumps into the hard soil and the rest of the fuselage continues to hurtle towards the runway. The plane is on its belly, momentum having taken us onto the runway, but it is sliding at right angles along the tarmac, burying the aircraft in an avalanche of sparks.

Every cockpit siren is blaring. The world outside is lost in a blur of vibrations. The harness is just about holding me in place, although there is intense pain in my ribs as my chest strains against its confinement. My head is banging away against the headrest like one of those rubber balls attached to a paddle that I used to play with as a kid.

Slowly, slowly, the mad ride is coming to a halt. Bit by bit the aircraft is drawing up. Before it has even stopped, though, I pull my aching body out of my seat and start moving to the door. I shout, 'I'm out of here,' and rip the headset off and persuade my long immobile legs it's time to spring into action.

All I can think about is that this thing could blow at any second and I have to find my way out of here. It's a long way to come to die in a fireball. I open the cockpit door and am reminded of something: all the death that this plane carries. In all the other madness I had put it out of my mind, but there is no escaping the grim reality now I have escaped the pilot seat.

I know it's a sight and a smell that will haunt my dreams and my nightmares for ever. Gagging, stumbling. Trying not to look at all the corpses, I find my way through the first-class cabin, somehow decide it's a good idea to stop and pick up my backpack, which is still wedged under my old seat, and head to the main entry door.

Remembering all the years of practice, I manage to open the door. It swings open with a gentle groan and I realise the plane is still moving. Not fast, but it hasn't quite come to a halt.

I think 'fuck it' and jump. I can't bear to be on this thing for another second. It's about three metres to the ground and I land roughly. A sharp, intense pain runs straight up my right leg, from the sole of my foot to my hip.

Too bad. I run. I run like my life depends on it. I have to get away from that plane. I don't want to be its last victim.

27

Eventually I stop and drop to the wet ground. Exhausted, out of breath. Crying. But relieved. I have made it. Somehow. I am safe again. I look around and see the broken, defeated 767. Missing a wing, nose down in the dirt. I give a silent thanks to that destroyed plane that will never fly again. It's taken me further than I thought was possible.

I follow the trail of destruction spread over half a kilometre. In the remaining runways lights, I can make out the perimeter fence. Flattened. I guess that's what I hit on the way in. One obstacle too many.

Lying on the runway, I see a large set of wheels. The landing gear. The 767's wheels either didn't lock in place or were just swept away by the force of my inelegant landing. I soon become aware of other activity. Sirens. Flashing lights. A series of fire trucks and ambulances are heading to the aircraft, while another set of flashing lights is heading my way. A convoy of police cars, by the look.

I stand. Then fall back down again. That pain in my right leg is intense. I carefully feel around the shin. The gentlest of touches and it feels like the skin is on fire. Broken. Definitely broken. It's a nice match with the bullet wound in my left arm.

The cars are on top of me now. A swarm of blokes in uniform jump out. They all have guns drawn; some are taking cover behind car doors.

I'm sitting up. Arms in the air. Trying to look as defence-less as possible, which, let's face it, doesn't require any great acting skills.

'I am on your side,' I shout as loud as I can. 'I am on your side.'

Three of the soldiers detach themselves from the rest and start to march toward me. Guns still out. This is fucking me off no end. I just want to get out of here. Get to hospital. Have a shower. Sleep. Please, let me sleep.

The lead goon is standing above me. He uses his black right boot to shove me down on the ground.

'Face down,' he yells. 'Hands behind your back.'

'Mate. Give it a rest. I'm on your side here. Help me up. My fucking leg is broken. I've been shot in the arm.'

He whacks me across the face with his gun. I feel an explosion of blood. Nose, I think, or could be mouth. It wasn't a precise blow. I go down. I understand this is a bloke running on fear and adrenalin. It's his chance to play with the big boys and he's not going to miss out.

The pain in my head has blotted out the pain in my leg for the moment. So that's a win, but I awkwardly rearrange myself so I can comply with the first instruction.

My arms are dragged behind me. Handcuffs are snapped onto my wrists. Two of them grab me, one by each arm, and drag me to the waiting car. I am thrown into the back seat. The agony in my leg has caught up and overtaken the pain in my head. I think I may have emitted a whimper.

Two giant men squeeze in either side of me, guns still out. I feel like the youngest kid on a family holiday. The one who always gets the worst seat.

'Where are we going?' I ask.

No answer. There are two armed and threatening army types in the front, two in the back and me. They can't seriously think I am going to make a run for it. There are three or four cars in front of us, I assume a few more behind. We leave the airport at speed in a swirl of red and blue bouncing lights, sirens on full volume.

'Where are we going?' I ask again.

Still no reply. On the bright side, they seem to have given up on beating me for the moment. The convoy screams out of the airport and onto the now-deserted streets of Queens. I close my eyes. The exhaustion is sitting on me like a dead weight.

Did I fall asleep? Maybe. Briefly. But now I am fully conscious again as the line of cars deviates from the public roads and sweeps through a large gate and into what looks like an army base.

I don't see much of anything. I have slunk down in my seat, the two goons beside me blocking my view of anything else. I am aware of a lot of bright white lights. Sounds in the distance that could be helicopters rotors either spinning into life or coming to a stop. There's an aeroplane engine some-where in the mix as well.

'Fucking hell', I suddenly think. 'They are taking me to Guantanamo.'

There's a quick, jolting stop. Tyres squeal. The whole bit. Even before we have come to a complete halt, my compan-ions have flung open the back doors, jumped out, managed to swing around, drop to one knee in some kind of shooting pose, guns pointed at my head. I'm clearly a very dangerous person.

The chap in the front passenger seat is on the move almost as fast. He comes at me from the right-hand side of the machine, reaches inside, grabs me and issues the order to 'move your fucking ass, mister'.

It seems to me I am suddenly the main character in the movie these fuckwits have spent their whole lives waiting to be part of. He grabs my arm and tries to pull me towards the door. I do my best, but it ain't easy. Broken leg. Gunshot wound. Busted nose. Handcuffs. You'd be surprised how difficult it is to get out the back seat of a car in such circum-stances. Eventually I'm dragged from my place. I give no resistance. I crumple onto a hard road and the order comes again. 'Get the fuck up.' Although it seems superfluous given two of the monsters have already grabbed me under the arms to bring me to my feet.

I look up, bewildered. We have stopped outside the usual cardboard cut-out building you find on just about every military base anywhere in the world. The kind that looks like the overriding imperative when building it had been that it should be cheap. But I don't have time to critique the architecture. I am propelled forward, up two small steps, through a glass door and into the building.

An anteroom. Some kind of reception desk. Two corridors leading into the body of the building. We take the left. One. Two. Three doors. Take the left and into a conference-sized room. Empty. Three bare walls. A picture of the president on the fourth. No windows. I'm put in a chair. Everybody leaves except the two heavies from the back of the car and the nice man who smashed me in the face. What a fine group we make.

There is no sound in the room except for a lot of heavy breathing. I focus on the one who hit me. Trying to make eye contact. Show him I'm not the type to be intimidated, even though I am sitting here shitting myself, wondering why the nightmare isn't over. Why having survived Khalid, Arzu and that plane ride I am still having to fight for my life.

He looks at me. This hulk in army fatigues. Huge, well over six feet. Fair hair, angry red face, thighs that rub together when he walks. The kind of lunatic who is a life member down at the NRA with all the other nuts.

'Where's Miller?' I ask him in my calmest voice.

He takes three steps towards me and smashes me again. Forearm to my busted nose. He follows it up by getting behind me, right arm crooked around my neck, and slowly squeezes the life out of me.

'You fucking shitbird,' he's shouting. 'You think you can get away with that shit again. I'm going to kill you, right here, right now.'

I struggle. Legs kicking. But he has an iron grip. And, let's face it, it's not that difficult to strangle a man with his arms tied behind his back. The world is turning black. The fight has left me. And then the pressure stops. Voices. Shouting.

'Get off him.'

'Stop that.'

'Fucking hell, he's killed him.'

The lights in my head flicker back to life. Colour. Vision. A face in front of my eyes. A voice.

'Come on, Ted, don't quit on us now.'

Miller.

'Thanks for showing up,' I whisper through my damaged throat.

Over his shoulder, I can see my tormentor. Now he has two blokes pinning his arms behind him.

Miller sees me looking and stands up from his crouching position. He walks over to his attacker, stops, his face up close.

'You stupid fuck. You big, brave warrior. Beating up on a defenceless man. A man who probably just saved about 10,000 lives. A man who is probably going to get just about every award for bravery this country has to offer.'

28

I wake up in a hospital room. Clean. Bright. White. A single room. Door closed. There is a small window. Outside I can see a patch of green, some grass, a tree, all bordered by a thin, grey road. It feels like I am in some sort of compound. There is a blue sky and I fancy I can smell the tang of salt in the air. Am I near the coast?

I'm alone. It's all very quiet. Peaceful, even. I can't see a soul outside my window. My right leg is hoisted at an uncomfortable angle, attached to a sling hanging down from the ceiling. My face feels strange, constricted. I bring up my right hand and discover most of my head is covered in bandages and sticking plaster.

I don't know where I am, or how and when I arrived. My last memory is still of that room on the army base. I must have passed out again.

The door opens. It's Miller. With a big bunch of flowers. 'How's my hero today?' is his opener.

Not in the mood for levity, I give no answer.

He puts the flowers down on the bedside table. I see in his other hand a wad of newspapers. The *New York Times*, the *Washington Post*, the *Wall Street Journal*.

'I thought there may be a few things you might want to catch up on while you're in here,' he says.

'The footy scores? Did Sydney win on the weekend?'

He looks puzzled and just holds up the front page of the *Times*. Front-page headline: *Australian Hero Pilot Saves NYC*. A picture of me. An old picture of me from several aeons ago when I was a lot less battered-looking than I am today.

'Where did they find that picture?' I ask.

'I think the Australian government gave it out. You know, when they realised you were a national treasure and not a national disgrace.'

'How long have I been here?'

'You've been out for a couple of days. We put your leg and your nose back together. Stitched up the hole the bullet made. It was the least we could do. You're still pretty ugly, although I'm not sure that's anything to do with the crash.'

'Funny. Where am I?'

'The army's finest hospital. Walter Reed. Washington, DC. Nothing but the best for you, my friend'

The memories are starting to emerge from the hidden, and probably heavily drugged, recesses of my brain. The words come out in a rush.

'What the fuck happened? Sydney. Rio. Paris. Have you got Khalid?'

'Who's Khalid?' is his first answer. This is a worry. 'Sydney was close,' Miller continues. 'Rio was hit. Don't know anything about Paris. We think that plane must have crashed out at sea somewhere. Christ knows where, though.'

'What happened in Sydney?' I ask quietly, still fearing the worst.

'Essentially, we got lucky. They missed. The plane got to Sydney Harbour without anyone noticing. It came in low, just like you did. It looked like it was aiming for the Opera House or the Harbour Bridge, but just got too close to the water. It ditched. One ferry got hit, 25 people on it dead.'

'Christ.'

'It was a horrible sight. The plane broke in two on impact. All those dead bodies floated to the surface. Just bobbing around in the water.'

I was appalled. But relieved as well. It could have been much worse.

'Rio?'

'We didn't get lucky there,' Miller mutters. 'The fucking thing just pancaked into that soccer stadium. At last count 5000 dead.'

'Fuck.'

We both go quiet for a moment and then I remember what he said about Khalid.

'So, you don't know who Khalid is?'

'No.'

'He is the one behind all this. The planner. The master-mind. I met him. You'd better make some calls. You are going to want to hear this.'

* * *

It took me the best part of a day to tell the story. The doctors wouldn't let me out of my room, so the best brains in the US military and secret services all crowded into my confined space.

Then I told it again. And again. The experts quizzed me on every detail. Forcing me to remember bits and pieces of the story I had forgotten the first time around. In some ways I couldn't tell them too much. I still wasn't exactly sure where I had been. I told them I thought I was high up somewhere on the northwest coast of Africa. Maybe in Western Sahara, if Arzu was to be believed.

I told them all about Khalid. My suspicions about his motives, his grand plan. They looked stunned. This was a full-blown terrorist network that had entirely escaped detection.

Two days after the briefings, and still in hospital, Miller came back for a visit. He looks beat. Like he had been sleeping in his suit.

'How goes it?' I ask.

'Not so well,' he says as he sits down in the chair beside the bed.

'What's been happening? Found anything?'

He lets out a long sigh. Right hand scrubs across his face. He looks pained.

'Nothing. We've been working off your memories, so it's taken a few days to piece everything together. The flight data recorder was switched off early in the piece, probably the first thing your pal Arzu did. Then we suspect it was ripped out of the plane entirely after it landed in Africa.'

'You haven't found the base?'

'No, I think we found it. Well, we found the place it probably was. Right on the coastal fringe of Western Sahara. You were right about that. Not far from the border with Mauritania. Given what you told us, we had a close look at every square inch of Africa's northwest via a bunch of satellites. We found what looked like an abandoned air force base. After some to-ing and fro-ing and not informing the government of Western Sahara, an ostensibly friendly nation, the president gave the go-ahead. And in we went. All guns blazing, as it were.'

'And there was nothing there.' I said it as a statement rather than as a question.

'Deserted. There were signs of recent activity. Footprints. Tyre tracks. Food in the kitchen. Quite a bit of bedding left behind. There could have been a couple of hundred soldiers there, we think. But they picked it pretty clean.'

There was a silence between us as we thought this through.

'Did you find out where the other planes were stored before they were sent back?'

'Still working on that as well. Getting closer. We're thinking the Garuda may have had a couple of hiding spots. Or, at least, a refuelling spot closer to Sydney. Hard to see how it could cut across the Australian mainland without being spotted.'

'So Khalid is still out there. Somewhere in the wind and we have no idea where?'

'That's about the size of it. It's not a pretty thought.'

'Did he ever claim responsibility? I mean, by any normal standards, this was a pretty successful operation. He managed to steal four planes, held the world hostage for days, brought the international aviation system to its knees, sent stock markets plunging, then sent the planes back to terrify Sydney and New York, and killed thousands in Rio. Not to mention all the dead in the four aircraft. It's going to be a while before the world goes back to normal, if it ever does.'

'Not a squeak. A few of the smaller groups have tried to claim some credit, but an operation of this scale would be beyond them.'

'That is pretty scary, then,' I say.

'Which bit?'

'That he's still out there. Khalid. Somewhere. We don't know where. But we can be sure he'll make himself known again at some point. He wants to put together a caliphate and he has just delivered the biggest calling card in history.'

'Yep.'

'What's next then? What's the plan?'

'We just keep looking. There is no other choice. It is the agency's number one target as of this moment. Possibly its only target. The resources being thrown at this guy are unlike anything I have ever seen. We need to find him. That's the bottom line.'

'Is there anything more I can do?'

'You have done plenty, Ted. Without you we still wouldn't know who was behind it all. Go home. Recover. We know where to find you if we need you. I suspect you haven't heard the last of Mr Khalid.'

EPILOGUE

They let me out of the hospital after another four days. Physically, I was relatively sound. The pain in the leg was still there, and I would need the help of a cane to get around for a while, but I was assured I would make a full recovery.

They had done a good job on the busted nose as well. Probably looked better than before, to be honest. At least it was straight now. The pain in the arm had receded to a dull throb, but the stitched-up wound still surprised me every time I looked in the mirror after a shower

It was not without trepidation that I boarded another plane to head home. I told myself I was being silly, that this was just another ordinary trip, but the mental scars may take a little longer to heal than the physical ones. They put me up in the comfy seats at the front, but it only brought back memories of sitting in the same spot when I boarded the Ukraine International flight out of JFK. Wherever I looked, I imagined I could see versions of the passengers

I had shared that flight with. I thought I would be seeing those ghosts for the rest of my life.

Still, if I wanted to go home, this was the only way it was going to happen. A sea voyage had even less appeal. I had the cane, but I still didn't think I was infirm enough to actually go on a cruise ship.

When I arrived back in Sydney, I was ushered out the side door of the airport. Media had been staking out the place for the last few days, but the government wasn't too keen to parade me in front of the cameras just yet. I went home. Back in Sydney, I walked through the front door of my Glebe house. Back into my version of normality. It was like nothing had changed in this part of my world.

My coffee cup was still on the kitchen sink where I had left it, residue hardened into a hard, black sheen at the bottom. It felt like I had been away for centuries, but when I opened the fridge I realised the expiry date on my milk carton was still a day away. I hadn't even been gone long enough for the milk to go off.

There was still one more person to see before I could consider all this over. I had spoken with Bob a couple of times on the phone from the US, but I had to go and see the old man face-to-face.

I took a cab into the city the next day. There is nothing like a night in your own bed to bring some restorative calm to your world. I paid the driver and again walked into the office where all this started. This time I paused before entering Bob's office to look out of those tall windows over Sydney Harbour. All the wreckage and debris of the plane that had ploughed into the water had been cleared away. Today it looked like just another day in Sydney. Ferries scuttling about, people going to work, going home. Tourists enjoying the sunshine and making their way to the Opera House, to the Bridge. I hoped it would be just as easy to clear away my debris and set me to rights, but I had my doubts.

Penny was waiting for me. She jumped out of her chair behind the desk and ran over to me. Didn't say anything at first, just grabbed me and hugged me. It felt good. When she raised her face from my chest and looked at me, tears were streaming down her face.

'It's so good to see you, Ted. I thought we'd lost you for a while there,' she said.

'I thought I'd lost me too,' I replied.

She hugged me again.

'Are you okay, though? Are you going to be okay?'

'I think so. They tell me I will be able to get rid of the cane in a couple of weeks and I'll be fighting fit again,' I said with a confidence I didn't really feel.

'You'd better go in. He's waiting for you.'

I opened the door to the familiar office and Bob was there behind his familiar desk. He rose and walked over to me. He ignored my proffered hand and instead enveloped me in a bear hug. This was a first. When he broke away he just looked at me.

'Ted, welcome home. How is everything?'

'Still a few aches and pains, but should be right in the long run I think.'

'Good, good. You take as long as you like, we all owe you a great debt of gratitude. The prime minister wants to meet you and give you some sort of award himself.'

'That's nice, Bob, but would you thank the PM for me and tell him I am declining his generous offer of the meeting and the gong. Not really for me. I just want to get away for a while and live the quiet life. There are a few things I really need to straighten out.'

'Okay, Ted. You do what you need to. But you will be back? We do still need you, you know?'

It was a question I had given a lot of thought to over the last couple of days. Would I be back? Could I really keep doing this kind of job? I'd arrived at no conclusion. Until now.

'No, Bob, I'm out.'

With that, I stand up, shake the silent Bob's hand, and walk away. There was someone I needed to find.